MW00625154

A NOVEL BASED ON THE LIFE OF
ARTEMISIA GENTILESCHI

WHAT A
WOMAN
CAN DO

Peg A. Lamphier, PhD

THE
M
MENTORIS
PROJECT

What a Woman Can Do is a work of fiction. Some incidents, dialogue, and characters are products of the author's imagination and are not to be construed as real. Where real-life historical figures appear, the situations, incidents, and dialogue concerning those persons are based on or inspired by actual events. In all other respects, any resemblance to actual persons, living or dead, events, or locales is entirely coincidental.

Barbera Foundation, Inc.
P.O. Box 1019
Temple City, CA 91780

Cover photo: Asar Studios / Alamy Stock Photo

Cover design: Suzanne Turpin

More information at www.mentorisproject.org

ISBN: 978-1-947431-34-8

Library of Congress Control Number: 2021932883

All net proceeds from the sale of this book will be donated to Barbera Foundation, Inc. whose mission is to support educational initiatives that foster an appreciation of history and culture to encourage and inspire young people to create a stronger future.

The Mentoris Project is a series of novels and biographies about the lives of great men and women who have changed history through their contributions as scientists, inventors, explorers, thinkers, and creators. The Barbera Foundation sponsors this series in the hope that, like a mentor, each book will inspire the reader to discover how she or he can make a positive contribution to society.

Contents

Foreword

First and foremost, Mentor was a person. We tend to think of the word *mentor* as a noun (a mentor) or a verb (to mentor), but there is a very human dimension embedded in the term. Mentor appears in Homer's *Odyssey* as the old friend entrusted to care for Odysseus's household and his son Telemachus during the Trojan War. When years pass and Telemachus sets out to search for his missing father, the goddess Athena assumes the form of Mentor to accompany him. The human being welcomes a human form for counsel. From its very origins, becoming a mentor is a transcendent act; it carries with it something of the holy.

The Mentoris Project sets out on an Athena-like mission: We hope the books that form this series will be an inspiration to all those who are seekers, to those of the twenty-first century who are on their own odysseys, trying to find enduring principles that will guide them to a spiritual home. The stories that comprise the series are all deeply human. These books dramatize the lives of great men and women whose stories bridge the ancient and the modern, taking many forms, just as Athena did, but always holding up a light for those living today.

Whether in novel form or traditional biography, these books

plumb the individual characters of our heroes' journeys. The power of storytelling has always been to envelop the reader in a vivid and continuous dream, and to forge a link with the subject. Our goal is for that link to guide the reader home with a new inspiration.

What is a mentor? A guide, a moral compass, an inspiration. A friend who points you toward true north. We hope that the Mentoris Project will become that friend, and it will help us all transcend our daily lives with something that can only be called holy.

—Robert J. Barbera, Founder, The Mentoris Project
—Ken LaZebnik, Founding Editor, The Mentoris Project

For Cameron Burke Gray

"Nothing can dim the light that shines from within."

—Maya Angelou

Prologue

I am trapped in the Netherlands. Well, not entirely trapped, but I had to flee London with Queen Henrietta's retinue and I appear unable to book passage on a ship out of here. The queen doesn't want me to leave her. She looks upon me as a kind of pet, much like the three dwarves and the monkey that travel with her. I don't like being lumped in with the dwarves and monkey—even though one of the dwarves is a very good painter of miniatures.

The Hague is a lovely city, or it would be if the sun ever came out. Although, after nearly four years in London, I suppose I should be used to gray skies and cold drizzle. I yearn for the blue skies and warm weather of Naples even more than I dream of a decent meal. English food ought not to be tolerated by anyone raised in Rome. They boil everything until it is gray and no longer resembles its original state. Most people in England, even the royal palaces, have never seen a fork, nor do they clean their knives between meals. I swear, if I have to eat one more bowl of boiled mutton or stewed sailfish, I shall howl in protest. The English also drink tankards of ale, a thin, bitter brew I never get used to. When they do drink wine they sweeten it with honey and whatever else they have on hand. Give me a cup of unaltered red wine, rich with the taste of grapes and soil and sun, and maybe a bit of aged cheese and some fruit and I'm a happy woman.

Forgive me. I complain about the weather and food to distract myself. I am most dreadfully homesick, you see. I came to England to help my papà finish a series of paintings for a ceiling in the queen's new house, but before I finished the paintings, Papà died. First, I stayed to finish the work, though I insisted only Papà get painter's credit for it. Later, I stayed because the political situation in England went to hell in a handbasket. King Charles and his queen kept me in England against my will. I don't think Charles even likes my paintings. It the king's politics that have trapped me—politics of the worst kind—religious politics.

I blame King Henry VIII almost as much as King Charles. Henry died a good fifty years before I was born, but my English captivity is still his fault. Long ago, he conceived an unseemly passion for Anne Boleyn and the only way he could marry her was to get his marriage to Catherine of Aragon annulled and the Pope wouldn't agree to that. So Henry took England out of the Catholic Church and made himself the head of the new Protestant Church of England. Once rid of papal authority, Henry put away his queen, married his mistress Anne Boleyn, and as a bonus, dissolved all the Catholic convents and monasteries. Of course, he kept their riches for himself. What a rat!

But what does that have to do with me, Artemisia Gentileschi, an Italian lady painter? More than you'd think. When Queen Elizabeth died without heirs, her cousin who was already King of Scotland became King of England as well. James' parents raised him Catholic but he had the sense to pretend he'd converted to Protestantism. Or maybe he didn't care one way or another, as long as he ended up king. This is the same man who had babies with his Protestant queen, even though everyone knew he loved the Duke of Buckingham. James was the English monarch for even longer than Elizabeth and by the time he died, England had been Protestant for over a century. His son Charles, as in King Charles, won't play his father's game. First, he tried and failed to marry a Spanish princess, then he successfully married Henrietta, a French princess, and both of those countries are as Catholic as Rome. Worse, Queen Henrietta never pretended to be anything but Catholic. Which is why she is so fond of Catholic painters like Papà and me and also why her subjects hate her.

England has stood on the precipice of revolution for years, with the king and parliament bickering about who has ultimate power and which religion is best. The problem came to a head when the Dowager Queen of France, Marie de Medici, visited her daughter Henrietta and tried to remove her from England. The plan was to flee and take all the Catholic courtiers (and painters) with them. Charles put a stop to it, knowing that if his queen left England, it would be the end of his rule.

I complicated my English purgatory by refusing to paint anything for either monarch. Though Queen Henrietta took possession of my *Self-Portrait* and a *Lucretia*, she never paid for either, nor has Charles paid me for the work Papà and I did at the queen's Greenwich house. I needed that money quite badly and thought I could force the monarchs to pay by refusing to paint anything new.

The queen never did pay me, but she did take me to the Netherlands and The Hague when she at last fled England, leaving her husband, Charles, behind. Supposedly, she's looking for support and funding to make war on those Englishmen who disapprove of their essentially Catholic monarchy. I'm not sure I care. Kings and queens are not like other people, and people who stand near them too often get hurt.

In the meantime, it may be months before I find a ship willing to take me home. My best chance is to hop-skip my way home from the Netherlands to Portugal or Spain, then to Naples. Luckily, Naples is an important port in the Mediterranean and I'm likely to find passage home once I get out of the North Sea. It's bound to take months, but I vow I will get there eventually, and when I do, I shall leave Naples no more.

Because I have neither painting supplies nor the heart to paint, I have decided to write my life story. Now, more than ever, I am grateful my friend Signor Galileo proved such a stern taskmaster. He taught me my letters, you see, then he taught me to write. And though he was always kind, he expected perfection from the start. At the time I wanted to strangle the old man after every lesson, but if I could go back I would kiss his cheek a hundred times. Last week, news of his death reached The Hague and I knew not if I should rejoice at dear Galileo's release from his travails or weep for the pity of it all.

But enough of that. I must tell this story in seemly order. I can begin writing while I wait for a ship and continue on the trip home. And should that not prove enough time, I shall write when I am between paintings. I do so not because I am important, but because I am unusual. I am a woman painter. Not one of those lady dilettantes who paints pictures of fruit baskets and bundles of flowers—not at all. I knew Caravaggio long ago and am considered among great Caravaggisti. I have sold paintings to popes and cardinals, dukes and duchesses, and even kings and queens (when they would pay). And I have done so while the world told me women couldn't be serious artists. Bah. Of course we can. We have to work twice as hard for half as much money, but we can be great. I have known a few great female painters and I find one in my mirror every morning. To all the men and women who told me I could not paint, I always said the same thing, though more often with my brush than my mouth, and I say it to you now: "I will show you what a woman can do."

Chapter One

"What do you think, Papà?" I could hear the anxiety in my voice, but I couldn't help it. So much depended on Papà's judgment. He stood in front of my first unsupervised painting, one I'd planned, sketched, and painted entirely on my own. I'd painted in my bedroom, rather than in Papà's workroom, so he wouldn't see it and advise on its progress.

Papà stepped back, stroked his beard, and tipped his head to the right like he was thinking hard. After a long moment, his lips curved into a faint smile. "You are a far better painter than I was at sixteen, Artemisia," he said.

I bounced on my toes, then caught myself and clasped my hands together. A grown woman did not bounce at praise. "I was afraid it might be too . . . common," I said. I thought my first *Madonna and Child*, which I painted with Papà's supervision, idealized and romanticized the mother-child bond. But Papà wanted it that way, so that's how I painted it. Every time I saw it, I heard the argument I'd had with Papà in my head.

New mothers never look like the Virgin Mary does in church paintings, all holy and serene; instead, they look exhausted and disheveled. But if you observe a mother, you'll see that look that says she'd die before she let anyone hurt her baby. That's what I tried to capture with my second *Madonna and Child*: the paradoxical mix of worn-out befuddlement and helpless adoration. Still, my choice to use our servant Tuzia as the model worried me a bit. Madonnas should be young and beautiful, and Tuzia had five living children and wrinkles at the corners of her eyes. She'd been a maid and housekeeper her whole life, so she wasn't the sort of woman who had her portrait painted. That was for rich ladies.

Papà shook his head at my concern. "The world is full of mothers no longer in the prime of their beauty," he said. "Our friend Caravaggio would approve of your realism. This looks just like a scene in any plain Roman house." Papà stepped right up to the canvas, so close his nose almost touched it. "I like the way she appears half asleep and rumpled from bed. I've seen your mamma look that way many a night, God bless her soul."

I stepped over and patted him on the arm. Mamma had died four years earlier, but we hadn't gotten used to her absence, though my little brothers didn't remember her as well as Papà and I did. I'd been twelve years old and nearly a woman when Mamma died, but poor Francesco had been only seven and Giulio had just turned five. Everyone in the Piazza di Spagna thought Papà should take another wife to raise his children and keep his house, but Papà said a wife would mean more heartache. One dead wife was enough for him. Papà is tender like that.

He took my hand and gave it a little squeeze. "It reminds me of how your mother looked when you children were young. We were happy then," he said. He turned his gaze back to my Madonna. "You have a marvelous way with hands—I should take lessons from you. And your drapery is every bit as good as mine."

"I had a good teacher," I said. Everyone said Orazio Gentileshi had a gorgeous way with fabric. Papà could make the folds look so real, you'd think you could reach out and feel the softness.

Papà laughed. "I have always had trouble with hands and feet, so you didn't learn that from me. My lady hands always look like silk gloves filled with sand."

"The trick is to paint dimples on the backs of the hands," I said. "It suggests knuckles, which in turn suggests bones. And you told me to think of the bones when painting faces. I do the same for hands."

Papà peered at the Madonna's hands, then stretched out his own before him. I touched the dimple on the back of Papà's wrinkled hand, then pointed at the Madonna's hand. "See?"

"I do, you clever girl. Run up to my studio and fetch the Madonna you painted last winter. I want to see them side by side."

I found my other painting sitting against the interior wall and snatched it up without really looking at it. I'd stared at it enough when planning the new painting, deciding which elements to keep, throw out, and improve. Papà was still staring at the new painting when I returned. I leaned the older painting against the base of the tripod that held the second Madonna so the two lined up, one above the other.

"Ah, yes, Artemisia," Papà murmured. "Many people would prefer the first painting, but they would be wrong."

I sighed in happiness. I thought so too, but hadn't been so sure Papà would. The first painting was sweet and easy to look at, though the baby resembled a tiny adult—you see that in paintings a lot and it's stupid. Babies didn't look like miniature adults in real life.

As if he knew what I was thinking, Papà said, "Your baby toes are magnificent. And the scale of your mother's legs and feet—my girl has been studying her Michelangelo."

I nodded, thrilled he'd noticed. "It was Michelangelo's s *Cumaean Sibyl* in the Sistine Chapel that made me realize I'd avoided the mother's legs and feet in this painting." I pointed at my first Madonna and said, "That, and the *Madonna and Child* sculpture at the Church of Saint Agostino. You remember, the one we visited on Ash Wednesday. That Madonna's body had gravitas like she connected to the ground in some earthy, rooted way."

Papà nodded. "I am glad you pay attention to our lessons, unlike your brothers, I must say. You perfected your draped fabric painting in this first Madonna, and that's a skill you'll need. But here," he said, pointing again, "you demonstrate *perfect* anatomy. And do not for a moment think I've failed to notice your homage to the *Madonna and Child* I painted last year for Cardinal Scipione Borghese. Tuzia didn't mind?"

Like Papà's painting, I had painted my Madonna offering

her breast to the child. So the painting wasn't about just maternal love, I had posed the child reaching for its mother's hair and looking up at her face, ignoring the proffered nipple. The child's gaze made the connection between the two figures more intimate, emphasizing a connection between mother and child that has little to do with milk.

Papà turned away from the paintings and sat on the edge of my bed. He patted the spot next to him on the mattress. "Come sit with me, my dear."

I sat, hearing the rustle of straw stuffing as I drew up one leg and turned toward Papà. He'd liked my new painting, but that didn't keep me from worrying. Before he could speak, I blurted, "I can do it, Papà. I know I can."

He sighed and stared at the wall opposite the bed. "It's a hard thing, this life as a painter, and it will be much harder for you than it's ever been for me." He shook his head. "If only you'd been born a boy."

I was ready for this argument. "Signora Fontana does well for herself. Why, just last month, Accademia di San Luca admitted her to its guild. And two popes have shown her favor—not just Pope Clement, but Pope Paul as well."

Papà sighed. "That is true, my dear, but we both know Lavinia Fontana is a high-born lady whose family is connected to the old Pope Julius, may God rest his soul. You are the daughter of a painter whose own father was a goldsmith. Smithing is a necessary and honorable profession, but your grandfather was a tradesman and people do not forget that. I wished we lived in a world in which social hierarchy does not matter, but we do not."

Papà wasn't wrong, but he wasn't right either. I pushed myself off the bed and stood before him. "Signora Fontana's family has money only because she earns it. Everyone knows her family is well-born but poor, and her husband is not a gentleman. He takes care of the household and grinds her pigments," I said. "She earns her family's living by painting, though it is true she's a portraitist."

Papà wagged a finger at me. "Have a care, Artemisia. Many a hardworking painter has made a living from portraits. There's no need to pour scorn on artists with less ability than Signora Fontana."

I frowned at Papà, refusing to be sorry for speaking the truth. "I just get so angry. Why should I not paint? Because I am not a man? You said yourself I paint the best hands in Rome. Lavinia Fontana has proved a woman can paint important paintings, even nudes. And there is also Sofonisba Anguissola."

"Another noblewoman and portrait painter."

"Yes, but the great Michelangelo recognized her talent, didn't he?"

"So you seek to emulate Sofonisba?" Papà smiled and waved his hand at my two Madonnas.

I put my hands on my hips in exasperation. "Well, no, Papà. You know as well as I do that she was the Spanish queen's pet painter."

"True," he said with a grin. "But there was that scandal, the one with the ship's captain."

I laughed. After contracting one respectable marriage to a Spanish nobleman, Sofonisba married a ship's captain. The news had been a seven-day wonder, even in Rome: the great Sofonisba had married a commoner. But the captain had turned out to be his wife's greatest advocate and promoted her paintings wherever he traveled.

"I have little hope of marriage to a wealthy, high-born man, nor to a devoted commoner. But I can make my living as a painter, I am sure of it," I said.

"As Signora Fontana does?"

"Yes, Papà. I admire her style of living, though I don't like the way she idealizes figures. You left Mannerism behind for Signor Caravaggio's naturalism, and you were right. It is a better sort of art." Because I couldn't help myself, I added, "And, like Sofonisba, she's wasting her talent painting portraits."

Now it was Papà's turn to laugh. "I already told you, there's no shame in honest work." He rubbed at his head until his thin gray hair stood on end. "I must concede that you have met every challenge I set for you. You learned to grind pigments and mix paint when you were no taller than a donkey's back, and you learned to sketch when you could barely hold a piece of charcoal. In fact, your current command of anatomical drawing has exceeded mine."

"And you never needed to beat me," I said with a wink. When I first learned to draw, he'd set me to some task and tell me that if I failed, he'd beat me with a stout stick. The threat always made me laugh. Unlike most fathers in the neighborhood, Papà never hit any of his children, not even Giulio, whose antics would have tried Saint Monica.

Papà kissed my cheek. "No, I did not. Perhaps I should have.

I would be a poor papà indeed if I didn't admit that despite being a woman, you have a great talent. And you're likely the only painting child I'll have—your brothers are worse than useless at anything but making trouble."

My heart soared at his words. There have been times when I thought he'd never give up on Francesco and Giulio. Most papàs expected their sons to carry on the family business while daughters married and went away, and mine was no different. Or he had been no different until my brothers proved they would never be real painters.

Papà took my hand to pull me back to sit next to him. "Here is what I propose," he said. "Signor Esposito has seen and admired my *Lute Player* and wants one of his own. But I have won a position with my friend Agostino Tassi, painting frescoes at the Quirinal Palace."

"Oh, Papà, that's wonderful. When did that happen?" I clapped in appreciation of my father's astounding coup. The Quirinal Palace was one of the great new buildings in Rome.

"I heard only yesterday. Pope Paul set aside money to finish the palace's decorations. He has commissioned a group of us to paint various scenes in the Sala Regia. The pope wants Greek Muses and lots of scenery."

"Really? The pope would allow non-religious themes? I thought the Council of Trent forbade superstitions in paintings."

Papà shrugged. "Pope Paul is a Borghese and they are an art-loving family. I've heard he finds the religious art of the last fifty years quite dreary. But you've gotten me off the topic, you wretched girl. My point is that I do not have time to plan and produce a copy of my lute girl, but the money is too good to leave on the table. I propose you paint it and we sell it as mine."

"Papà!" I gasped. Painters passed off their assistant's paintings as their own all the time and no one thought much of it, but Papà had never done it.

"We'll get a much greater sum for your painting if Signor Esposito believes I painted it. Then I shall give you half the commission. With that money, you must paint a large-scale, multi-figure painting as a sample of your talent. It should announce to the world that you are available for commissions."

I threw my arms around his neck and thanked the Holy Father for giving me the best papà in the world. "What shall I paint?" I asked.

He kissed my forehead and stood to go. "That is for you to decide. It will be *your* statement to the art buyers of the world, not mine."

When Papà had gone, I walked to my bedroom window and pushed back the shutters. Below me, the piazza bustled with activity. Women washed clothes at the fountain, a baker's boy wheeled a cart piled high with golden loaves, and gentlemen strolled about, notable for the swords they carried at their hips. I watched, marveling that no one knew that up in this window stood a girl whose life had changed. *I am no longer an apprentice,* I thought. *I am a painter.*

"Now tuck it away where a cutpurse can't get at it," Papà told me. He shook the small leather pouch so the coins inside jingled like bells. "It's quite a tidy sum of money for a young woman just past her seventeenth birthday."

We stood on the street in front of our house, waiting for a hired carriage. For the occasion I wore my best gown, made of green linen with a square-cut bodice and a split skirt, showing an embroidered underskirt. I am burdened with unruly hair, thick and curly and brown, but I had braided a green velvet ribbon into it and pinned it around my head in a crown. Francesco had whistled at me when I came downstairs, and because neither of my brothers is free with compliments, I took it to mean I looked my best.

Dear Papà had arranged the day as a reward for the work I'd done on the two copies I'd painted. He'd meant me to copy *Lute Player*, but then Signor Esposito decided he also wanted a copy of Papà's *Judith and Her Maidservant*. At first, I'd been annoyed at the delay, especially because my *Lute* painting hadn't been an exact copy of Papà's. But Signor Esposito had liked my variation (though he thought it was Papà's, not mine) and wanted more. This turned out fine because Judith paintings are a wonderful way to portray women *not* being saintly. If you've ever seen a Judith painting, you know why—they're wonderfully violent, especially the ones where she's beheading Holofernes. Papà's version showed the moment just after Judith cut off the Assyrian general's head. In it, Judith and her maidservant held Holofernes's decapitated head between them, Judith still clutching the sword she'd used for cutting. I painted it pretty much that way, except my Judith didn't look a bit afraid.

"I am always careful, Papà," I said. I tucked the little pouch down inside my bodice, where no one would get it. It felt good to know I could go into any apothecary that specialized in colors and buy whatever I needed for making paint. Papà had a magnificent book on how to make dyes and paints, but I'd never learned to read. By the time Papà discovered I was going to be a painter and not a housekeeper, it was too late to learn. Papà taught me the formulas for nearly fifty colors, from the galls that make grays to the orpiment that makes yellow and gold, and all the colors in between.

I'd need to buy a large frame, canvas for stretching, and a pot of white lead glaze. But first I must decide what to paint. The Judith had been fun, but I didn't want anyone to confuse my work with Papà's or Caravaggio's, and both had painted famous Judiths. So, something else. But what, and just how big? It needed to be large enough to make an impression, but not so massive that it was impossible to move around. At least I could afford whatever I chose.

"The carriage will take you first to Signora Fontana's studio," Papà said. "The good lady has consented to give you some time. The pope has just appointed her as the official portraitist of the court, and as a consequence she is very busy, so do not linger. After that, you'll visit Saint Peter's Basilica and the Sistine Chapel to examine the paintings there. I'm aware you've seen them several times, but I want you to look again with an eye to our sample painting. Oh, and I've arranged a surprise for you at Saint Peter's."

I knew better than to question Papà about the surprise. He

loved arranging treats for his children, and no matter what I said, he'd keep his secret.

The hired carriage came around the corner and stopped at the house. As I climbed in, I spared a glance at the horses before turning back to Papà. "And then I'll finish the day at the Quirinal, where you're working?" I asked.

Papà nodded. "I'd like you to see the work and meet my friend Signor Tassi. Go, now. I'll see you in a few hours."

No more than fifteen minutes later, the carriage came to a narrow, three-story house. I felt a little disappointed at the sight of it. Such a famous lady painter should live in a grander building. When I knocked, I was admitted by a man who introduced himself as Lavinia Fontana's husband, Gian Zappi. "She'll be right down," he said as he showed me to a small sitting room. "She likes to work in the morning when the light is best, but I will tell her you are here."

The room had shelves on two of the four walls, each filled with interesting artifacts and books. A third wall held a small spinet, its keyboard open as if someone had played it only moments ago. I tried not to feel intimidated, but we Gentileschis certainly couldn't afford books and instruments.

After a few minutes, a small, dark-haired woman bustled into the room. "You must be Orazio's daughter," she said with a gentle smile. "He says you have the gift, and so I think we shall be friends."

I leaped to my feet and introduced myself, feeling quite stupid as soon as the words came out of my mouth. Of course Signora Fontana knew who I was. She just said so.

"You may call me Lavinia," the lady said. "We are sister painters, are we not?" Lavinia motioned me back to my chair and sat nearby. We talked of inconsequential things for several minutes before she brought up the topic of my painting. "Your father tells me you are planning your first great work and could use some advice about the subject. Is that true, or have you already decided what you're going to do and you're being polite?"

I shrugged, feeling embarrassed again. "I know and I don't know. I like to paint women but I don't like most of the paintings of women I've seen." Realizing my error, I added, "Not yours, of course, but . . ."

Lavinia sat back in her chair. Her eyes crinkled in thought. "I understand," she said. "Most painters paint women as objects—things men look at. They see us and don't see us." She rose and beckoned me to follow. We walked down a short hall and turned into a man's study. "Zappi's room," Lavinia explained. She gestured at a painting on the far wall. "I keep this painting in here to remind myself what I'm up against." A nude woman looked straight at the viewer, inviting them to gaze at her naked body, while also seeming aware of the two leering old men outside her window. Near her foot, a fountain gushed water, while a tubular strip of cloth lay between her legs.

I knew it immediately. Cavaliere D'Arpino's *Susanna and the Elders* was a much-reproduced painting and d'Arpino visited Papà's studio on occasion. "I know d'Arpino," I told Lavinia. "It's scandalous, isn't it? The painting, I mean."

"It's no better than erotica," she said, her mouth twisting with scorn. "You know the story, do you not?"

"Two older men spied on Susanna, a virtuous and beautiful wife, while she bathed," I told her. "When she refused their advances, they denounced her as an adulterer. The very men who accused her found her guilty and sentenced her to death. Then, at the last minute, Daniel questioned the elders and proved they were lying. So the judge found the elders guilty of bearing false witness."

"And executed *them*, not Susanna," Lavinia said. "Yet you'll see countless paintings of this parable as only an opportunity to display a naked female body. Men want this art in their homes, but it is little more than pornography. It matters not that no woman wants old men to watch her bathe." Lavinia dismissed the painting with a wave and left the room. I followed, considering her point.

When we took our seats again, I said, "You are right, but the problem isn't just naughty pictures." I described the Judith painting I'd copied for Papà. "It was very good, but he used me as his model for Judith and made me-Judith look nervous about cutting off Holofernes's head. And afraid in general."

"And how should Judith look?" Lavinia asked, leaning forward a little.

"Any woman brave enough to sneak into an enemy general's tent to slice off his head with a sword wouldn't be timid. She'd be wary but excited, and very, very dangerous."

Lavinia grinned. "She'd be jubilant too, don't you think? Wouldn't you, if you'd killed a man you hated? I haven't seen your father's Judith, but I've seen Signor Caravaggio's and I thought he got it all wrong. Not that anyone agrees with me. That painting took Rome by storm."

She was right. Caravaggio painted Judith leaning away from the knife, as if she was trying to distance herself from the violence inherent in slitting a man's throat. "Men want to believe women are meek," I said. They don't want to show a woman being strong. Maybe they think it will give us unseemly ideas."

Lavinia was still laughing at this when a servant interrupted with a tray of fruit juice and small cakes. After we'd served ourselves, Lavinia returned to our discussion. "Are you thinking of trying a new kind of Judith?" she asked.

"Oh, heavens no." I nearly spit out my lemon cake at the idea. "I don't think I should challenge those paintings when I have no reputation of my own."

"I agree," Lavinia said. "There's too much history. Of course, you must do a Judith at some point in your career, but not yet. I'd almost like to try one myself, but my appointment to the Papal Court has me painting cardinals and their mistresses. No, you need some known subject upon which you can work your point of view, but not one recently painted by anyone of note."

"Must it be religious?" I asked. I wished I didn't already know the answer to this question. "It would be great fun to make one of the Greek goddesses do something heroic or scandalous. Diana hunting bad men with a pack of vicious dogs or something like that."

"No Greeks or Romans. You know better." Lavinia frowned at me. "And remember, there's religious and then there's biblical, if you take my meaning. I'd advise against any sad-faced saints or perfect Madonnas, but the Bible is full of stories of strong women. You could take your pick."

Just then, Signor Zappi came in and kissed his wife's cheek. "Darling, Casoni is here to take your silhouette. I've taken him up to your studio," he said.

"Tell him I'll be right there," Lavinia said. She tipped her head so her husband could kiss her on the lips, then watched him as he left the room. "The pope desires a medallion struck in my image and Casoni is here to start the work. It's a bit embarrassing."

I thought it sounded grand and entirely thrilling. Maybe one day a pope would want my image on a medallion. Wouldn't that be something?

We stood to make our goodbyes, and Lavinia clasped me in a light hug. "You will have to work twice as hard and for half as much money, but you'll do fine if you stay true to your art. And before I go, here is my best piece of advice."

"What?" I blurted like some great fool.

Lavinia chuckled. "Marry a good man who is also a bad painter. He'll be only too glad to give up his career and manage the household so you can paint. And because he once himself painted, he'll understand your work and take care of you as well as my Zappi does. I've had eleven children; did you know that?" Her expression turned downcast. "All but three have passed on to heaven, but I still have my dear Zappi."

"Marry a nice man," I repeated. If only I'd known how difficult it would be to follow that simple advice.

~

I watched out the window as the hired carriage next took me to Saint Peter's. I could have walked the distance, but respectable women did not walk about Rome alone. The city was safe enough, but rules like that are often about something else, aren't they?

I saw the grand dome of Saint Peter's towering above the rest of the buildings around the Vatican. Like any Roman, I knew Emperor Constantine the Great had ordered the original Saint Peter's built. That first Saint Peter's formed the basis for Vatican City, built on the former site of Nero's Circus. The insane Emperor Nero had crucified the Apostle Peter right where the basilica stood today.

A hundred years ago, Pope Julius had the old church torn down and began a new one. Everyone said Saint Peter's was the greatest building in Christendom, and I believed it. I'd visited Saint Peter's several times with Papà, but each time I saw the great basilica I felt a kind of awe—it was like no other building in Rome, and that was saying something. Rome had a multitude of great churches.

The carriage driver stopped just inside the Vatican walls, at the front of the piazza that spread before Saint Peter's. I was wondering if it would be decent to cross that great, sacred space alone when I heard someone call my name. The carriage door swung open to reveal Michelangelo Buonarroti the Younger. "Uncle Michaelo!" I squealed.

He hugged me so tightly, he squeezed the breath out of me.

Uncle Michaelo isn't a real uncle to me, but he's one of Papà's good friends and we consider him family. He is also the great-nephew and heir of the same Michelangelo who was the architect for Saint Peter's and painted the ceiling of the Sistine Chapel.

"I didn't know you were in Rome," I said when he released me. "Have you finally admitted Rome is a far greater city than Florence?"

"Never." He smiled a thin-lipped smile. "I've nearly finished my dictionary and the Vatican has agreed to publish it. The Republic of Venice has also offered to publish it, so I'm deciding which city shall have the honor. But no dictionary today. Instead, I shall serve as your guide as we tour my granduncle's greatest works."

As we walked across the piazza toward the massive colonnades that fronted the basilica, I saw the ongoing construction. It was the same all through Rome. Pope Julius and Pope Clement had been great builders who had filled Rome with grand new churches and public buildings. Saint Peter's was by far the largest of the city's building projects and it seemed as if it would never be finished. "Can we go inside the basilica, or just the chapel?"

"Ah, the work on the facade is nearly complete, and Cesari is working on the mosaics for my granduncle's dome as we speak. But neither project should impede our tour, and it is the chapel to which we must devote most of our time. Dear Orazio tells me he wants you to pay particular attention to the Sistine paintings." He grinned at me again, then held out his crooked arm. I took it with pleasure.

We spent an hour inside Saint Peter's, though the massive scale of the basilica made it impossible to see even a tenth of its exquisite beauty in such a time. Michelangelo had redesigned the building's astounding ovoid dome so it was the largest in the world. Workers had completed the dome not quite twenty years earlier, but Uncle and I agreed its grandeur made it worth the three-decade effort. We spared a few quiet minutes in the Pieta Chapel, gazing at Michelangelo's sculpture of Mary with her dead son draped across her lap.

"He was only twenty-four when he carved it," Uncle Michaelo whispered. That anyone could make such reverential beauty, let alone someone so young, astounded me. I sighed a little.

Uncle Michaelo leaned in close. "I know just how you feel," he said, whispering again. Everyone whispered when they stood before the *Pieta*. "To stand in front of such greatness is to confront one's mediocrity."

We left Saint Peter's feeling chastened and small, but the Sistine Chapel's brightly colored frescoes swept away the gray in no time. Every time I visited this chapel, I marveled at the contrast between the building's plain exterior and exuberant interior— like Lavinia's house, but on a monumental scale. Michaelo and I walked up and down the long central aisle, reviewing the wall frescoes. The frescoes had been divided into three tiers, interrupted by six windows on each side. The lowest tier contained mostly paintings of gold and silver draperies, offering little for the eye, while the topmost tier featured cranky-looking popes.

But the middle tier, that's where you found the real art—vibrant portrayals of Moses and Jesus going about their holy business in paintings so vivid, so detailed, they looked like real life.

I stopped in front of Pietro Perugino's *Christ Giving the Keys to Saint Peter*. "I love the blues and greens in this. Everyone says the Botticellis are the finer paintings," I said, waving at the *Temptations of Christ* at the other end of the chapel's north wall, "but he overcrowds his works."

"Botticelli's colors are not so vibrant as Perugino's either," Uncle Michaelo said. "Granduncle liked the bright colors too." Uncle waved his hand at the ceiling. "I'll tell you something few people know. My dear Granduncle didn't want to paint this ceiling. He hated leaving Florence, so he told Pope Julius he'd only take the chapel ceiling job if he could paint God's creation from Genesis. He'd heard the pope wanted scenes from the lives of saints, so he thought the pope would refuse him and hire another artist. But the pope liked the Genesis idea."

"It sounds like Pope Julius tricked Michelangelo," I said.

"Maybe," Uncle Michaelo said with a grin. "You know, my granduncle never really considered himself a painter. He always said he was an architect and sculptor."

I turned my eyes up to the chapel's barrel ceiling. It had once been painted blue with scattered gold and silver stars, or so Papà said. Now it was an overwhelming visual feast. Most of the images were male, though there were some female prophets scattered here and there. All of Michelangelo's women looked like men with breasts, and I wasn't the only one to say so. Roman gossips said the artist had spent too much time with men to understand the female form. I thought that might be true of many men. They also said Michelangelo had no interest in women in general. It didn't matter much to me; anyone who could paint like him could do as he pleased.

I pointed to a figure seated on painted steps. "See the scale of his Cumaean Sibyl?" I asked. "Her arms are as muscled as a blacksmith's and her legs and feet are massive, as if she sprung from the earth like some old forest god. I tried to do something like that with my second Madonna's lower body, though she's nowhere near so formidable. I also like the hands on the male figure next to her—it looks as if he was fending off a blow, though from where I don't know."

Michaelo stared upward. "I'd never noticed that. He's curiously vulnerable, isn't he? So unlike the Sibyls. The Libyan Sibyl might be a man, she's so muscular and commanding."

As we stared up at those juxtaposed figures, I had a kernel of an idea for my painting. What if I could contrast female vulnerability with womanly strength? That might set me apart from other painters of women. I tucked the idea away for later consideration and returned to my examination of Michelangelo's greatest work.

After a few hours, Uncle Michaelo left me at the piazza gates, claiming he couldn't look at any more paintings. "My brain will explode if I go with you to the Quirinal Palace," he said. "I shall take to my downy bed and contemplate my failures." He kissed me on the cheek and sent me on my way, assuring me he'd join Papà and me for dinner before he returned to Florence.

The papal summer palace lay across the Tiber River, atop one of Rome's famous seven hills and not far from the Coliseum. The air around the river felt hot and heavy and smelled like rotten fish, but as the carriage climbed the hill a breeze freshened and cooled the air. No wonder the last three popes had made the Quirinal Palace their summer home.

A maidservant took me to the Sala del Concistoro, where I found Papà working on a border near the ceiling. When he saw me, he shouted with joy and climbed down the scaffolding quicker than a man his age ought to.

"Agostino, come down," he hollered to a man working on another scaffold. "You must meet my daughter."

The man clambered down and strode over to where we stood. He was a portly fellow, not much taller than myself, with dark hair that curled around his ears. He bowed to me with a dandyish flourish and kissed my hand, his lips lingering wetly a second or two longer than was usual. I resisted the urge to pull back my hand, an impulse Signor Tassi must have sensed. He squeezed my fingers briefly but roughly, then let go, only to meet my eyes with a bold stare. A thinly lashed eyelid slid down into a wink. I was too shocked to do anything but take a step back.

Papà missed the entire exchange, having turned toward the nearby fresco. "Look at this, my daughter," he said. "See how Signor Tassi excels at architectural painting?"

Tassi waved a hand. "Bah, it is nothing. Painting people is the real artistic challenge, and you, Orazio, you are my superior in that."

Despite Tassi's modesty, the work was quite good. It showed

steps and a colonnade in the foreground, then another building behind that, with a fleet of ship masts behind the second building. "It looks so real, I feel as if I could step onto the street," I admitted.

"It's his mastery of perspective that creates that illusion," Papà said. "I could never do that well."

Tassi rocked on his heels. "It is a simple matter of mathematics, architectural drawing, and certain tricks of shading. I could teach it to you in a matter of months."

Papà shook his head. "I am too old to learn, but my daughter is not."

Tassi turned to me. "Your father says you are talented." The man's eyes made me nervous and my lips clamped together so no words could come out. "Ah, a modest young woman," Tassi murmured. "I congratulate you, Signor Gentileschi. So few women these days know to keep their tongues behind their teeth. And she is so beautiful."

Papà chuckled. "She is not usually so quiet. I suspect your talent silences her."

"Perhaps I could give your daughter lessons?" Tassi said, stroking his chin.

"What a fine idea," Papà said. "Don't you think so, daughter? You would be more employable if you could paint the sort of landscape frescoes our friend Tassi does so well."

Before I could answer, Tassi spoke up. "Sir, you don't mean to suggest your daughter would paint in a public place such as this palace. It would be most inappropriate and unladylike."

Papà agreed. "But there are plenty of private houses that might prefer to hire a woman painter." Papà waved at Tassi's fresco and said, "What do you think, Artemisia?"

Tassi took advantage of the fact that Papà had turned his back to stare at me. His eyes began at my chest and traveled down my body, then back up. I wanted to refuse Tassi's offer, but I had no good reason to. "That sounds fine, Papà," I said.

He didn't notice how my voice wavered as I spoke.

Chapter Two

I wiped the sweat from my brow and stepped back to appraise the work. There were several more layers of color to apply, but my *Susanna and the Elders* was coming to life. Paintings are like that. First, you sketch, then lay in the outlines and blocks of color, and then you begin the laborious process of layering paint. You work on it for months and it sits there on the easel like a dead thing. Then one day you walk into the workroom and find the work has experienced a kind of alchemical miracle. You can almost feel it breathe as it comes to life and becomes real. *Susanna* had done that this morning.

My initial sketches had been of a more defiant Susanna. The Susanna I'd seen at Lavinia Fontana's house showed Susanna at the moment of her bath, with the elders looking on. I meant to shift Susanna to the moment when she refused the elders' advances. I sketched her standing by her bath, largely covered by a drying sheet, clearly refusing the men. I planned a Susanna who would be heroic in scale and build, like Michelangelo's

Cumaean Sibyl, who looked so strong and unassailable. But that had been before Agostino Tassi made my life living misery.

Tassi had started coming to the Piazza di Spagna house not long after I first met him. Papà would show him to our shared studio, then leave us alone. The father I knew would never have left me alone with a man, but Tassi was my painting instructor and Papà didn't want to interfere with my lessons. At least, that's what I told myself. At first, Tassi confined himself to teaching me perspective—which was hard because I had to learn some math. But even in those early lessons, there'd be the occasional sly touch of my hand. In only a few weeks, he'd progressed to lewd remarks about his sexual prowess and my attractiveness. It was disgusting, but I tried to ignore it or pretend I was too innocent to understand his meaning.

One day he leaned against me as I stood at the easel. He pressed himself against my back so I could feel his manly appendage pressing into my skirts. I tried to squirm away, but he knew how to trap me against the drawing table. After several weeks of leaning and touching, he began to bring his friend Cosimo Quorli to the house. Signor Quorli had a position in Pope Paul's court and Papà thought it was a great honor that he visited our humble home. Papà didn't know Quorli was nearly as aggressive as Tassi, and twice as oily.

Tuzia, our housekeeper, should have been in the room with us whenever Signor Quorli came to call, but most days she let the two men come upstairs alone. I began to suspect the men were paying Tuzia to stay away, though I couldn't bring myself to ask her about it. Once, Tuzia had been nice to me—a mother, almost—but not anymore. It was like she'd decided I was a bad woman and didn't want to associate with me.

It was all so confusing. What had I done to encourage these men? How had I become a bad woman? I would lay in bed at night, thinking about how it started and trying to figure out where I'd gone wrong.

The worst of it was that I couldn't tell Papà. Even if I didn't feel so ashamed, I still couldn't tell Papà. He needed Tassi right now. Poor Papà had troubles of his own. It started last summer, when news of Signor Caravaggio's death reached Rome. When the great painter first came to Rome years ago, he had revealed his dramatic yet realistic painting style with two genre-changing paintings from the life of Saint Matthew. They were unlike anything anyone else had ever painted, all extremes of dark and light and figures that looked flawed and real. People went wild for Caravaggio. Cardinals and rich merchants alike vied for his works, and every painter in Rome declared either for or against his new style of painting.

I'll never forget the day Papà took me to the Contarelli Chapel to see *The Calling of Saint Matthew*. Its stark contrasts of light and shadow, the beam of light that pointed at Matthew like the finger of God, the common room setting—it mesmerized both Papà and me. This was no Matthew on a cloud surrounded by angels and bathed in golden light. No, he was grubby and penitent and confused and so very real. We stood before the painting for over an hour, letting it wash over us and quietly pointing out its remarkable aspects. After that, Papà shifted his technique to emulate Caravaggio's. He even made friends with the brilliant painter, though it hadn't taken long for Caravaggio to reveal himself. How a man of such low moral character could paint such inspiring paintings, I'll never know. As Papà said, Caravaggio painted like an angel and lived like a devil. He drank too much, dallied with attractive young men, and had a fondness for duels. He even embroiled Papà in a lawsuit. Something about public brawling, but I am not sure—Papà was so ashamed, he wouldn't speak of it.

Then Signor Caravaggio killed a man in a sword fight, which was doubly bad because duels were illegal. Only noblemen were supposed to carry swords in the first place. The painter left Rome to avoid murder charges, then resurfaced in Naples the next year. It didn't take long for Caravaggio's Roman problems to catch up with him there, so the artist fled again, this time to Malta. There he'd joined the prestigious Knights of Malta and for a time settled down to a sober and Christian life. Or so we heard. It's hard to know for sure. All that had been bad for Papà, who'd gotten a reputation as Rome's leading Caravaggisti. Papà weathered the storm only because his idol kept painting works that shook and delighted the art world.

After that, Signor Caravaggio either wounded or killed one of the Maltese knights—no one seemed to know the real story—and the ruffian painter disappeared. He later showed up in Sicily, where everyone said he acted crazy for months, before moving back to Naples. Caravaggio died there, where it was said his behavior had reached new heights of outrage. Gossips said syphilis, contracted in low bawdy houses, made him crazy and killed him.

As a result, starting last summer, no one wanted anything to do with the Carvaggisti style. When Papà's commissions dried up, we had to move, first to Villa della Croce and then to an even more dilapidated place across the Tiber River. We settled in Sassia, near the Santo Spirito church. The neighborhood may once have been nice, but in those days it housed a great number of Rome's prostitutes. Nightly the streets filled with that species of men who availed themselves to fallen women. Sword-carrying gentlemen roamed the streets in the arms of their current favorite, drinking and fighting and generally causing an uproar. The irony that Rome disapproved of Caravaggio but tolerated Sassia was not lost on Papà and me.

Now we'd nearly run through the money from Papà's *Saint Jerome*, which he'd finished just before news of Caravaggio's death came to Rome. That's when Tassi found Papà a job painting frescoes at Cardinal Scipione Borghese's new palazzo. The cardinal had a great fondness for the disgraced Caravaggio. Because Cardinal Borghese was the nephew of Pope Paul, he had the political power to ignore Caravaggio's scandals. Borghese hired Tassi, who brought in Papà and several more Roman painters, most of them Caravaggistis, to paint *A Musical Concert Sponsored by Apollo and the Muses*. Tassi had gone so far as to paint me into the ceiling as a fan-wielding concertgoer. No doubt he thought the image was so sufficiently flattering that I'd give up my virtue to him. Papà delighted in the flattery that comes with finding your daughter's image in the cardinal's grand palazzo. I played along with the farce, though the painting wasn't at all flattering. I'm no great beauty, but nor am I a thick-waisted matron with dull hair.

I'm sure Papà would kill Tassi if he knew what he'd been up to, and Quorli too, if I'm honest. Caravaggio, with his connections to the pope's favored nephew, might get away with murder, but not Orazio Gentileschi. And then where would Papà and I be? If they executed Papà, he wouldn't be around to stop the wretched Tassi from making good on his threat to force me into marriage. And Tassi has said often enough that when we marry, he'd share me with his friend Quorli. How disgusting is that?

And so my Susanna painting changed. All I could think about was this situation with Tassi and I didn't have the heart to paint Susanna defiant, not when I felt sick and frightened. I threw away my sketches and despaired. Then I had an idea. I turned back to tradition, except instead of a Susanna whose eroticism implied she enjoyed the male attention, my Susanna curled defensively before them, her hands upraised to ward off the old men. And the elders, rather than innocently enjoying themselves, hung above Susanna in a predatory and menacing manner. I'll be honest, I took my cues from Rubens's *Susanna and the Elders*. He too had painted predatory elders and a frightened Susanna, but I like to think my Susanna was more obviously terrified.

To make my point clearer, I'd painted Susanna in pearly pinks and creamy yellows, so she glowed with an inner light. The men, on the other hand, I painted in umber and shadow, with dark storm clouds looming behind them. I shaped the composition as an inverted triangle, with the men creating a strong line across the top third of the canvas and Susanna's foot the downward-facing point. The arrangement created a pleasing balance at odds with the uncomfortable dynamic between the three figures.

I'd briefly toyed with the idea of painting Tassi's face on one of the men, but decided that was a step too far. The thing was distressing enough just as it was, and if I was too obvious, I'd be announcing Tassi's behavior to the world—and with it, my shame. That wouldn't be good, not for me or Papà. Still, maybe Tassi would get the message. Or maybe Papà would see how it was with me. Maybe.

As I dabbed more ochre on the second man's cloak, I heard a door slam downstairs. My heart jumped. *Not today. Please, not today*, I thought. But Papà was at the palazzo and my two admirers nearly always came when he was away. "Tuzia, is that you?" I called out. I silently damned myself for the quaver in my voice.

"No, it's me," came Papà's voice.

I took a deep breath to steady myself and put down my brush. Then I picked it up again when I heard Papà's footsteps on the stairs. *Act like nothing's wrong*, I told myself.

Papà burst into our small studio in a flurry of flying cloak and waving hair. "I came home early because there was nothing more I could paint today. Would you like to take a walk? It's not very hot out. We could stop at that place you like and have a glass of cold wine." He kept his eyes on my face as he talked, as if he feared what he'd see if he looked at my canvas.

I stifled a sigh. He never really looked at the Susanna. It was as if he didn't want to see the truth, and I could hardly blame him. I didn't like it much either.

~

By the end of the summer, my life had become a nightmare I couldn't escape. Quorli would come to the house while Papà and Tassi were working at the palazzo. Despite his favored position in the pope's court, I found Quorli entirely repugnant. He seemed to never wash, only rub more and more perfumed oils into his hair and skin. He reminded me of a glistening roast piglet, a resemblance not helped by his pug nose and protruding yellow teeth.

Just this afternoon, he'd come into the kitchen while I was peeling lemons and Tuzia was at the baker's shop picking up tomorrow's bread.

"More than all the stars in the night sky, that is how much I love you," he stammered. He gripped the rough wood of the kitchen table and leaned across it as if he thought his lips could cover the divide.

I stood my ground on the opposite side of the table. "If you loved me, you would leave me alone. You frighten me and I want you to go away," I said coolly, fighting the urge to yell. It would ruin my reputation if the neighbors heard me talking to him without a chaperone.

"I cannot leave you. I yearn for your touch." He spat a little as he spoke, and dashed around the end of the table.

I skittered left to keep the table between us. "I will never love you. Go away before you ruin me."

"Bitch," he hissed. "You have bewitched me, and now you torture me."

"This is the way you talk to the woman you love?"

He slammed his hand on the table so hard, the cups and plates jumped. "Foul temptress, I will ruin you, you wait and see. Some slut of a painter's daughter will not deny Cosimo Quorli."

He stormed out of the kitchen, leaving me alone. I wanted to yell after him, "I'm a painter, not just a painter's daughter," but it seemed beside the point.

The next day, both Tassi and Quorli arrived at the house just after Papà left for the palazzo. I was still in bed when I heard them in the kitchen with Tuzia. *Not good, not good*, I thought. I grabbed my everyday dress, the one I wear for painting, and pulled it over my head. Jamming my bare feet into a pair of wool slippers far too warm for the morning, I rushed down the stairs to head them off.

"Agostino, what brings you here so early?" I asked him, ignoring Quorli. He didn't get to insult me one day and expect civility the next. I also ignored Tuzia, who stood just outside the kitchen door, grinning like someone had given her a present. I spared a moment to wonder when Tuzia had had become my enemy before I turned my attention to the two men.

"We came to break our fasts with you," Tassi replied with a courtly bow. Behind him, Quorli scowled and made a rude gesture.

All the rage I'd slept off overnight instantly bubbled back up. I pointed first at Tassi and then at Quorli. "Why do you bring that terrible man here?" I demanded.

Tassi pulled his silken flat cap off his head and slapped it against his leg. "Be quiet, woman," he said. "You should be grateful such a great man pays you attention."

Quorli stepped up beside his brother in sin and said, "You should also be nicer to Agostino. You'd be lucky to get him for a husband."

"Lucky? I'd be lucky if he left me alone. Even luckier if both of you did."

"When you give yourself to every man who gives you a look?" Quorli said.

Tuzia cackled in glee as her eyes darted between the three of us.

I snorted in a most unladylike manner. "I am a maid and a virtuous woman. Your friend Tassi doesn't treat me as a gentleman treats a lady. Neither of you should even be here," I said, sparing a scowl at Quorli. "And you, sir, are a scoundrel. Do you think I've forgotten yesterday?"

At that moment, our neighbor Signor Barberini poked his head into the kitchen. "What's all this racket?" he squawked in his rusty old man voice. "I haven't even had my morning wine and I hear the quack-quack of a flock of unruly ducks. Go away and leave this girl alone." He waved his shirttail at the men and glared at them from beneath lowered brows.

As the two men pulled on their hats and scampered away like chastened children, I lowered my eyes, knowing men didn't like women to see them in ignominious defeat. When I looked up, Signor Barberini had disappeared. I made a note to kiss the old man's balding head later that day and maybe even listen to one of his interminable jokes. He had only three and told them over and over, each time as delighted as the first.

The next day, Tassi gave Tuzia a piece of cloth big enough to make a cloak for her oldest boy. It was a bribe. He wanted her to talk to Papà and get his permission to take me for evening walks. I know this because she later told me while she showed me the length of fabric.

Papà thought walks were a delightful idea. "It's not healthy for you to stay in the house all the time, my dear. Signor Tassi will walk in the vineyards with you," he said.

I didn't know what to say to such a repugnant idea, so I tried to retort with propriety. "It's not proper for unmarried women to go out in the evening," I said. Papà thought I was being difficult, but I insisted, so he withdrew his consent for the walks.

My victory was short-lived. Tassi redoubled his efforts to get me alone. He followed me home from church each evening. I'd catch glimpses of him loitering in the graveyard and though I was careful never to look back, I sensed him behind me like a starving wolf trailing a deer. One night, Papà saw Tassi outside our house, but Tassi told him some men had been bothering me and he'd protected me. He even told Papà he'd beaten several men on my behalf, which was total nonsense but seemed to impress Papà.

It went on like that for a long while. Weeks later, Tassi caught me working on a painting of Tuzia's oldest son, a boy of only eight years old, and flew into a jealous rage. He told me he didn't want me to look at any other men but himself, then he threw my paints against the wall. He even broke my best brush. It sounds foolish now, but it was frightening at the time. I never knew when he'd appear or what he'd do when he did. I would jump at the slightest sounds and couldn't sleep at all.

On the morning of the worst day of my life, Tassi appeared in my studio just as I began to paint. He knew Papà wouldn't be home for hours and he was acting weird. He walked around the room two or three times, his heels thumping on the floorboards. He'd stop to look out the window, then circle and tip forward paintings he found against the wall, look, let them go with a thump, and walk again. After about ten minutes of this excruciating behavior, I broke the silence. "I've been ill today," I said. "I have a fever." It was my way of telling him to go away.

"Oh, I have a fever far hotter than yours," he said. He grabbed me by the neck and dragged me toward the door. I struggled against him, but his arm was like steel against my throat. I grabbed the little table where I kept my paints, I don't know why, and tipped it over with a great clatter. He dragged me out of the studio and into my bedroom. There he put his hands between my shoulder blades and shoved me across the room. I stumbled onto the bed as he locked the door. Then he was on me, tearing and hitting and howling. He tore at my bodice, exposing my breasts, and grabbed one and squeezed it until I heard myself squeal. This is not happening. *This is not happening*, I thought.

Next he thrust a knee between my legs and levered me up until I could not close my legs. I screamed, and before I knew it he'd stuffed a corner of my blanket into my open mouth. He let go of me to unbutton his pants but he kept his lower body pinned to mine. I turned my head so I wouldn't have to see his face.

That's when I saw the little knife I kept for sharpening my sketching pencils. It lay on the little table next to my bed, where I'd left it last night after using it to clean paint from under my fingernails. I grabbed it and swung it at his back, but he was wearing too many clothes to make much impact. Still, he screamed with rage and wrenched the knife from my hand. He held it to my throat and kept on with his business. Of the next few minutes, I can say little. The memories of pain and humiliation have never left me.

When finished his business, he hit me across the face. "That's for the knife," he said. He stood to button his pants.

I rolled onto the floor. "I wish I'd killed you. You've ruined me."

He laughed at me then. *Laughed*—as if it had all been a game. He opened his coat wide and said, "Here I am."

I grabbed my little knife up from where he'd dropped it on the floor. With all my might I threw it at him, but it bounced off his shirt and fell to the floor. I am ashamed to say I burst into tears.

He kneeled next to me on the floor. "Give me your hand." In a hard voice, he said, "I promise to marry you as soon as I can. But I warn you, when I take you as my wife, I will not tolerate any of this foolishness with knives and crying." He rose to his feet and left me there, bleeding from what he'd done to me.

~

My troubles did not end with my rape. Tassi would not be content with dishonoring me once. No, not he, the devil he was. The first time he came to me after the rape, he found me in the tiny garden behind our house. The day had been cloudy and dark and bad for painting. Instead, I had my sketchbook open, though I could not concentrate well enough to draw even the simplest flower. My body was still as sore as my heart and I could not get the images of that horrible day out of my head. And then I heard steps. I looked up and he was there.

He held out his hand. "Come, my wife. I require your services."

"I am not your wife," I whispered.

He smiled, dropped his hand, and said, "But you are, for who else would have you now? My first wife is dead and I have claimed you as mine."

I shook my head, unable to say anything.

He took several steps closer to me, his smile never leaving his face. "You know what you must do. You are ruined for any other man and I have marked you as my own. Why must you fight me? Do you want me to tell your father you have given yourself to me?"

"I did not," I protested. "You forced me."

He frowned. "I understand you are a modest woman, but between you and me there must be no lies. Not if we are to be man and wife. You wanted me but could not admit it, not even to yourself. I sensed your longing and answered with my own.

And now you still play reluctant maiden when we both know the truth."

I could only stare at him. It hadn't been that way, of that much I was sure. Everything in me rebelled against this man.

He took another step closer and again raised his hand to me. "Come. You have no choice. Act the wife with me or I shall tell Orazio you are a whore. I shall tell everyone and give you to Signor Quorli, and anyone else I am pleased to bring here. You can be my whore or you can be my wife. Come with me and be my wife." He thrust his hand at me.

God help me, but I took it, rose, and followed Tassi into the house. What choice did I have?

After that, Tassi came every few days. After Papà had gone to work, Tassi would enter Papà's house through Tuzia's apartment and do what he would to me.

Once, after Agostino left, I found Tuzia in the kitchen and asked her why she let this happen.

"You and your father," she spat. "You think you are so fine, but you are peasants. You serve the rich just the same as if you cooked their food, emptied their chamber pots, and washed their dirty undergarments."

I peered into her brown eyes, set in a tired, lined face. "Why do you hate me so?" I asked.

"Do?" She wheezed a dry sound of amusement. "It is what you are. Fine Signora Gentileschi, who doesn't have to cook or clean or learn anything a respectable young woman would learn to make herself fit for marriage. You walk around this house with your nose in the air while I, Tuzia, do all the work."

Without thinking, I said, "But that's your job!"

"Job, bah." She pursed her dry lips and spat on the floor. "It is true that you pay me. With that money I keep my sons and daughters fed and clothed, but none of them will ever be as fine as Signora Artemisia Gentileschi. Yet you are no better than the granddaughter of a dirty blacksmith. Do you think I can afford to apprentice my boys with the pittance your father pays me? At least Signor Tassi recognizes my worth." She turned back to the stove, where she had been stirring a large pot of white beans with garlic.

I stared at her back, unable to comprehend the depth of her hatred. Her husband had died four years before, just after the birth of their fifth child, leaving her an aged woman with too many children and not enough money to support them. But we paid her and treated her kindly, and still she sold me to Tassi for thirty pieces of silver, knowing what he did to me? Were we not both women? I would never understand her betrayal.

Months went by and nothing changed. Agostino continued to insist we would marry someday. He just had to clear up some legal problems with his first wife's death, or so he said. Sometimes Agostino, for so he insisted I call him, sent his sister-in-law Costanza to fetch me to his house. Costanza had married Agostino's brother, who died several years before. She remarried an older man who didn't seem to care what she did. I'm sure she had carnal relations with Agostino, but knowing what I knew of him, I didn't know if he forced her or if she liked it. Not that I cared. What good would that do me?

Costanza would arrive in a hired carriage and pretend to be my friend. Papà would let me leave with her, glad I had a friend as elegant as Signora Tassi to take me places. Sometimes Quorli would be at the Tassi villa, and if Agostino had not yet arrived, Quorli would say terrible things and try to get me to bed. I refused time and time again, both because I found the man repugnant and because, as much as I hated the idea, marriage to Tassi was now my only hope. He had ruined me and only he could save me from public disgrace.

My relations with Agostino eventually reached a kind of settled place, at least as far as he was concerned. He would take me to bed and I would let him. I would make myself dead inside when he touched me and I'd send my mind far away. Thinking about paintings helped, though invariably I'd see Holofernes's decapitated head in the Judith I'd painted for Papà—only it wasn't Holofernes's head anymore; it was Agostino's.

Each month, I anxiously awaited my womanly courses, terrified they would not come. But they did. Quorli told me Agostino's wife left him because he could not give her babies. Quorli thought this fact would turn me toward him, which shows you how dumb he was. How could he imagine I would want children from this situation?

One afternoon, Agostino burst into my studio and, without a word, slapped me. He hit me so hard, I fell against the wall. "Bitch! Whore! What have you done?" he shouted.

Stunned, I focused on the blue daubed paintbrush I'd dropped on the floor. Azure is too expensive to waste.

He stood over me and screamed, his eyes wild and utterly mad, "Why would you do this to me when I love you so? Why?"

Keeping my eyes on the paintbrush I asked, "Do what?"

He kicked my leg and shrieked, "You betrayed me with Signor Quorli." He kicked me again.

I tried not to shudder. I should have seen this coming. I looked up into Agostino's eyes. He needed to believe me. If I failed, he would surely beat me until I died. "I did not. He is a worm compared to you, my darling."

Agostino balled his fists and bounced them off his thighs, but I could see tears in his eyes. "You have never before called me your darling."

I pushed myself up and kneeled before him. "But is that not what you are? My soon-to-be husband and protector? My one and only man? Why would I share myself with that toad Quorli when I have you?"

He burst into tears and lifted me to my feet. He pinned my arms to my side and shook me. "If you ever give yourself to another, I shall kill myself, but not before I kill you first," he seethed. "Understand?"

I did. All too well.

Chapter Three

ROME, THE PAPAL STATES
1612–1613

From downstairs came the sound of a knock on the door. I glanced out the window to confirm the time. In midsummer, the sun doesn't set until just before the ten o'clock bells and it was nearly full dark outside. Who would come calling this late? I started down the stairs when I heard Papà's voice.

"Thank you for coming, Agostino," he said.

My heart began to pound. Did Papà ask Agostino to come to the house? At this time of night? Did he know?

The sound of my tormentor's voice, smooth as oiled paper, sounded on the night air. "Your message made it sound urgent. Of course I came. What can I help you with, old friend?"

"Come out of the hall," Papà said.

I heard the sound of shoe heels clicking on the floor, then the thunk of a closing door.

I crept down the stairs barefoot, careful to avoid the third step from the bottom. I didn't want the squeak to alert Papà to my presence. I'm sure he thought I was sleeping and I wanted to keep it that way.

Four steps took me across the front hall to the door of the small room Papà used as a study. I pressed my ear against the wood, my heart beating so hard it felt as if Papà would surely hear it.

Papà's chair creaked like it did when he leaned back in it. I had time to wonder why Papà had not offered Agostino a glass of wine or grappa when I heard the younger man speak.

"You look troubled, my friend."

"I am," Papà said. "I have been speaking with a friend and have heard things that do you no credit."

"Gossip. It's so unreliable," Agostino said. "And after all this time we've been working together, you understand what sort of man I am."

"I begin to think I know nothing at all."

"Come, tell me what you heard so I may put your mind at rest."

Papà's chair creaked again as he said, "The most worrisome is about your wife."

"My wife? I have no wife," Agostino said. "Much to my distress, she died two years ago."

"Ah, but did she? Your neighbors all say that one day she was there, and then she was gone."

"Because she died. Of course she wasn't home anymore. My poor Valentina sickened and died in the night."

Papà sighed. "But your neighbors say there was no funeral

feast or death rites. She just disappeared. And there is more gossip, as I'm sure you're aware, that you caused her death."

I couldn't believe what I was hearing. Had Agostino done something nefarious?

Agostino gasped. "Sir, do you accuse me, your old friend, of some crime?"

"My source says you hired bandits to kidnap Signora Tassi and murder her."

"What? Who is this source? Clearly, he is a bad man who has led you astray. We've been friends for a long time, Orazio. Would I do these things?"

I knew the answer to that question. Agostino was selfish, violent, and more than a little crazy. He could certainly kill his wife or have her killed.

There was a pause before Papà's voice came again. "I have heard these things and more from Giovanni Battista Stiattesi. He is a good and honest man."

Papà wasn't wrong. Signor Stiattesi was a good friend who brokered all of Papà's painting commissions and notarized the sales. He also walked to mass every morning and gave alms to the poor, and he fed stray cats in his garden. There was no kinder, truer man in Rome than Giovanni Stiattesi.

"I cannot believe I have to say this, but I swear on your daughter's head that I did not kill my wife," Agostino said.

After another long pause, Papà said, "Signor Stiattesi tells me others say your wife is not dead but merely ran away from you. They say you beat her and worse."

"Worse?" Agostino screeched. "Worse than beating and murdering her?"

"Yes," Papà said with a hint of steel. "On Signor Stiattesi's advice, I checked with the Papal Court. Last fall, you were charged with incest with your sister-in-law, Costanza. Her testimony was that you had violent relations with both your wife and herself after your brother died."

"Yet I was not convicted." Agostino's voice had turned to the sneering tone he so often took with me. "I am guilty of no crime."

"Perhaps not. I thought you were a good man when I agreed to let you court her."

I jerked my ear from the door and stepped back. No. I must have misheard. Papà had agreed to a courtship? Did that mean he knew about Agostino and me? And what was this about Costanza? Utterly confused, I put my ear back to the door.

"I still intend to marry your daughter, just as we agreed," Agostino said. "It's just this difficulty with my wife—it is some mix-up about her death. Until I get the paperwork straightened out, I am not free to marry. But the second I am, I will take her straight to the church door."

"I fear I made a great mistake with you," Papà groaned. "In my eagerness to find my daughter a good husband who would ignore her lack of dowry, I delivered her into the hands of a villain. Now you've ruined her and have not married her, as you promised."

"I have *not* ruined her. You must trust me, Orazio. I have

many enemies and they lie about me. I am a good man and I will make your daughter my wife as soon as I'm free."

I heard their chairs scuffle and, fearing discovery, fled back up the stairs. I couldn't stand many more revelations anyway. How much could a poor girl know before her head and heart exploded from shock and dismay? I sat on the edge of my bed and thought. All this time I'd been keeping my secret, letting Agostino do what he would to me, all to protect Papà, and he'd known the whole time? Could it be?

A night of contemplation left me with several uncomfortable realizations. First, however much Agostino professed otherwise, he wasn't ever going to marry me. Whatever the reason for his wife's disappearance, she wasn't legally dead and he wasn't free to marry. Second, Agostino was a monster, and not just with me. He'd preyed on at least three women and God knew how many more. Third, I was irrevocably tied to this monster, and sooner or later, everyone in Sassia would know I was no better than his mistress.

By dawn, I'd formulated a plan. When Papà left for the day, I sprang from bed and dressed in my best dress, the same one I'd worn last year to meet Lavinia Fontana. I tied my hair back with a yellow silk ribbon and dabbed a bit of lavender oil behind my ears to give me confidence. Then I found Tuzia and told her I'd run out of red paint and needed more realgar crystals. Tuzia didn't like to go to the color shop with me—she thought the place reeked of bad magic, which was pretty stupid. Paint pigments are indeed made from a lot of odd minerals, plants, and even animal materials, much like magical materials, but paint is paint, not magic. For example, the color bone black is pretty much what it sounds like; charred bones make a much blacker black than does lamp char. That doesn't make bone black bad though. It's a color. Not that Tuzia agreed with me, and a good thing too. I didn't need her along for this errand.

I made my way to the other side of the river, near our old neighborhood. Signor Stiattesi answered the door himself, though he was dressed in a house robe and looked as if he hadn't brushed his bushy gray hair. He looked surprised to see me, though he disguised it as best he could. "I am sorry, my dear. I wasn't expecting such lovely company," he said. "Come in, come in."

He motioned me into the house and shut the door behind me before turning and frowning, his brown eyes crinkling in sadness. "My poor dove, you must be so exceedingly upset."

My throat closed at Signor Stiattesi's fatherly sympathy. I opened my mouth to speak and burst into tears. He opened his arms and I stepped into them. I sobbed on his shoulder while he patted me on the back and whispered wordless sounds of pity. When I was done crying, he took me into the room that served as his office.

"Tell me everything. Hold nothing back," he said. "But wait just a moment, I have forgotten my manners." He rang a small bell and, when a kitchen boy appeared, he ordered fruit juice and cheese. When the boy was gone, he motioned me to sit before taking a chair himself.

"Now, tell me. Leave nothing out for modesty's sake. If I am to help you, you must tell me the worst of it. And before you begin, let me assure you, I believe Signor Tassi is one of Rome's greatest villains. Your father does not see the evil in others."

I gathered myself, let out a long breath, and told Signor Stiattesi everything. It took half the morning to get the whole tale out, though it would have taken less time if I hadn't kept stopping to cry. When I got to the part about Quorli's harassment, Signor Stiattesi held up a hand.

"You mean to say both men?"

I felt myself blush. "No, not that," I said. "Signor Quorli says bad things and threatens me, but he has done no more than that."

"No more than threatening a young woman of good family? The man is a scoundrel and should never have been admitted to your father's house. Why does your father allow it?"

I shrugged. "I haven't told him. I was afraid he would do something awful to one or both of the men. Then he would lose his place at the Quirinal or to jail—or be executed."

Stiattesi's face went carefully blank. He took a sip of juice and opened his mouth, then shut it again. His struggle confirmed my suspicions. Papà had known all along. My papà, whom I loved more than anyone in the world, had thrown me to a wolf named Agostino Tassi to advance his own career. "This tale of yours is most distressing, my dear, but I do not see what I can do to stop it if you can't or won't tell your father. You must decide. Do you protect him? Or yourself?"

The truth of these words hit me like a stone falling from a great height. I stood, stammered a hasty goodbye and fled Stiatessi's house.

I walked home under the glaring light of self-realization. There was no hope for me now. And, God help me, I also thought about what my disgrace would do to my life as a painter. Who would buy a painting from a woman who was no better than a courtesan? No one, that's who.

Life went on for several months. Tassi continued to plague me, Tuzia mocked me and Papà pretended all was well. And for him it was. I couldn't bring myself to speak to Papà and he certainly never spoke to me. In the mornings, when the light was good, I worked on the Susanna, feeling more and more like I was painting myself: one woman naked and alone, fending off the advances of two men, unable to do anything to stop them.

Signor Stiattesi came to the house on several occasions, but he acted as if we never had our talk. In fact, he barely acknowledged me when he saw me. He and Papà would closet themselves in Papà's study for an hour, sometimes longer, and emerge looking cranky with each other. I didn't bother to listen in. I was trapped. Listening at doorways hadn't made my situation better. No, it only alerted me to how bad my situation really was.

Then one day in March, arriving home several hours later than usual, Papà called me into his study. I sat in the chair in front of his desk and watched as he fiddled with sketches and generally ignored me.

After several long, awkward moments, I spoke. "Papà, you

asked me to come here, but if you have nothing to say, I would like permission to return to my bed. The sun rises earlier and earlier, and I'm trying to finish the Susanna."

Papà looked up at me, then shifted his eyes to the left. He reminded me of a dog that had just peed on the rug. Finally, he said, "I have come from Lord Decio Cambio's office. I have sworn out a lawsuit against Agostino Tassi."

Lord Cambio was the Vatican's chief notary and the highest legal authority in Rome. I didn't know what to say. "Why?" I asked.

Papà wiped his brow with the back of his hand. "I have charged Signor Tassi with property damage and lost value stemming from his rape of my daughter." Papà paused. "You, I mean."

I shook my head as if to clear my ears. "Why now? It's not as if you didn't know what he's been doing to me the past year."

At this, Papà looked startled. "My dear, I am your father. Do not speak to me this way."

"Just because I am a young woman does not mean I am stupid, Papà. All this time, you had to know and you did nothing. And now you want to protect me?"

He shrugged. "That is my problem. People talk. Everyone in Rome knew that scoundrel was already married—everyone but me."

"And me," I added. "I didn't know." Part of me wanted to tell Papà how I felt when Tassi first raped me. I could explain why I had kept my mouth shut about the whole affair, including Quorli's harassment, but I was still so angry with him that I could hardly speak.

Papà had enough grasp of his shame to blush red. "Lord Cambio has had previous dealings with Agostino and is eager to bring the man before the court once more," he said. "Did you know his real name isn't even Tassi? It's Buonamici, and he comes from a family of common furriers. He wanted people to believe the Marchese Tassi had adopted him."

I shook my head but kept silent. Papà failed to notice the similarity between himself and Tassi's lies about his name. Papà's family name was Lomi, but he'd changed it to Gentileschi to curry favor with a rich Roman uncle. His stepbrother Aurelio, who'd recognized Papà's talents and taught him to paint, still used the Lomi name despite the family's lowborn origins.

"Lord Cambio contends Tassi raped a woman in Livorno and as punishment was sold as a galley slave," Papà said. "Livorno! The man's not even a Roman, though he says he is."

My mind raced and came up with a question. "Why isn't he still rowing a galley somewhere in the Mediterranean?"

"The devil escaped after the sailors took him out of his chains to paint something on the ship. Lord Cambio has no jurisdiction over Tuscan criminals, but he's eager to throw Tassi in a deep, dark dungeon for his Roman transgressions. They're arresting him right now."

I slumped in my chair, unaware until that moment how much I spent each day dreading Tassi's visits. If the authorities had him in custody, he couldn't bother me anymore. For now, at least.

Papà tilted his head and watched me. "I thought I was doing the right thing by arranging your marriage to Signor Tassi. He is a highborn man with a bright future and you are the grand-daughter of a tradesman with no substantial dowry."

I stared at Papà in disgust. "He's not highborn. You just said so yourself. And you didn't arrange a marriage so much as give him access to my body so you could force him to marry me. And you never talked to me about it. You just decided to let things happen. Bad things, Papà. Really bad things."

Papà shook his head. "I was doing my best for you, as a father should. How could I know my friend was a liar and forni-cator? I wanted you to be happy."

I leaned over my lap and rubbed my forehead. There was no use arguing. I had to get out of this predicament with my repu-tation and honor intact. My relationship with Papà was another matter altogether.

The trial began nine days after Agostino's arrest, on March 18, with Papà reading his petition to the court. He stood before Lord Cambio, Pope Paul's representative in Papal Court, wearing his best black velvet tunic, shook out a roll of parchment, and read:

"Orazio Gentileschi, painter, and most humble servant of His Holiness, respectfully reports to you. I explain how, through Madame Tuzia, my tenant, and as a result of her complicity, my daughter has been deflowered by force and carnally known many, many, many times by Agostino Tassi, a painter and close friend and associate of mine. Also taking part in this obscene business was Cosimo Quorli, your orderly. And because this is such a nasty deed, giving such serious and great injury to the plaintiff and his sons, and because it was done under the trust of friendship, it is like murder. And even worse crimes have been perpetrated by Cosimo Quorli. I implore you in the name of Christ to take action, and by your action keep the poor plaintiff from disgracing his other children."

I listened to my father with mounting dismay. *He* was the injured party—not me? Of course he was. No one cared what happened to women, but Rome should care that Papà's property had been damaged. And Papà was worried about the damage to my two brothers, but not me? As if being the brother of a disgraced woman was worse than being the disgraced woman herself. Papà really was after money. In cases such as these, the man who voided a marriage contract, even a verbal one, was forced to compensate the father. The money could be used for a new betrothal.

Papà continued reading from his petition. He described how Tuzia let Agostino into the house when Papà was away, and how Tassi brought Cosimo to the house and later took me to his sister-in-law's house. He didn't mention the rape but did describe how Agostino promised to marry me after he deflowered me. Papà also described a conversation he'd had with Tassi about how the latter's wife had died.

Papà shared other details I'd never heard before. That was probably what he and Signor Stiattesi had been discussing in Papà's office. Signor Stiattesi had been gathering evidence for this very trial. For example, Papà said the signor had letters proving Tassi had murdered his wife. Supposedly, he'd hired bandits to kill her as she traveled from Rome to her parents' house in

Florence. The Tassi household maid, a woman named Vincenza, would testify that these bandits had come to the house to receive their payment.

Papà also shared written testimony from Filippo, Costanza's second husband, that Tassi had fathered children with his now-wife. Most surprising, Tassi and Tuzia apparently interfered with a marriage proposal to me from a man from Modena. I could hardly believe it. Who did we know from Modena, and why had I never heard of this proposal? Oh, Papà.

Last of all, apparently Cosimo Quorli had broken into Papà's house and stolen a Judith I'd painted. That painting had been curing in Papà's bedroom, waiting for the customer to finalize payment. I didn't even know it was gone. My heart broke to think of my beautiful Judith with the despicable Quorli.

Papà finished his reading with some harsh words for Quorli. He told the court that Agostino had broken his promise to marry me because Quorli told him to. That doesn't make sense if Agostino's wife was still alive and he wasn't free to marry, but it does make sense if Agostino had his wife murdered.

After Papà's recitation of charges, I was called to the fore of the room. I looked out on a room full of people, some I knew, most I did not. This was my one chance to tell Papà what I'd been through since he had given me over to Agostino. I steeled myself to tell the truth, whatever the cost to my dignity, and I told it all, leaving out no fact, no matter how embarrassing or graphic. Lord Cambio interrupted me with questions several times. It quickly became clear that His Lordship was establishing the legal basis for stuprum, a particularly nefarious category of rape. For a man to be convicted of stuprum, three things must be proved: The woman must have been a virgin, she must have been deflowered, and she must not have consented to the deflowering. I confirmed all these conditions with brutal detail.

When I told the court about Cosimo Quorli, the judge asked me if I had ever acted carnally with Quorli. I answered most firmly, "No, sir. Signor Quorli took all sorts of efforts to have me, both before and after Agostino did, but I never did give consent, even when Quorli threatened me. He said he would boast about having sex with me even if he didn't, so the deed was as good as done."

When I was done speaking, His Lordship ordered my examination by two midwives, telling them he required evidence that I had been deflowered. The two women, one older and stick thin and one younger and plump, took me to a nearby room, where they asked me to remove my skirts. I felt ashamed at first, but they spoke to me in soft tones and examined me gently and with surprising swiftness. Back in the courtroom, the older midwife testified that she had been a midwife for fifteen years and could say with authority that I was no virgin.

His Lordship looked at me with pity in his eyes. "I order you, Signora Artemisia Gentileschi, to go home and not return to this court until I send word for you to present yourself."

I left, however reluctantly. Tuzia was scheduled to give her testimony the next day and I was anxious to discover what lies she would tell to excuse her treatment of me. As I left, I looked at Papà to see if he would come with me, but he would not even look at me. Instead, Signor Stiattesi rose and accompanied me from the courtroom. He kissed my cheek and smiled sadly.

"You did well today and your father and I are proud of you," he said. "There is a hired carriage waiting outside to take you home."

"But—" I began, but he stopped my words.

"No, dear. Go home and do of something else. You should not be here to hear the lies of Tuzia and Agostino. Those lies cannot be unheard and your father and I would not have that for you."

When I arrived home, I crawled into bed in the clothes I'd worn to court and fell straight into sleep. I vaguely remember Francesco and Giulio coming into my room, but I was too far down the well of forgetfulness to speak to them. I didn't wake when Papà came home either, and in the morning it occurred to me that he had made no effort to wake me.

The trial took many days. Each evening, Signor Stiattesi came to the house and explained what had happened that day in court. He said my betrayer Tuzia told many lies. She told the judge that Agostino and Cosimo came to our house with both Papà's and my permission. She denied taking any payment from either man, though she did admit Cosimo had found her good-for-nothing son a job. Not that she called her son names in court, but he is; he has never kept a job for more than a few days and he is often drunk. When Tuzia said Agostino was a kind and good man who loved and protected me, the judge yelled at her. Signor Stiattesi said the judge told her she'd been sworn to tell the truth and he knew she was lying. He sent her home for the day and told her to be prepared to tell the truth the next day. My heart lifted. Clearly, Signor Stiattesi was correct when he said the Lord Judge understood Agostino was a bad man.

The next day, Tuzia continued lying. She said she'd seen me holding hands with Agostino many times and that I willingly gave myself to him. She described her version of the day Agostino first raped me, saying I'd told her to leave the house because I wanted to have carnal relations with Agostino. When she dared to say she didn't like my hot pursuit of Agostino, the judge stopped her and sent her home again.

The judge didn't call Tuzia back for a week. I suspect he thought if he gave her time to consider the evil of her lies she would begin to tell the truth, but that's not what happened. Instead, she invented more lies. She claimed I'd left Rome with Agostino on several occasions and shared my favors with so many men that Cosimo urged Agostino not to marry me. This time, the judge ordered her to spend the night in jail.

The next day, the judge called Signor Stiattesi. The signor explained how he'd come to be involved in the case and how he investigated after I told him of my rape. My friend spoke on two successive days, answering dozens of questions the judge asked and putting into evidence the letters that proved Agostino had paid men to kill his wife. He also entered court documents from when Agostino raped his sister-in-law, Costanza. And as if that were not enough, Signor Stiattesi had dozens of letters written by Agostino, begging Stiattesi to take his side in the trial. Some notes threatened Stiattesi while others tried to bribe him with papal favors. Stiattesi also had written proof that Cosimo had removed my Judith from Papà's house and now had it in his salon. The theft of the painting was important—if Cosimo could be proven a thief, nothing he said could be taken as true, not as far as the court was concerned.

"I am exceedingly pleased with how the trial is going," Signor Stiattesi told me on the evening of his second day of testimony. "The judge listens carefully to everything I say and, more importantly, has little patience for Tuzia's nonsense."

Though I desperately wanted to be at court listening to witnesses, Signor Stiattesi's nightly visits helped me feel less weak and helpless. Papà, on the other hand, continued to pretend I didn't exist. He would come home late and leave early in the morning, though where he was when the court was not in session, I do not know.

Finally, the day came when the judge called Agostino from his jail cell. After ordering Agostino to swear to tell the truth, the Lord Judge began his questioning. He asked about Agostino's prior run-ins with the law, then about his birthplace and name. Agostino tried to say he'd been born in Rome and lived here his whole life as a Tassi, but the judge knew Agostino's real name wasn't Tassi. Having established the witness had already lied, the judge asked Agostino when his wife died. Agostino said he didn't know exactly because he'd lived with her in Lucca, in northern Tuscany, and left her there when he moved to Rome. The judge then pointed out that Agostino had just said he'd been in Rome his whole life. Signor Stiattesi told me it went on like that the whole first day of Agostino's testimony. The judge would ask a question, Agostino would answer, then the judge would point out his errors and ask more questions. Things came to a head when Agostino insisted that Papà and Signor Stiattesi had lied about his relations with me because he had loaned them money and they did not want to pay it back. When he said that, the judge stopped the testimony and sent Agostino back to jail.

The trial resumed on April 6 with more Tassi testimony. This time, the devil insisted I'd been unchaste with Papà's apprentice. He said he'd been loath to teach me because I was so notoriously dishonorable, then he claimed Papà had hired Tuzia to keep an eye on me because, he said, I was "leading a bad life."

When Signor Stiattesi repeated that to me, I barked out a laugh. Tuzia wouldn't know bad if it hit her in the face. The judge pressed Tassi for details on what he meant by that, and all Tassi said was, "I don't remember, sir." He also he claimed he'd never been alone with me, because I was always chaperoned by Tuzia or one of my brothers. At this lie the judge once again stopped his testimony and back to jail Tassi went.

Still, Tassi didn't learn his lesson. The next time he appeared in court, he brought with him a long list of men I'd supposedly had carnal relations with. Geronimo Modenese, who'd once worked as a painter's assistant for Papà, was on the list. Tassi told a story about how he and Papà once beat up Geronimo for defiling me. Papà stood up and declared it had never happened, and once again the judge sent Tassi back to jail for lying.

Tassi testified on and off until the middle of May. Before he was done, he'd accused me of having inappropriate relations with a dozen men, including my own Papà. On Tassi's final day of testimony, the judge asked if Tassi would cease his obstinacy and tell the truth about the rape. Tassi insisted he'd never touched me, so the judge asked if he'd be willing to say that in front of me. Naturally, Tassi said he would.

So, one May day, Signor Stiattesi showed up at my house and took me back to court for the first time since the trial began. As we rode across the city, he told me what to expect. I was frightened, but I resolved to do what had to be done. At the court, I was placed in front of the chair in which Tassi sat and the judge made me swear to tell the truth. Then the judge asked, "Do you, Artemisia, daughter of Orazio Gentileschi, confirm before the witnesses here that all your previous testimony is true?"

I looked around the room at all the male faces staring back at me and said, "I am ready to confirm my testimony here, in front of Agostino Tassi."

The notary read aloud my testimony from back in April and I again testified that it was true. Agostino leaped to his feet and yelled, "Signora Artemisia is lying! That I raped her is not true, nor did I have any relations with her, because so many men already did." He shouted and waved his arms about his head for a minute or two before the judge stopped him.

The judge looked from Tassi to me. "Are you prepared to confirm your aforesaid testimony under trial?" he asked me.

My heart skipped a beat, even though Signor Stiattesi had warned me I'd be physically tested to assure the court I was telling the truth. Men liked to believe women couldn't lie while they were in pain. It's why magistrates would questions an unmarried woman in labor about the identity of the baby's father. I wasn't so sure the theory was a good one, but I knew nothing the court could do to me would be worse than what I'd already been through. And should I do well in my 'trial' people would believe me. It would be worth it, even if the thumb press crushed my thumb. I would learn to paint left-handed. I took a deep breath, pushed back my shoulders, and said, "Yes, sir."

The judge called a skeletally thin prison guard to bring the sibille, rather than the thumb press. I repressed a smiled at this news. It meant two things. The judge was already inclined to believe me by choosing the less painful instrument and I would not lose my right thumb this day. The guard pulled small iron rod from his pocket. Around it were wound strands of rope not much thicker than the cords used to tighten a woman's bodice. He unwound an arms length of cord and wove it around the fingers of my right hand. He pulled the cords tight, narrowing his squinty black eyes in pleasure as he did. At first the pain was no worse than a pinched finger, but then he pulled again, this time so hard that the cords dug into the skin between my knuckles and my fingers began to turn pink. Tears sprang into my eyes, but I did not cry out. I would not cry out.

The judge asked me if my testimony was true.

"It is true, it is true, it is true," I said between gasps of pain.

Agostino yelled, "It is not true! You are a liar and a whore."

The guard tightened the strings again. My fingers turned bright red and began to swell.

"It is true, it is true, it is true," I repeated.

The judge motioned squinty-eyed jailers to loosen the strings, but Tassi stopped him. "I have a list of questions I want to ask the witness under trial and it is my right to do so," he said.

And so began a torturous back and forth between me and my tormenter.

"Tell me how I came to your house and supposedly had relations with you," he asked. He wore a nasty little half smile as he spoke.

I looked down at my swollen fingers, knowing I had already won. "I have spoken of this already. It should be enough." From the corner of my eye, I saw the judge nod.

"Tell the truth. Tell about the men who visited your house and had relations with you."

"There were no other men. There was only you," I said. "You know this to be true, Agostino."

"Were you ever alone with a man?" he asked.

I grunted out a laugh in spite of the pain in my hand. "Yes, you. Several times a week."

"Did your father deflower you?"

From the gallery, Papà shouted, "No!"

The jailer turned the wooden screw that tightened the strings a quarter turn. My fingers protested with a shriek of pain.

"My father provided for my needs only as a father should."

"Tell me about the indecent letters you wrote to men," Agostino demanded.

I nearly laughed again, though my poor fingers were in hot agony. "I cannot write, nor can I read. I have never learned, though I will so I might better defend myself in the future."

His face had turned bright red and his fists shook, rattling his chains. "Why do you speak this way in court?"

"I hope you are punished for at least one of your crimes, for the wrong you did to me." The jailer peered at me from under his eyelashes and turned the screw so the pressure on my fingers infinitesimally lessened.

Agostino paused and examined his list. "You say you were forced by me. Did you make any noise?"

"I screamed once, then you gagged my mouth." My outrage was such at this memory that I entirely forgot my throbbing fingers. "You held me down and forced yourself on me."

He widened his eyes, as if surprised. "Were you deflowered?"

"You were there and you know I was." My fingers had turned a grayish blue color and throbbed in time with my heart.

"Were you hoping to have me for a husband?" he asked.

"Not until after you raped me, and then only to save me from ruin," I said. I felt a red ball of rage build in my belly. Even should I win this trial, I would be ruined. What sort of man would take me as wife now? What respectable family would want one of my paintings in their house? I would be alone and dependent all my life. All because of this loathsome, selfish, lying worm. "I hate you."

He reddened anew and squinted at me. "Who told you that if you lied about me I would marry you and save you from your bad life?"

The judge had enough. He pushed back his chair and came over to me. He unwound the cords from my swollen fingers. Needles of pain shot through my hand, but with the judge's next words, I knew it had been worth it.

"Guard, take Signor Tassi back to his cell. And you, Signora Gentileschi, you are dismissed with the court's apologies."

After the sibille, the trial's outcome was all but assured. No one in Rome thought a woman could lie under torture, not even a young woman put to a device as mild as the sibille. It seems silly now, all these years later, but at the time people believed such things.

The judge continued interviewing Tassi for several months. Signor Stiattesi later told me Tassi wrote a handful of inflammatory letters from his jail cell, accusing Papà of all sorts of bad deeds. In response, the signor called two of Papà's old apprentices to court. Both men testified that the Gentileschi household had been a proper one and they had seen no improprieties while working there.

As the weeks dragged on, I became angrier and angrier with Papà. I wouldn't be in this fix if not for him. I wouldn't have had to stand up in a crowded room and speak the words that described my worst day and darkest shame. He should have found me a good husband, not a devil named Tassi. And it wasn't as if no one wanted to marry me—there was this man from Modena, a man my father had never once mentioned to me. And when it became clear that Tassi would not marry me, had Papà done anything to protect me? No, he had not. He'd waited until gossip pushed him to file a lawsuit, waited until Signor Stiattesi stepped in to protect me, waited until my honor was besmirched past saving. Worst of all, he'd waited while Tassi and Quorli humiliated and harassed me day after day after day.

In September, seven months after the trial began, Signor Stiattesi came to the house with a bottle of wine and a huge smile. "Lord Cambio has found Agostino guilty and sentenced him to two years in jail," he said.

Papà whooped with joy and grabbed Signor Stiattesi into a hug. I stood by and watched them. I guess I was happy—it was hard to tell and even harder to feel. Tassi's guilty verdict might lighten the stain on my reputation, but I'd never be rid of it entirely. People would look at me and think, "There is that girl who was raped." What man would take me now? I hadn't wanted to marry Tassi, but I had wanted to avoid the public humiliation of having been used without marriage. And the trial hadn't fixed the pain and fear. I still had bad dreams all the time and felt afraid each time I saw a strange man. Papà and Signor Stiattesi did not understand. They had won, but I never would. I trudged up to my room and left them to celebrate without me. I'm not sure they even noticed my absence.

The next morning, Signor Stiattesi came to the house and once more closeted himself in Papà's study. I know because I was in the kitchen with our new housekeeper, a wrinkled woman named Thomasina, kneading bread dough. We would set the loaves out to rise in the morning sun, and after lunch she'd take them to the baker to be turned into crusty loaves.

As I was brushing flour off my hands, Signor Stiattesi opened the kitchen door and motioned for me to come into the study. A little part of me wondered what the two of them could want with me, but the larger part didn't care. I didn't care about much these days. It was easier not to feel.

When I'd seated myself on Papà's third chair, a rickety affair that squeaked when I moved, Papà pushed a piece of paper across his desk toward me. "The signor and I have arranged a marriage for you," he said, looking down at his desk.

I took up the paper, though why I do not know. I really needed to learn to read.

Signor Stiattesi leaned toward me from his chair and said, "My youngest brother, Pierantonio, has agreed to take you in marriage." Seeing my blank look, he hurried to explain. "He's been living in Florence, trying to make a living as a painter, but with little success." Stiattesi frowned. "I'm afraid he has more enthusiasm than talent. You shall give him some purpose."

Papà spoke, keeping his eyes on his desk. "He's best suited as a painter's assistant. You must be the painter, my daughter."

I remembered Signora Lavinia Fontana and her advice about husbands: "Marry a nice man, one who will take care of the household while you paint." I found myself daring to hope.

"Will he come here, or does he have a house in Rome?" I asked.

Papà glanced at Signor Stiattesi. "Pierantonio is very poor, but Signor Stiattesi has agreed to give you a dowry." Papà smiled. "It will pay for your new life in Florence."

"Florence?" I heard my voice rise. "I am to leave Rome?"

Papà looked me in the eye for the first time in weeks and said, "The Gentileschis will all remove themselves from Rome for a time. Your brothers will go to Pisa to apprentice with my Uncle Aurelio, and you are off to Florence, where Michaelo will guide your entrance into the art world. I had thought to send you to Pisa as well, but Michaelo has more power than Aurelio and your talent is too fine to waste in Pisa. Florence is the best city for you. And I will give up this house in the hope that the stain upon the Gentileschi name will be washed clean with time and distance. I've taken a commission with a family outside Rome. They require frescoes, which I do not enjoy painting, but who will pay for my paintings now? The scandal you caused has ruined the chances for myself and your brothers in this city."

I gaped at Papà in an open-mouthed mix of bewilderment and fury. *Do you blame me? You rotten old man. You did this to me*, I thought. *Only a fool would have trusted Agostino Tassi.* It occurred to me then that Papà understood all too well his culpability in the Tassi scandal—it's why he'd been avoiding me.

Realizing I had no more choice in this than I'd had in my malignant relationship with Tassi, I only asked, "When?"

Signor Stiattesi took the paper from me and said, "This afternoon. This is a special license."

And that's how I came to be standing in the church hours later, marrying a man I had met only moments before. He had a dark beard that matched his earlobe-length hair. He wore a brown velvet doublet that didn't quite fit him, which didn't surprise me, as I'd seen his larger and older brother wear it several times. The ceremony took only a few minutes before afternoon mass. Afterward, Pierantonio kissed me dryly on the cheek and whispered, "You may call me Pietro." Then he turned to take his older brother's arm and walked away. That's when I learned Papà had arranged it so we would not live as husband and wife until we left Rome. There would be less talk about my private life that way, or so I supposed. Papà never explained.

The next few days, Papà and I lived in the uncomfortable spaces between things not said. My eighteenth name day came and went unremarked. Four days after my strange marriage, a carriage came for fourteen-year-old Francesco and twelve-year-old Giulio. They were off to Pisa and my uncle, and if you asked me (which, of course, no one did), not a moment too soon. The boys had had too much freedom the last few months with Papà distracted by court. It was a wonder one or both hadn't been taken up by the authorities for any one of a dozen minor crimes.

Neither boy showed much promise as a painter, but Papà thought Uncle Aurelio could teach them to be painters' assistants. This plan had the advantage of getting them away from their gang and our problems in Rome. Uncle Aurelio did much the same for Papà many years ago after Papà refused to learn his father's trade.

I watched from my window as my brothers crawled into the carriage that would take them north to Pisa, envying their chance to start anew with our kindly uncle. It got me thinking: Moving to a strange city might be good. Pierantonio might be a good husband. Maybe we could live like Lavinia Fontana and her husband, in a companionable partnership. Maybe everything would turn out fine. Maybe.

I turned away from the window and confronted my Susanna, taking in her cowed posture and pleading hands. It was a good painting—technically proficient, vibrantly colored, and well balanced. And I was done with it. I turned the painting around so it faced the wall. At four feet wide and five feet tall, it wasn't easy, but I did it. It was time for a new painting, one that declared the end of my victimhood. I smiled to myself as an idea came to me. I'd paint a Judith, but a new kind, one that would send the art world and Papà a message. I'd make sure he couldn't miss the meaning this time.

Chapter Four

FLORENCE, THE GRAND DUCHY OF TUSCANY
1613

Florence turned out to be good for my life as an artist. As a native Roman, I grew up believing Rome was the greatest city on Earth. I may yet be right about Rome, but Florence ran a close second. There's a reason Florentine art is in demand, not only in the Italian Peninsula but in France, Spain, and the Germanic states too. The credit must go to the Medici family, whose great wealth supports painters, sculptors, and architects.

Pietro and I traveled to Florence early in the year. We brought two wagons full of art supplies and household goods, as well as my Susanna and the two Madonna paintings. We set up our small household near Uncle Michaelo's new palazzo, Casa Buonarroti. Our rooms were small and the building quite old, with tiny north-facing windows that made painting nearly impossible. Still, it was a pleasure to establish my own home away from Rome and its gossip, and I soon found myself expecting my first child. It was all terribly exciting.

Uncle Michaelo showed me his new palace not long after we

arrived. He promised he would hire me to paint a frescoes in the galleria he was having built to honor his granduncle Michelangelo. "I also have this for you," Uncle said with a grin. He held out a folded piece of parchment.

I took it, noting the thickness of the paper and the wax seal of the Medici family. Before I could open it, Uncle blurted out, "It's an invitation to an audience with the Dowager Duchess Christina of Lorraine, a week from today."

"What?" The great and powerful dowager duchess knew I existed and wanted to meet me? I ripped open the seal, half hoping Uncle was wrong. Christina of Lorraine was the granddaughter of a Danish princess on one side and of Catherine de Medici on the other. Catherine had been the queen of France and mother to three French kings, and was by all accounts a formidable woman who married her daughter Christina to Ferdinand, the Grand Duke of Tuscany. When Ferdinand died four years earlier, their son Cosimo II inherited the duchy, but Cosimo was young and chronically ill. His mother, the Dowager Duchess, was the real power in Tuscany. If she liked me she could make my career, but our meeting could just as well go the other way. If she knew of my scandalous past she would surely condemn me and then no one would ever buy a painting from me. No one.

I scanned the document, my heart beating like a snare drum. I was indeed commanded to appear before the dowager duchess next Wednesday at the tenth bell. I said the only thing that came to mind: "I have nothing to wear!"

Uncle laughed. "It's all right. My darling Francesca has agreed to loan you something."

"Francesca? Do you mean Francesca Caccini, the court composer?" He smiled and nodded. "But she's married, isn't she?"

"Yes, but unhappily, as is often the case. We met earlier this year when she set my comedy *La Tanzia* to music." He wagged his finger in my face. "Before you go frowning at me, I should say she is a great favorite with the Dowager Duchess Christina. You would do well to make friends."

I did end up making friends with Francesca, though I hadn't meant to. It would not do my uncertain reputation any good if I associated with a woman who openly broke her marriage vows. But Francesca won me over with her kind manner and open heart. She also had a wardrobe full of sumptuous court dresses and I was happily not so pregnant as to exceed the limits of a pretty dress. She chose for me a gold-and-green gown made of wool so light, it felt like linen. The low, curved bodice exposed rather more of my breasts than I was accustomed to. It was lined with gold lace, while the green and gold brocade overskirt was cut in the Florentine style, in two separate pieces, one for the front and one for the rear of the dress.

"You're lovely," Francesca said when she had me laced and tied into the dress.

I waved at my décolletage. "Are you sure this won't offend the dowager duchess?" I asked.

Francesca laughed lightly. "The dowager is part French and the French are daring, at least when it comes to fashion. You will see."

Francesca also advised me on how to behave in front of

the dowager. "She's exceedingly grand but also practical. Be respectful but don't overly humble yourself, and for goodness' sake, don't scrape and bow. One curtsy, then look her in the eye and speak frankly. She'll like that."

A hired carriage dropped me in the Palazzo Pitti's courtyard. Courtiers and magistrates stood about the ducal palace's interior space, talking quietly. I showed my letter to a velvet-dressed page, no more than ten years old, who directed me to the far end of the courtyard. There stood over two dozen columns with arched arcades between them. A large double door stood in the center. I presented my letter to the guards who flanked the door. They called another page, this one older but no less richly dressed, who led me inside through a large echoing space with marble floors and statuary on every wall. We walked up a stone staircase and down a long hall, along which I recognized several paintings by Michelangelo and Leonardo. The page, who spoke not one word to me, opened that door and stepped back with a bow. I entered, feeling as if I'd rather turn and run back the way I'd come.

And so, wearing a borrowed dress, I found myself standing before the dowager duchess of Tuscany and one of the most powerful women in Christendom. I was surprised to find she looked like a regular woman, though with the bone structure of someone who had been a great beauty. She sat at a small table, surrounded by papers, and was smaller than I'd expected. She smiled when I entered.

After I made my curtsy and said the appropriately polite things, the dowager duchess took a paper from a courtier standing behind her. "I have a letter from your father, Orazio Gentileschi, here. He writes that you are unique in your profession. Is that because you are a woman or because you are a painter of unusual talent?"

Remembering Francesca's advice, I answered, "Both, Your Highness. The two are not unrelated. Because of my sex, I could not train at the academy in Rome, nor take lessons from great painters, yet I am as proficient as any painter my age."

The dowager duchess smiled at this. "It is nice to hear a woman say she is good at something other than household management." She waved her hand around her head and said, "I am a much better ruler than either my husband or son."

I looked the older woman in the eye and said exactly what I thought. "I agree, Your Highness. You are an exceptional woman."

She laughed this time, then made an infinitesimal motion to her attendant. He stepped out from behind her chair, pulled out a second chair from the table, and indicated I should sit. I tried not to collapse from relief, knowing I'd passed some kind of test.

"I admire your answer, but you are wrong," the dowager duchess said once I'd settled my skirts. "Only my circumstances are exceptional. I believe many women would make good rulers like myself if only they were given a chance. My birth has given me opportunities most women will never have. Much as your birth has done for you—if you had not been born to a father who painted and was willing to teach you, your talent would have gone undiscovered."

"That is true, Your Highness. In many things, I have been

lucky." I found my hands twisting the brocade of my borrowed finery and forced myself to stop.

The dowager duchess inclined her head toward me. "And yet, in many things you are unlucky. Is that not true?"

I felt myself blush. She knew. Of course she did. How could she not?

The dowager duchess leaned forward, put her index finger under my chin, and pushed it up. "Do not be ashamed. We live in a world that blames women for men's failings, but you and I both know how few choices women have." She tapped the letter from my father, where it lay on the table between us. "Your father describes this Tassi fellow as a great villain. Was he?"

"Yes, Your Highness." I wanted to say more but found my tongue would not let me.

"Hmm." She looked at me like a hawk watching a rabbit and I knew she saw the truth of my relationship with Tassi. "Your father says this man is skilled at eluding punishment for his crimes. He urges me to issue a writ that will keep your seducer in jail until his sentence is fully served."

I didn't know what to say. I was still angry with Papà and it surprised me to hear he'd been trying to help me from afar. Or maybe he was helping himself by using this opportunity to establish a relationship with the immensely powerful Dowager Duchess of Tuscany.

The dowager duchess sighed and pushed Papà's letter onto the floor with a firm shove of her forefinger. "Did you know I am the patron for a half-dozen female monasteries?"

I shook my head. "No, Your Highness."

"There is opportunity for women who remove themselves from the world of men. And yet, monastic life isn't practical for all women. I shall view your paintings, and if they are as good as everyone says they are, I shall have you paint something for me. Expect me at your place of work tomorrow, midday." She waved at the anonymous courtier, who pulled out my chair. I stood and he led me away. My heart pounded in my chest like a wild thing at the prospect of so grand a personage as Christina of Lorraine visiting my humble rooms.

My life as an independent painter began that day, though I did not know it. Christina came to our dingy rented rooms and prowled my studio, examining paintings with the critical eye of a true connoisseur. Her rich velvet dress and pearl head dress looked as out of place as anything I'd ever seen, but she appeared to care not one whit about the modest surroundings. She paced, peered and said nothing for nearly fifteen minutes, which made me so nervous I thought I might wet myself.

She leaned in to my Judith, so close her nose nearly touched the canvas, then stood back "This is an exceedingly powerful painting, but if I hang something like it in Palazzo Pitti, it will make my sons and advisors exceedingly nervous." She looked sideways at me and winked.

I grinned back at her. She'd gotten the gist of the painting with one glance. "Is it too violent?" I asked.

"Bah," she said with a wave of her slim hand. "Many paintings are violent. It's the female nature of this violence. Judith's face is that of a woman who has no qualms about cutting off a man's head; it is business to her. Men would prefer to see us as weak and gentle and your Judith is a warrior knight in a dress." She pointed to the maidservant in the painting and said, "That's an interesting choice for Abra. I like how you painted the general's fist as nearly as large as Abra's head, yet she holds him down with such force."

That was exactly what I'd been aiming for. The story of Judith is old. The Assyrian general Holofernes, in his war on the Israelites, besieged Bethulia. The widow Judith went to Holofernes and pretended to betray their people, promising to help him enter the city. Holofernes invited the beautiful widow and her maid, Abra, to his tent, where he intended to have his way with Judith. Instead, she got him drunk. After he passed out, Judith, with Abra's help, severed the general's head with his own scimitar and took Holofernes's head back to Bethulia. Frightened by their general's gruesome death, the Assyrians lost the next battle and abandoned the siege. Naturally, Judith became a heroic figure in Jewish lore.

Painters have been depicting Judith and Abra for hundreds of years. Generally, Judith is portrayed as either seductively beautiful, emotionally repulsed by the beheading, or both. Her servant, Abra, is nearly always portrayed as a passive old woman who stands by her mistress. My Judith was in the bloom of her womanhood and she did not look ashamed or afraid. I painted Abra not as a crone, but as a second figure in the fullness of her womanhood. She held down the struggling Holofernes so Judith could cut off his head, and she looked determined to have the job done.

The dowager duchess turned toward me. "Did you know the Protestants took the Book of Judith out of the Old Testament?"

"I heard," I said. For all their professed modernity, Protestants dislike powerful women a great deal more than Catholics, and that's saying something. "I could not have painted this in the Netherlands or England without earning the ire of powerful churchmen."

"True, true," the dowager duchess murmured. "They have no nuns, no female monastic communities, no veneration of Mother Mary. They've taken all the stories of strong women out of the Apocrypha. In my opinion, a religion that accepts the divinity of only men seems a dry, bloodless sort of belief system."

She stepped over to my Susanna, appraised it, and glanced back at the Judith. "I would not have had to read your father's letter to see a story in these two paintings." She pointed at the Susanna and said, "This woman is acted upon by men. She is more defiant and less seductive than the usual Susanna, but she is nonetheless a victim. This, on the other hand," she said, stepping back to the Judith, "is two women acting decisively for a moral purpose." She sighed. "It's astounding."

My heart lifted at this praise. The piece needed more paint and several layers of lacquer to finish, but I liked the choices I'd made, even if they were unconventional. "What is it Ecclesiastics says? 'Let us now praise famous men and our fathers that begat us.'"

The dowager duchess threw back her head and laughed. "That line has always irritated me. It ignores motherhood, which is ridiculous. But you are correct. Women in paintings are only famous for their beauty. Your Judith's beauty is entirely beside the point. In fact . . ." Her voice trailed off.

She'd finally seen it. I nearly laughed in delight.

She looked from the painting to me, and back again. "You've painted yourself as Judith, haven't you? Is Holofernes that awful man? What was his name—Signor Tassi?"

I nodded.

"And the blood?"

I nodded again. I'd painted the sheets under Holofernes's head to look like the sheets on my bed after Tassi first raped me.

She stroked her chin. "Beheading would be as bloody as childbirth, though most painters don't paint it that way. Have you ever seen an animal with its throat cut? They spray great gouts of blood. Beheadings are like that."

I suddenly felt unsure. My painting was far more violent than any Judith I'd ever seen. Yet this great woman, who held my future in her hand . . . Did she think the painting not bloody enough?

Then the dowager duchess spoke again. "Not that you'd dare paint a man that way." She grabbed my arm. "You must paint a Judith for me. Will you?"

"Of course I will." Did anyone turn down the Dowager Duchess of Tuscany? "I could reproduce this in a matter of months."

She shook her head. "Oh, no, you misunderstand me, my dear. I don't want a copy of this painting, however much I admire it. I told you, it would make every man in the palace wilt with fear. No, what I want is the next moment. Do you know what I mean?"

I did. While many Judith paintings captured the beheading, many more portrayed the two women leaving Holofernes's tent, usually with the general's head in a basket. "You want that moment, but with this attitude, correct?" I swept my arm in front of the beheading image.

"Exactly, my dear. No fearful Judith, nor reproachful Abra, but two women getting away with murder with a minimum of fuss and fear. With this use of light and dark, and the same realism. It's utterly masterful. I've never seen the like, not even in Signor Caravaggio's paintings."

I didn't have the heart to tell her that I'd painted it that way, with a dark background, because I'd never learned perspective. In my sketches, I couldn't figure out what to put in the background, so I painted it dark. It made sense thematically because the subject was dark in nature. And given my painting's tangle of arms, with Holofernes reaching up to push off Abra, Abra pushing down, and Judith with the sword, I didn't want anyone's legs or skirts in the painting. It would have been over-busy. The action, like my Susanna, was contained in an inverted triangle with the blood dripping off the bed as the point. In trying to avoid a technical problem with the background, I'd made the picture better. By setting the figures in close up, illuminated against a pool of dark, the image became more dramatic. I liked it so much that I used the technique my whole career, always to great effect.

My good luck continued when a few weeks later I received an invitation to the Florentine Academy of Arts of Drawing. I have no doubt the dowager duchess saw my living quarters and understood how difficult it was to paint in that place. Happy, but wary of the invitation, for most art academies didn't allow women, I hired a carriage to take me to Santissima Annunziata, where the academy made its home.

The main building had the look of an old Roman temple, with its double row of twelve columns. I entered through the center of three doors, stepping into a dim and cool chapel. I momentarily forgot myself as I walked the walls, gazing at frescoes as fine as any I'd ever seen. There was an *Assumption of Mary*, a *Journey of the Magi*, and more. The artists were all minor painters, but then again, so was I. The church's main body contained more frescoes, each lovelier than the last. I stood in the center aisle, lost to the visual richness before me.

"May I help you, sister?"

I startled at the soft voice at my elbow and tore my gaze from the ceiling to see a friar standing feet from me. His head came only to my shoulder and his face was as wrinkled as a winter apple. He wore the dark brown robes of the Servite Order. The Servites, who made this cloister their home, were an order of friars and nuns dedicated to serving Holy Mary, which I thought might explain their willingness to tolerate not just artists, but female artists in their midst.

"Wonderful, is it not? Are you new to our church?" His voice was as gentle as a mother's touch.

I nodded. "I'm looking for the Academy of Arts."

"Ah," he said, nodding. "The dowager duchess sent a letter saying a young woman would come to us for help. I assume you are Signora Stiattesi?"

"Yes, I am she." For brevity's sake, I did not explain that I had not taken my husband's name. Nor did I tell him I intended to sign my paintings with Lomi, our old family name. The friar led me up the aisle, where we made a right turn and passed into a large, light-filled atrium. Two men, one dark-haired and at an easel and the other gray and seated with a sketchbook on his knee, looked up as we passed. They smiled. We passed through this space into a hall with half a dozen doors on each side.

The friar waved at the doors. "These are our private painting studios, or you may paint in the atrium, as your needs require." He walked halfway down the room, opened a door, and stood aside. "This shall be yours, if it meets with your approval."

I stepped into the room. It was about the size of my studio back in Rome, twelve square feet. A large window filled with clear glass dominated the back wall. A sturdy table and chair stood in the middle of the room as if waiting for my sketchbook. "It's glorious," I said, and I meant it.

The friar, who said his name was Brother Peregrine, explained that as an adjunct member of the academy I was allowed to run an account for painting supplies. He left, then reappeared with the younger of the men in the atrium. "Signor Allori, allow me to introduce to you Signora Stiattesi." Brother Peregrine smiled fondly at Allori. "Signor Allori is one of the finest painters in Florence."

The painter laughed and clapped Brother Peregrine on the back. "Brother, you will go to hell if you keep up this bad habit of telling lies." The two men smiled at each other before Allori turned his eye toward me. He stepped forward and kissed the back of my outstretched hand. The hairs of his jet-black beard, which he wore trimmed into a Spanish point, tickled my knuckles. "The abbot said he would be joining us. You will be our first woman member."

"She is not a full member," Brother Peregrine hastened to add. "That honor yet awaits the signora."

"If she's half as good as the dowager duchess says, it is only a matter of time." Allori turned his black eyes on me and asked, "Are you?"

The twinkle in his eye allowed me to reply, "Why, yes, of course I am."

As we chucked at each other, the older man from the atrium stepped into the hall, sketchbook under his right arm. Signor Allori waved him over. "My friend, come meet the newest addition to our academy."

I watched the man approach, not knowing I was about to meet one of the greatest minds of our time. Nothing in his dress or demeanor gave him away as anything but an aging artist. He was slightly built, dressed in unadorned clothing, and wore his hair in a rough tumble as if he cut it himself.

He bowed to me and kissed my hand. "Galileo Galilei at your disposal, Signora Stiattesi," he said.

I opened and closed my mouth, not unlike a fish pulled suddenly out of water. What did one say to the man who'd observed the moons of Jupiter and the rings of Saturn? More impressively, he was the man who insisted the sun, not the Earth, was the center of our universe. The cardinals who took the Bible literally were not amused.

He saw my reaction and patted his head. "See? No horns. I am but a harmless old man."

"Forgive me, Signor Galilei," I said. "I am only astounded to be meeting a learned man so famous as you. And you are an artist too? Is there no end to your talent?"

"Ha!" He shared a grin with Signor Allori. "We must keep this one around, for she is both beautiful and an artful flatterer. You must call me Galileo and he Cristofano, for I am sure we will all be great friends."

It was my turn to laugh; the two men made such merry faces that I had no choice. Brother Peregrine excused himself and left me with Cristofano and Galileo. I thought about asking the two of them into my new studio, but the space had only one chair, so we talked in the hall.

Galileo explained that the academy made him a member based on his skill as a draftsman. "I am no artist, though I am a great appreciator and collector of paintings. The dowager duchess tells me she has given you a commission."

Allori widened his eyes at the news. "What? Newly in town and already you've caught the biggest fish in Florence?"

I felt myself blush. "She liked my *Judith Slaying Holofernes* and wants something like it," I said.

Allori leaned back and stroked his beard. "And what shall you give her?" I explained what the dowager duchess wanted. "Ah, a *Judith and Her Maidservant*. I have always thought to paint something on that subject as well, but I am generally kept busy with court portraits."

Galileo clapped his hands together. "You were just telling me you have nothing after you finish the portrait of Cosimo. And your mistress wants a portrait. I propose a contest: You paint a Judith using your mistress as the model. Signora Stiattesi will paint her own, using whatever model she chooses. And I and Brother Peregrine shall judge who has the best Judith."

"Oh, what fun," Cristofano half shouted. "Do you mind, signora? A harmless contest with no stakes—there can be no sin in it."

I smiled at the two men. It was hard not to like them—little did I know we'd remain friends until distance and death parted us. "I will allow it, on one condition," I said. "You must quit calling me Signora Stiattesi. My Christian name is Artemisia."

You will note that I have said little of my husband and home life. My mother used to say that if you had nothing good to say, you should keep your lips together, and I have little good to say about my husband. He was lazy, profligate with money, careless of my feelings, and jealous of my talents.

Pietro's jealously began nearly the moment we arrived in Florence. On the journey from Rome to Florence, I could see he fancied himself the heroic knight who saved me from shame and ignominy. As long as I was in his debt, he acted tenderly and kindly toward me, so much so that, as I have said, I was pregnant with my first child by the time we arrived in Florence. However good Florence was to me, it was correspondingly bad for Pietro.

I should have known something was wrong long before I did. When we were to leave Rome, he came to my father's house with a wagon. I thought him sweet for helping to pack his wife's household goods and paintings, though he knew me not at all. Pietro said nothing of my Susanna as we wrapped it for travel, though at the time I thought he was being tactful about my troubles. But then we wrapped my *Judith Slaying Holofernes* and still he said nothing. Even half finished, the painting was too large and powerful to ignore. I thought perhaps the violence of the painting made him uncomfortable. Seeking to reach out to this stranger to whom I found myself married, I asked him about his own work.

"I have no paintings to show you," he said in a lofty tone. "I have sold everything I painted."

I thought this was odd. Every painter has studies or rough versions of important works, as well as paintings we do only for ourselves, for pleasure, or to show prospective patrons. Still, I did not press him, knowing it would be unseemly for a wife to question her husband. I smiled and said, "Then perhaps you could show me your sketches sometime."

Again he shook his head. "I lost my sketchbook and have not replaced it."

This seemed incomprehensible. I'd been sketching since I

could hold a charcoal rod in my fingers. Papà used to say he had to sell an extra painting a year just to keep me in parchment. What kind of artist was Pietro that he did not keep a sketchbook?

While I tied the Judith's wool wrappings with twine, I spared a glance at Pietro. His lower lip stuck out like a cranky baby's. Seeking to mollify him, I said, "It's probably for the best, what with so much to pack." I stopped myself from adding, "We can buy you a new sketchbook in Florence." I was not entirely stupid about my new husband.

As we packed up my pigments and oils, I tried another conversational tack. "With whom did you apprentice?" I asked. "You see, I am jealous of anyone who had a real apprenticeship because I only trained with Papà."

He chewed on that lower lip like I'd asked him a difficult question. "I apprenticed briefly with Federico Barocci, who was himself a student of the great Taddeo."

His answer confused me. I'd heard of Taddeo, of course, but I thought he'd left Rome years ago. Maybe I'd heard wrong. "Then you're a Mannerist? Of the old school?"

"What is the point of painting reality? We can see that with our eyes. Painting should be about ideal forms and high ideas, not darkness and sin." He gestured at my wrapped *Judith Slaying Holofernes.*

I ignored the slight. "So you are no fan of Signor Caravaggio?"

"The man's life was as disordered as his paintings. We live in a time when there is a market for dark art, but that does not make it holy, and art must be holy." Pietro picked up one of my smaller chests and marched it from the room, boots thumping on the floorboards as he made his way down the stairs.

I didn't agree at all. Art must be what it need be, both to the artist and to the audience, and our needs are not always holy.

I worked on my *Judith and Her Maidservant* most of the summer. At home, life was tense and uncomfortable as Pietro became increasingly resentful of my success. Remembering Lavinia Fontana and her husband, I suggested Pietro make use of his time by acting as my painter's assistant. "I could make us more money if I could complete paintings faster," I explained. It turned out to be a bad idea.

"Assistant to a woman?" he screeched. "Do you take me for a eunuch?"

"No, it's not that, darling," I protested with a shake of my head. "I just thought . . ."

He stepped right up to me and yelled into my face, "I am a man, damn you, not your lackey!" before storming out of the house. That was the first time he stayed away all night.

After one particularly vicious fight, I confessed my problems to Brother Peregrine. He counseled me to greater patience, which wasn't very helpful, but he also found Pietro an empty studio for his use, which *was* helpful—for a time. Pietro came to the academy most afternoons and busied himself in his studio. At the start, he seemed happy, but after a few weeks he became increasingly short-tempered. Then he began disappearing in the late afternoons and arriving home late at night or early morning, reeking of wine.

One afternoon when he was out, I snuck into Pietro's studio. The room was strewn with torn parchment and canvases badly sketched and daubed with mismatched colors. Dried paint stuck to the table, muddled with breadcrumbs and spilled sour wine.

"It's worse than you thought, isn't it?" a voice said behind me.

I whirled around, my heart pounding in fright, to find my friend Cristofano. Relieved Pietro hadn't caught me, I said the first thing that came to mind: "It's the space of a madman."

"No," he said with a shake of his head. "It's the space of a man who wishes he had one-quarter of his wife's talent. Your husband is no painter."

I had to agree. Nor was Pietro an assistant, and lately he was barely a husband.

Pietro was the only dark spot in Florence. Uncle Michaelo visited me in my studio once or twice a week, sometimes more. Uncle often brought Francesca with him and sometimes she came on her own. Like me, Francesca traveled about the city without a chaperone.

"Of course I travel alone. I am no lady. Neither are you," she said as she watched me add layers to the drapery of Judith's headcloth.

"Francesca!" I startled. Even though I was losing the afternoon light, I sat my paintbrush down and faced her. "How dare you say such a thing."

She smiled and waved her hand languidly. "My darling, like me, you must work to earn your living and you must work hard. How much does your lower back hurt?"

I admitted that it hurt quite a bit. It is not easy to stand for hours a day while increasingly pregnant. The bigger my belly became, the more my feet swelled and my back ached. I tried to paint sitting down, but I couldn't do it. Painting is not a sedentary art. That it was summer and grossly hot, even within the thick church walls, did not help.

She nodded. "And yet you paint. A lady would take to her bed and rest until she delivered the child, then she would have a leisurely lying-in. And why can she do this, this lady?"

"Because she does not have to earn her own money," I sighed.

"Exactly. Yet you and I do. Ergo, we are not ladies. You should not be ashamed to be self-sufficient."

Each time she visited me, I liked her more, though I tried not to. After Tuzia, I mistrusted female friendship, and for good reason.

The dowager duchess also visited the academy occasionally, though only for a few minutes at a time. She was always polite and pleasant, but far too grand to stand around chatting with a woman who had paint on her skirts. Sometimes Pietro was there for the dowager duchess's visits and he was always extra nasty afterward. He would disappear, sometimes overnight, though he always returned full of remorse and promises to be a better husband. And for a time he would be—until something set him off again.

One morning in September, I awoke with a terrible ache in my lower back. I wrote it off as exhaustion, then dressed and set off to walk to the academy. You see, the midwife had told me the baby would not come until near November, and I needed to finish the Judith so I could pay my paint bill and the rent. I had walked no more than two blocks when a lightning bolt of pain ripped through my abdomen. I cried out and grabbed a nearby tree. A woman on her way to the market took pity on me and helped me home. Pietro hadn't come home the night before, but our landlady was home and sent for Francesca and the midwife.

About the next few hours I wish not to write. All mothers have their tales of sweat and pain and blood and loss. Mine is no different. The midwife assured me the birth went exceedingly well, though it did not seem so to me. I suppose it never does to the laboring mother.

As dusk fell, I was safely delivered of a tiny, quiet boy. Francesca took him immediately to the church of Saint Maria Novella, where the priest there baptized him Giovanni Battista, after my two brothers. Neither of my brothers named Giovanni had survived childhood, though the oldest lived six years and the youngest two. My poor little Giovanni lived only a night and a day. I prayed my heavenly mother would take care of him, as she does all babies too small and too sweet for this world.

Of Pietro, I saw nothing until well after that terrible moment when Francesca took my poor baby from my arms and wrapped him in his funeral shroud. When my husband did come home, he seemed genuinely distressed at the news of his dead son. He wept in my arms like a little boy, as if his was the greater pain.

"I will get a job," he said, "or mix your paints and prepare your canvasses. This is my fault, my darling. You worked too hard and became too tired. I will change so our next child may live to grow old and have their own children."

I stroked Pietro's dark head and tried to hope for the future as he wept upon my breasts. Then my husband told me where he'd been.

"I had a letter from my brother," he said after wiping the tears from his face. "I was so upset by its contents that I sought comfort in a *taverna*."

"What did the letter say?" I asked.

He grasped my hands in his. "You must brace yourself, my wife."

"What is it?"

"That devil Agostino Tassi has been released from jail. A new judge gave him a choice between five years of hard labor and banishment from Rome. Of course, he took the latter."

I stifled a whimper. "He's not even in Rome?" What if he came here, to Florence, and it all began again?

Pietro sighed. "No, he is not here. He's painting frescoes with your father in a small town outside Rome."

My ears buzzed and my head whirled. My father and Agostino, working together as if they were friends? The world fell away for a moment. My son had died this day and now my father was dead to me too.

Chapter Five

Pietro's promises to reform were, as the English playwright Shakespeare wrote in *Hamlet*, honored more in the breach than in the observance. I don't know if you've heard of him, but Romans love Shakespeare. I think it is because he so often set his plays in Italian cities. Papà took me to see a translated *Hamlet* more than a decade ago and I often thought of poor, troubled Hamlet during those years in Florence. I am no prince, but I had an honored position in the Medici court and all the painting commission I could wish for, and still I had trouble. My husband was often away from home and just as often spent the money I made on drink and loose women. Pietro also charged exorbitant amounts at the colorist shop, or he did until I told the shopkeeper to allow him no more credit. I shall not describe the tantrum that resulted, but there was no point in indulging Pietro's pretentions as a painter. He never produced anything worth leaving the studio, and I couldn't afford *all* his vices. As a consequence, Pietro humiliated himself and his hardworking wife by asking Uncle Michaelo for money. Of course, Uncle gave it to him, which I told him was no better than hurling ducats into the Arno River.

In November 1615, I had another son. I named him after my friend Cristofano Allori. Baby Cristofano lived longer than Giovanni, but not by much—only long enough that I grew to love him more than myself. I found him in his cradle one morning, cold and blue. Pietro didn't blame himself for his second son's death, though I had no more rest during this pregnancy than the first. No, Pietro blamed me, saying my sons paid for my past sins. I tried not to believe my husband's words, but sometimes in the dark of night, I thought he might be right. I am no delicate flower of a woman, but built of sturdy peasant proportions, with strong arms, wide hips, and a goodly bosom. I was built to make babies, yet I had no live children.

Instead, I had painting and my math lessons with a wispy acolyte from my local church—which is not so bad, I suppose, for both skills would eventually allow me a measure of independence. I could mix my own paints if I was better at math. It is through painting that I met Cristofano and Galileo. Speaking of which, Cristofano and I painted our dual *Judiths* and dear Galileo acted as the final judge in our silly contest silly. My *Judith and Her Maidservant* was a sister painting to my *Judith Slaying Holofernes*. I painted both Judith and Abra in the flower of their womanly strength. Abra stood with her back to the viewer, holding a shallow basket in which lay the head of Holofernes. I will admit that this time my Assyrian general bore a strong resemblance to Agostino Tassi. Judith's torso faced the viewer, her sword resting against her shoulder, like a soldier just home from war. Thus the two women faced each other in sisterly complicity, caught in a moment in which they hear some danger and glance behind them. Neither Judith's expression nor the set of Abra's shoulders suggest the women are afraid or ashamed. Though I later gave up the painting to the dowager duchess, I regard it as one of my best paintings. Indeed, I confess that I painted another version of it for my own pleasure some years later.

At first glance, Cristofano's *Judith and Her Maidservant* was much the same as mine, but as our judge Galileo pointed out, the similarity was only superficial. In the months the two of us worked on our paintings, Cristofano did something awful to anger his mistress, La Mazzafirra, who was a famous—or shall I say, infamous—courtesan. On the subject of his misdeed, he had few words, so I couldn't tell you what he did, but all of Florence knew of her fury. By way of an apology, he painted his Judith as La Mazzafirra and put his face on Holofernes's head. His Judith, like his mistress, was frankly sexual. She stared out of the canvas and straight into the viewer's eyes, her face and posture promising seduction. She grasped Holofernes's hair firmly in her fist, challenging the viewer to disapprove of her.

"Why, it's danger and sex all in one painting," Galileo commented when he first saw Cristofano's canvas. Cristofano and I had stood our paintings side by side in the church atrium so they might be judged, while a half dozen members of the academy gathered around, eager to hear the great scientist's judgment.

"Love and death," Cristofano said.

I sighed a little. I liked Cristofano quite a lot, but I was sick and tired of seductive Judiths and Susannas. Why must women always be portrayed as either saintly Madonnas or rapacious Magdalenes? I consoled myself with the fact that his Abra wasn't a dried-up crone.

Galileo stroked his beard and glanced between the two paintings. "Cristofano's is an exceedingly alluring painting, to be sure. But Artemisia's is truer to the Biblical story. The Apocrypha tells the tale of a virtuous and strong woman who saved her people through an act of physical daring." He gestured at my painting and said, "That is exactly what you've expressed here."

And so, as the academy looked on, I bested an exceedingly good painter and won my point about Judith and Abra. Whether I affected any long-term change in the way my male colleagues thought about female subjects, I cannot say. I will say that the following year I became the first woman to be invited to become a full member of the Academy of Arts and Drawing. Papà heard of my singular honor and wrote to me asking if he could attend the induction ceremony. I wanted to write a letter to himself, but even with Signor Galileo's writing lessons I had not the skill to avoid making a fool of myself. Instead, I dictated a letter to Cristofano, telling father he was much too busy painting frescoes with Agostino to come to Florence. I didn't need Papà in my life, or so I told myself.

One fine spring day when I was newly pregnant with my second son, Cristofano, who I hoped would help heal the hurt of losing sweet, departed Giovanni, Uncle Michaelo came to me and announced his palazzo was ready for decorations. "Come with me, my darling one, and I will show you the gallery I wish painted first," he said.

We took a carriage to Casa Buonarroti. It was a magnificent palace in the middle of Florence, built on land left to Michaelo by his granduncle Michelangelo. Michelangelo died before he finished the house, and Uncle Michaelo took the abandoned building and turned it into a structure fit for kings. Michaelo intended the building to be a museum and library for his famous relative's works.

We entered an airy central courtyard. As he walked me across the space, he waved at the doors that opened onto the yard. "I intend the ground floor to be living space, but the upper floor I shall dedicate to not only my uncle, but to the ideas of science and logic and beauty by which he lived."

We walked up a wide marble staircase, where we came upon a large, plain room. "I intend to hang paintings here, so I shall leave the walls and ceilings unadorned," he said. Then he motioned me through a set of doors on the far side of the room. "Over here. I want you to see this."

Beyond the doors lay a magnificent space. Woodwork framed bare panels on the wall and ceiling as if they were richly carved frames. "Oh, this is lovely, Uncle. What are your plans?"

He beamed at me. "On the walls I shall have important moments from my granduncle's life, while on the ceiling will be events from after his death. My friend Sigismondo Coccapani has agreed to paint a *Michelangelo Crowned by the Arts* here in the center to symbolize his treatment in heaven. Anastasio Fontebuoni, Giovanni Biliverti, Matteo Rosselli, and several others have also agreed to paint either wall or ceiling panels. And I shall have a figure at each corner of the ceiling to represent Michelangelo's personal virtues: tolerance, piety, inspiration, inclination, virtue, moderation, and honor. They shall be painted as beautiful Muses. I know you are busy, but I would like you to paint one of these virtues. You may have your pick." He rocked back on his heels at the pleasure of his offer.

"I will be the only woman painter?" I asked.

He stroked his wispy gray beard. "Do you know any other women who paint? It would give me great pleasure to send for Signora Fontana, but as you know, she died last year."

We shared a sigh at the passing of a great painter and lovely woman. Then suddenly, I knew which virtue I'd paint. "I'll take inclination. Lavinia Fontana and I would not be painters if it were not for the same inclination we share with male painters."

Uncle Michaelo rubbed his hands together in glee. "So it shall be," he said. Then he held up his index finger. "I ask only one thing of you as you make your choices. Paint in the Florentine style of my granduncle's time. I am aware that you are a Caravaggisti, but I want no natural realism."

"Like the Sistine Chapel?" I felt that thrill of a painting not yet sketched and decided. This would be an interesting experiment in old-style Mannerism, and if I did it well, it would show the world I was the master, so to speak, of both the ideal Florentine style and the realistic style popular in Rome.

Uncle Michaelo threw an arm around my shoulders and

pulled me to him like a father would a favored daughter. "Once again, my dear, you understand perfectly. This ceiling, like Michelangelo's ceiling, will represent the heavens, and its images should be celestial."

That summer I worked on my *Allegory of Inclination* in the afternoons and on a painting for the dowager duchess (of which I shall write more about later) in the mornings. After the midday meal, I worked in Michaelo's gallery. Some afternoons I painted alone, but often two painters worked with me, Biliverti and Coccapani. Both men were a decade older than me, but they painted as if they'd been born fifty years earlier. I suspect that was because they had both apprenticed under the great Roman Mannerist Cigoli, who in turn trained under Cristofano's father, Allesandro Allori, who worked with my Uncle Aurelio Lomi, who trained my father, who trained me. Oh, what tangled webs of connection we artists make. Both men also belonged to the academy, painted for the Medicis on occasion, and considered themselves friends of Galileo.

So, you see, we knew the same artists, worked for the same patrons, and were congenial with each other. I know this sounds unlikely, but we did not squabble. Sometimes I compared my life in Florence to my life in Rome and marveled at my good fortune. True, my husband was no prize, but he mostly stayed out of my way and my married status allowed me freedoms I would not have had as a single woman. In Rome, I had lived entirely within my father's household, meeting very few other painters—with the notable exception of Agostino Tassi, who turned out to be less painter and more monster. In Florence, I mixed with dozens of painters, each talented in their own way and all polite to this lady painter. I painted for the city's most powerful family and held conversations with the most intelligent people in the world. Who could ask for more?

Signor Galileo, for example, always took time to speak to me, both at the academy and at Uncle Michaelo's, where he frequently visited. That he took notice of me at all was entirely remarkable, made more so because he was in trouble with the papal authorities in those years. It began the summer I first met him—or more accurately, perhaps, it began a decade earlier when the then-dowager duchess hired Galileo to tutor her son Cosimo. Cosimo and Galileo got along so well that the Medicis invited the scientist to Cosimo's wedding to Maria of Austria. Galileo even named the four moons of Jupiter after Cosimo and his brothers.

So that was all well and good, but then the dowager duchess invited one of Galileo's students, Cosimo Boscaglia to court. I've never met the fellow, but he sounds like an ungrateful wretch, for he convinced the dowager duchess that Galileo was wrong about the sun being the center of the universe. Boscaglia even had mathematical formulas to prove both Copernicus and Galileo's calculations about the Earth's movement were wrong. Then he wrote a public letter announcing the dowager duchess agreed with him that the planets revolved around the Earth, which did not move. To suggest otherwise, he wrote, was a direct contradiction of the Bible, making it heresy.

Offended at the temerity of his former student, Galileo wrote his own public letter. In it, he corrected Boscaglia's math and, more importantly, argued that one could be a Copernican and not a heretic. He reminded the letter's readers that both Aristotle and Ptolemy agreed the Earth spun on an axis, so the idea that the Earth moves was not a new one, nor did it originate with him.

Galileo and I discussed it one day at the academy, in part so I could better understand the problem. It didn't feel to me like the Earth moved, nor did it seem like the sun did not, but I trusted in Galileo, who was a much smarter person than I.

"What frustrates me," he said as we sat in the atrium, he drawing and I painting, "is this nonsense that a man of science cannot also be a man of God. As if God gave us our nimble brains and expected us not to use them. Would God be that foolish?"

I set down my paintbrush and gave the question more consideration than he expected. "I want to say no. God would not be that foolish, but the Bible also says God wants women to be submissive and be only wives and mothers. And yet here I stand, as good a painter as any man. If you ask me, God expecting women to be inferior when we are not is foolish. Thus God can be foolish."

Galileo frowned. "I think you confuse God with Saint Paul, who quite hated women. God gave his only son to Mary to birth and raise, and God would not have done that if he hated women. I don't think it is God who hates women; it's the so-called men of God," he said. "But back to my argument. How is the universe less perfect if the Earth moves and the sun does not? If God made it so, then ipso facto, the Earth's movement is perfect. It is we, puny and foolish humans, who misunderstood God's system for so long, who are imperfect—not God and not the universe."

Considering this argument, I took up my paintbrush again and said, "The problem with your reasoning, my friend, is that you think logic should rule the day. If you are correct that humans are imperfect, then they can be illogical. Your heliocentrism, as you call it, is no less alarming to people because it is factually or morally correct. Most people care little for facts they can't or won't understand."

He stubbornly stuck out his lower lip. "It is so. But rational beings must embrace facts, not fancy."

"In what world?" I laughed. "In the world where a man may abuse and dishonor a maiden girl, be convicted of rape and jailed, only to be freed to live his life?"

"Hmm. While the girl trails the violence done to her behind her like a wedding veil in the wind. I see your point, but I am still right. I know I am."

I laughed again. "You miss the point entirely, my friend. The world does not care that you are right."

And he *was* right, or so I believe to this day. But right has nothing to do with life in a world in which church leaders have as much power as kings, and minions with bad math have curried their favor. Galileo's letter brought attention to the issue, attention the church did not want. That summer, the Inquisition declared Galileo's position on heliocentrism violated a Council of Trent decree that said no man outside the church could interpret Christian doctrine to distort scripture. The church would consider anyone who did so a heretic.

One day, as I was putting the finishing touches on the clouds in my *Allegory of Inclination*, Galileo came storming into Uncle Michaelo's gallery. He waved a piece of parchment around his head like a madman.

"They've gone and done it," he yelled. "That worm Cardinal Sfondrati has proclaimed my stance on heliocentrism presumptuous. *Presumptuous.* That puppy, I'll show him presumptuous!"

Signor Coccapani, who was working on his allegorical figure that afternoon, climbed down from his ladder to stand next to the raving Galileo. I stayed where I was. Anyone who has ever climbed a ladder in a skirt knows the perils, even when the woman in question isn't in her sixth month of pregnancy. Besides, I liked looking down at the men.

The painters gathered around Galileo and undertook a loud and fruitless discussion of the mental weaknesses of the cardinals in charge of the Inquisition. It went on for quite a while, but I kept painting. I wanted to finish my piece of the ceiling so I could move on to other projects, ones that did not require standing on a ladder or holding my brushes above my head. Below me, Galileo bravely declared that he would not change his position.

"Truth is the truth," he yelled, throwing his arms in the air. "I need a large jug of wine."

He stalked from the room, painters following him like ducklings after their mamma. One of the advantages of being a lady painter is I am never asked to interrupt my work for an afternoon of public drunkenness. In the end, the Inquisition decided to ignore Galileo, and Galileo most assuredly ignored them, so nothing came of it. At least, not then.

~

I had all the work a painter could desire during my time in Florence. In addition to the work I did for Uncle Michaelo, the dowager duchess commissioned several paintings from me. The first was a Saint Catherine. The dowager thought I might use the saint's allegory in conjunction with painting my self-portrait, in part because her son Cosimo collected images of artists he liked. She'd come to my studio at the academy, mostly to argue with Galileo about the Earth and sun controversy. I'm not sure the dowager duchess really objected to heliocentrism; she argued with Galileo like a woman who enjoyed verbal jousting. Anyway, one day she suggested I paint myself as Saint Catherine of Alexandria.

"Why her?" I asked. "And why a self-portrait?" I didn't want to paint myself, but I knew better than to argue with the dowager duchess. Galileo could argue with her, but not me, a young, relatively unknown female painter with a scandalous past.

She took a seat on my best chair, the one that didn't wobble, while I kept to my feet, as I always did in the dowager duchess's presence. "Ah, you don't know," she said. "This is what comes of women having so little education. I thank my Lord above that my father saw fit to educate his daughters alongside his sons. So, let me sum up. Saint Catherine's story is two stories. In the first, Catherine is a martyred princess and scholar, unjustly accused of heresy by the pagan Emperor Maxentius."

I nodded, seeing why she would want me to paint myself as a woman unfairly accused, even if it was more than a little presumptuous. "I know Joan of Arc claimed Saint Catherine appeared to her before her martyrdom," I said.

The dowager duchess squinted her eyes in approval. "Yes, but there's more. Many scholars believe the story of Catherine is, in part, based on the life of Hypatia. May I assume you have not heard of Hypatia?" I nodded, and she continued, "Well, she was a woman of the late Roman Empire, famed for her knowledge of mathematics, natural philosophy, and astronomy. She also ran a school where she educated both sexes. Then Christians arrived and objected to a woman of such learning and power. One night, a mob of Christian men tore her to pieces. Some stories say they flayed her first."

I gasped. It was hard to imagine such cruelty.

"I'd like a Saint Catherine with your face," she said. "I shall hang it for all to see and it will do more for your reputation and career than all your vengeful Judiths, no matter how good they are."

The dowager duchess did just as she promised. When the painting was complete, her son, Grand Duke Cosimo, liked it so much that he asked for his own. So I painted the second *Saint Catherine* like the first, as a mix of my naturalist inclinations and Florentine Mannerist idealism. I varied the work by using more vivid colors than the first; Cosimo had a great fondness for bright colors. Those two paintings led to other female saint—themed paintings, some for the dowager duchess and some for other prominent Florentines.

Over the next few years, I painted many more works for the dowager duchess. A portrait of Anne of Austria as the goddess

Minerva ended up being my least favorite painting, but it didn't start that way.

The dowager duchess asked me to attend the installation of the *Judith and Her Maidservant* in her public audience chamber. It was an exceedingly grand event and my first experience with public adulation. Once all the kind words had been said, the dowager duchess dismissed all her courtiers but me.

Once again, she invited me to sit with her. She called for wine before pulling a heavy piece of parchment from a pile and setting it before her. "I have here a letter from my sister Marie, Queen Regent of France."

"The queen of France is your sister?" I asked. I felt foolish the second the question was out of my mouth. Thankfully, the dowager duchess resisted pointing out my stupidity. "Of course she is, by marriage," I corrected myself.

"You are correct, my dear. Marie is a Medici by birth, daughter of Grand Duke Francesco, my late husband's brother, while I am a Medici by marriage. Though I regard us more as sister-rulers than as family, if you take my meaning."

I did. Marie de Medici was perhaps the most famous woman in Europe. She'd married the King of France back at the turn of the century. Then, only two years ago, she forced him to crown her queen, and the very next day the king, who was a Protestant, was assassinated by a Catholic madman. I don't mean all Catholics are madmen, only that this Catholic assassin was one—as all assassins are. No one blamed Queen Marie. People had been trying to kill her husband since the Edict of Nantes granted French Protestants rights in France, a country as Catholic as

Spain or any of the Italian kingdoms. The new king, their oldest son, Louis, was only nine when his father was killed, so Marie acted as ruler in his stead. When the French king came of age, Marie remained regent and firmly in control of France.

"I hear she is a formidable woman," I said. I couldn't resist adding, "Much like yourself, Your Highness."

"Bah," the dowager duchess said with a wave of her hand. "Don't you become a bootlicker. I have far too many worthless flatterers." We shared a smile. "And no doubt you've heard she's married the king to Anne of Austria, the King of Spain's daughter? To shore up her Catholic credentials, no doubt, while creating a powerful Catholic alliance, should she wish to make war on French Protestants."

"The marriage should be good for the royal treasury too," I added. Everyone knows the Spanish have more gold than they know what to do with. It's all thanks to their adventures in the New World, though it was an Italian ship captain who first got them there.

"Just so." The dowager duchess slid a hinged wooden frame over to me. "You'll see poor Anne was not chosen for her looks, though of course royal brides never are, and the Hapsburgs are not a handsome family."

The portrait she showed me was no more than five inches square. Anne was a Hapsburg on her mother's side and it showed in her heavy-lidded, protuberant eyes, lumpen nose, and weak chin. I looked from the portrait to the dowager duchess. There was only one reason Queen Marie would have sent this portrait from France to Florence. "Surely not?" I asked.

"Oh, yes," the dowager duchess snorted. "Word of your talent has reached the queen regent. She is a great patron of the arts and she wants one of your paintings. But, ever the political animal, she wants a particular painting for particular means. The king and his bride are both fourteen years old and of an age when France might expect heirs, but Marie writes that he refuses to consummate the marriage and he's quite vocal about it."

I looked again at the small portrait. It was true that Anne was not pretty, but she looked gentle and kind. How hard it must be for her to be so publicly rejected. "I fail to see how a more flattering portrait will help," I said. "Even if I were to paint her prettier, the king would still have the real Anne before him."

The dowager duchess nodded. "I'm sure the queen regent knows this. What she seeks is a more heroic version of Anne, not a prettier one. Marie surrounds herself with Minerva iconography and her son is fond of the goddess as well."

Ah, that made sense. Minerva was a Roman goddess of wisdom and peace. She was also the patron goddess of art. Minerva promoted peace through military preparedness, so she was often portrayed in armor or armed with a pike, and sometimes bare-breasted, sometimes not, like the Amazons of legend.

She picked up the letter and waved it at me. "Of course, Marie pretends she is conveying the king's wishes, which is nonsense, but you can say you've painted for the King of France. It is no small thing and the value of all your work will go up."

That's how I came to paint poor, unloved Anne of Austria as Minerva. I worked from that tiny portrait, particularly for her head, and a live model for the rest of her. I didn't think a fourteen-year-old girl in armor was a good idea. Besides, I'd never painted armor before and wasn't about to do it the first time for the queen regent of France. Instead, I put Anne in a silky dress so I could work my draped fabric magic. I did give her a pike and a wreath of laurel leaves for her head. Minerva is the Roman version of the Greek goddess Athena. All I knew of Athena was that she had a Gorgon head on her shield, so I painted a rather silly one into the side of Minerva's chair. I also painted her breasts bared, thinking the sight of his bride semi-nude might induce the young king to lust. The dowager duchess disagreed and made me paint over the nipples. Such is the life of a lowly painter working on a commission. The great and powerful, who can so easily bear the poverty and suffering of their people, cannot tolerate the sight of a woman's nipples.

As if to make up for the Minerva, the dowager duchess next asked me to paint a *Jael and Sisera*. Jael is an Old Testament heroine who helped defeat Sisera, who led the enemies of the Israelites. She drove a tent peg through Sisera's ear while he slept, after which the Israelites defeated Sisera's army. Like Judith, Jael is often painted as a reluctant heroine or as a madwoman. As you might guess, I painted her much as I painted my Judith, as a strong woman doing what must be done. Sisera curls on the floor, asleep, his head almost in Jael's lap. She holds the tent peg to his ear with one hand, the hammer raised for its strike in the other. I gave Jael a tender half smile, almost as if she were a mother looking down at her babe. The dowager duchess took such pleasure from the finished painting that she insisted I paint my name on the column behind Sisera so it appeared carved into the stone.

Through all this talk of Florence, I have neglected to mention my dear friend Francesco Maringhi. I met him when I first came to the city, though at the time I thought him no more than a dilettante. In fairness, I wasn't far wrong. Francesco inherited a large fortune from his merchant father and used his money to buy influence with the Medici court. Grand Duke Cosimo, a gentle and kind young man, took a shine to the fatherly Maringhi because they shared a love of art. Indeed, both Cosimo and Maringhi painted a little themselves. Maringhi was good enough to win a commission to paint the dome of a minor church in Rome. When I met Maringhi, as he liked to be called, he'd just returned from Rome. Cosimo, who had more daring taste than his mother, the dowager duchess, liked to visit Uncle Michaelo's gallery and see the progress of various naked ceiling muses. On one such occasion, he brought Maringhi with him.

I was high on my ladder, and pregnant with my doomed second son, when I first saw him. Our eyes locked and time stopped for a moment. I know that sounds like romantic twaddle, but that's how it happened. It might surprise you, but Maringhi was the only man I ever loved. And because I was married and already in possession of a dubious reputation, we could never do more than love in secret.

Maringhi was an unlikely love interest, being twenty years older than myself and portly. But he had the loveliest gray-blue eyes, eyes that saw the real me. It did not escape my notice that my dear Maringhi somewhat resembled Papà, but Maringhi never betrayed me or threw me to the wolves. At first, he visited me at the gallery, then he visited the academy. Cristofano always pretended Maringhi came to see him, and in this way we were never found out. My sweet man would come in the mornings and stay for an hour or two. Sometimes we talked while I painted, but other times he read. Our companionable silences made me feel safe and understood.

In the summer of 1617, my dear daughter Prudenzia, named after my dear mother, came into the world, dark-haired and red-faced in indignation. A little over a year later, I gave birth to my fourth child and second daughter, a perfectly pink creature I named Lisabella. And lest you think otherwise, both children were my husband's, for Maringhi and I never consummated our relationship. I may not be the most religious woman in Florence, but I wasn't so fallen as to break my marriage vows.

Most mornings, Maringhi would come to me at the academy, close the door, and push me into a comfortable chair (which Cristofano kindly provided). While I sat with my swollen feet on a stool, he would paint my backgrounds, prepare a canvas, or even grind pigments, like a lowly apprentice. He brought me cooling drinks and bits of food, in all ways doting on me as if the children I carried were his own. Pietro enjoyed the process of getting me pregnant, but he didn't much care for me as the mother of his children. I found my love for Maringhi expanding along with the love I felt for my daughters. After the birth of my second daughter, I felt as if dear Maringhi deserved better than a chaste relationship. But when I tried to ignore my marriage vows, my sweet Maringhi would not have it.

"I love you and I will not ruin you as others have done," he said one morning after I threw myself at him in a most passionate and inappropriate manner. He grasped my shoulders in his hands and held me at arm's length. "A man is only a man if he can control himself."

"But I love you," I whispered, trying not to cry.

He smiled at me and led me back to my chair. "I love you too, my sweet girl, but I am a man of many decades and have learned to curb my passions. I will be strong for you, my dear."

"No one would ever know," I said, pointing at my studio's closed door.

He leaned forward and kissed my forehead. "Of course someone would know. *We* would know. And then Cristofano, and Galileo, and . . ."

"But they would keep our secret."

He shook his head. "They would mean to, but affairs of the heart never stay secret. Only one person can keep a secret, and ofttimes not even then."

So, we continued with our platonic romance. If anyone suspected, they never said a thing.

The year I carried Prudenzia, I painted a *Penitent Magdalene* and a new version of *Judith Slaying Holofernes* for Grand Duke Cosimo. Having heard that monster Tassi had returned to Rome, his banishment entirely ignored by the authorities, I was happy to paint a second, even bloodier version of the painting. *My Penitent Magdalene* took longer than I'd planned, in part because I didn't want to paint Mary Magdalene the way everyone else did, as a vain courtesan. Caravaggio's *Conversion of the Magdalene* set the standard twenty years ago. That painting featured a richly dressed woman before a mirror, in discussion with a dowdy Martha. The moral was that the domestic Martha had less value than the seductive but regretful Magdalene. I didn't want anything like that, objecting to the impulse that made women into either temptresses or saints.

I first determined I would paint the Magdalene alone, without Martha, thus avoiding prioritizing one type of womanhood over another. It took a while to work out my Magdalene's attitude. I finally settled on a figure who was richly dressed but contemplative, as if she were on the verge of the revelation that would transform her into a saint. I used a rich palette of yellow-gold that would eventually become my signature color and juxtaposed this brightness against dark green and burgundy backgrounds. Liking the way the strong colors contrasted with the quietness of the seated Magdalene, I resolved to paint more paintings in that style.

The evolution of my paintings, the strong colors and increased use of light reflected the happiness of my life in Florence. I had interesting friends, rich patrons, and two little girls. I lived in Florence for eight years and loved it as I had no other city, not even Rome. Like Rome, Florence has a river running through it, making it a city full of gardens and fruit trees and singing birds. The Medici family, who rule Tuscany and thus Florence, think nothing of spending their immense fortune on new public buildings, churches, and art to adorn it all. Florentine bankers, renowned through Europe for their acumen, brought more wealth to the city, which in turn kept merchants and artisans well employed. Oh, the city had its poor, crippled beggars, and poxed whores, but not like in Rome, where the papacy's riches failed to trickle down to the populace.

Yes, Pietro was an imperfect husband, but he was gone from home so often that I operated as an independent woman much of the time. He drank too much and made too little money, but I had work aplenty and kept a roof over our little family's heads without him. And I had my dear Maringhi.

And then disaster struck. My near-perfect life fell apart and I was forced, for the second time, to leave a city I loved and start over in a strange place. Such was the story of my life.

Chapter Six

My time in Florence ended the first day of June in the year of our Lord 1619. I was accustomed to waking at dawn and tending to my two daughters, who were only fourteen months apart in age. I would dress and feed them, then leave them with the neighbor woman, whom I paid to watch them while I painted at the academy. The system worked because my husband continued to bless my life with his absence.

Then came that June morning. I walked into the small room that served as a nursery and found Prudenzia, who was not quite two, and Lisabella, who was eight months old, burning with fever. Spring is a perilous time for city dwellers, though the miasmas that bring disease do not generally peak until the long, hot days of late summer. I always kept their shutters closed while they slept to keep out the unhealthy night air. I was careful not to take my small daughters out about the city, for cities are unhealthful places. Despite my caution, I found both of them burning hot and listless. I put Lisabella to my breast, but she thrashed her little head back and forth and refused to take the nipple. I could feel the heat coming off her like a bread oven. Prudenzia would not take the breast either, and yellow mucus ran from her tiny nostrils.

I ran downstairs, caught up a water bucket, and dashed down the street to the common well, thankful the water was still quite cool this time of year. My neighbor Maria found me two hours later. I kept applying damp rags to my baby girls in an attempt to cool them, while also trying to keep them clean as their tiny bodies emptied of seemingly everything they'd ever eaten or drunk. Maria and I battled with the sickness through the day and into the night, though the harder we worked, the sicker the girls became. By evening, Lisabella had red spots all over her body and was as limp as her favorite rag doll. Prudenzia had spots too, but only a few scattered across her chest.

My sweet Lisabella slipped from this world just before the midnight church bells. Maria took her from her cot, washed her, and wrapped her one last time. While she ministered to my daughter who had gone, I attended to Prudenzia. She took a bit of broth and some lemon water sometime in the night. I focused on my living daughter, fearing that if I thought too much of Lisabella, I would come undone.

When the dawn came, I still had one daughter left alive. I tried to give thanks to God for that small favor, but I did not feel as grateful as I should have, I fear. We took tiny Lisabella to the church, where a kind priest said the last mass over her before burial. By we, I mean Maria and myself. Pietro was nowhere to be found.

Four days after Lisabella's death, I woke to a pounding on my door. I pulled on my brown dress and stumbled downstairs, fearing it was Pietro, come home so drunk that he could not open the door. Instead, there stood on my doorstep a large man wearing the official seal of Florence. Behind him stood four roughly dressed men and a large, empty wagon.

"Are you Signora Stiattesi?" the one nearest me asked.

When I nodded, he thrust a piece of paper into my hands. "I am ordered to confiscate your household goods for payment of debts."

I shook my head, not understanding. Debt? I didn't have any debt; I had another dead child. He ignored my confusion, pulled me out on the street, and flung me to the ground.

As I lay in the dirt and horse muck, I realized what had happened. This was Pietro's doing. It explained why he hadn't been home for days. The wretched man knew and was in hiding.

I picked myself up and brushed the mess off my skirts as best I could. Just as I was about to ask if I could retrieve my daughter, one of the men stepped through my front doorway with Prudenzia in his arms. He pushed her at me and smiled sadly. It was stupid, but that stranger's regret made me feel slightly better.

My daughter and I stood in the street with a crowd of neighbors and watched as the men loaded up and carted away everything I owned, from my old friend *Susanna and the Elders* to our two dented kitchen pots. While I stood there in a kind of dream state, Maria had the sense to send a boy to the academy to alert my friends. Cristofano arrived just as the men drove the wagon away. He took us to his home, where he and his housekeeper took care of Prudenzia and me. I had my daughter, my skill as a painter, and good friends. I could survive this latest indignity.

Before the week was out, my dear Maringhi helped me instigate a lawsuit against the city, and he represented me in court. We discovered that my husband's profligacy was much worse than I'd ever imagined. Pietro had debts in every tavern and whorehouse in town. He also had bills with three different tailors, two color shops, and one stable, where he kept a horse I hadn't known about. In court, Maringhi argued that the debts were not my own, but my husband's. The court contended that it didn't matter which of us had run up debts; the household goods, including my paintings, belonged to my husband by right of law. It took months to negotiate the terms of a debt agreement, and through it all Pietro never once made an appearance. He had vanished. Cristofano and Maringhi asked around at the city taverns but found only rumors. Some said he fled to Mantua, others said Milan.

Finally, the court allowed dear Maringhi to buy my property back. He soon after sold it all to me for one florin (a coin he had given me moments before I gave it back to him). The dowager duchess wrote me a kind letter, telling me she would recommend me to patrons in any city of my choice. It was her polite way of telling me I should leave Florence. I don't think she was being cruel—she wanted me to get away from my husband before he utterly ruined me. Of course, I am just guessing, because one so grand as the dowager duchess of Tuscany does not explain herself to twice-disgraced painters.

I packed my paintings, supplies, and clothes for Prudenzia and myself, and hired a coach to take us to Rome. The thought of Rome made my stomach lurch, but I didn't know where else to go. My twenty-three-year-old brother Francesco kept a small house in Sassia, and though I hadn't seen him in eight years, we had exchanged several warm letters. I knew he would take us in.

It turned out that Francesco lived with several other painter's assistants in the sort of genial squalor young men everywhere seem to enjoy. I minded, both for myself and my living child, and soon set the place to rights, but in the three months I lived with Francesco, I painted not one stroke. The double loss of my youngest daughter and my life in Florence left me feeling paralyzed. I drifted through my days, saying and doing the sort of things a widowed sister would (though I was not widowed, only shamed and abandoned). In my head I heard only the dull buzz of nothingness.

Then one day Francesco brought me a letter. "It's from Papà," he said. I took the letter and saw the broken seal. He shrugged with his whole body. "I didn't want to give it to you unless I knew he was . . ." Francesco paused. "You know, if he were going to be mean to you, I would have thrown it away. But it's not like that."

I smiled at my brother and opened the letter. Papà had

found work in Genoa and wanted me to join him. I looked up from the letter and into Francesco's eyes. "What do you think? Should I go?" I asked.

"I do." He scuffed his left foot on the flagstones. "There's nothing here for you, and you can't go back to Florence. Not if Pietro is there racking up more debt. Is he?"

It was my turn to scuff at the floor. "I don't know. He fled the city to avoid the lawsuit. He could be here, for all I know."

"Is that why you don't go out? You're afraid of your husband?"

I told my brother it was, though my reasons were more complicated than the simple fear of running into my husband. The problem was, Francesco was young during the rape trial. He probably remembered very little about the whole debacle.

"Go to Genoa," my brother said. "Maybe your life is there. If not, it's somewhere. Go looking for it, because you're not going to find it keeping house for me."

My brother is a smart man. My life wasn't in Genoa, but the road to finding it started there. Genoa is not a great art city, not like Florence or Rome, but it has a bustling port, and for reasons too complicated for me to understand, Genoese bankers control the debt of Europe's most powerful countries. This makes the city prosperous. Genoa looks out on the Mediterranean Sea, roughly in the center of the Republic of Genoa, on the northwest coast of the Italian Peninsula. In theory, Genoa is independent, but in practice, it depends mightily on the nations in debt to its bankers. France, particularly the Duchy of Savoy, would dearly like to take control of Genoa, including the island of Corsica, but for now, Spain helps hold France at bay. Thus, much in the city is influenced by the Spanish, including the art scene.

Papà's letter said he'd met a man who introduced him to several important patrons in Genoa and that I should come share in the riches. Papà doesn't have the kind of fame that leads to the meeting of great men, but luckily for Papà, Pope Paul V sickened and died, triggering the election of a new pope. Rome filled with rich men lobbying for their choice for the next pope, including the exceedingly rich Genoa banker Giovanni Sauli. I do not know if he supported the new Pope Gregory XV, but while he was in town he saw Papà's *Saint Francis Supported by an Angel* at the papal palace and liked it (for which I give the man credit. Papà's Saint Francis is a masterpiece of light and shadow).

As a consequence, Sauli enticed Papà to Genoa to paint frescoes at Palazzo Sauli. Sauli also introduced Papà to other rich bankers, each of whom was eager to have paintings that would demonstrate how rich they were. And Papà, in turn, invited me to join him.

Papà had tried to heal the breach between us a half dozen times while I was in Florence, but as long as he was working with Tassi I wasn't interested. Then I heard Papà and Tassi had a falling out after Tassi tried to blame Papà for some badly painted frescoes at the Quirinal Palace. Papà can't be friends with a man who smears his reputation, though he never had any trouble with the ruination of mine. But thinking like that wasn't going to help me find work, and it was time Prudenzia met her grandpapà.

Our carriage arrived in the mid-afternoon at an address

supplied by Papà. Hot and exceedingly dusty from the road, we came to rest at a small but neatly kept house. From our driver's remarks, I discovered it stood on the square behind Sauli's magnificent palazzo in what is a very good neighborhood. Lime and lemon trees grew both on the street and in the house's central courtyard, where a fountain tinkled merrily in counterpoint to the singing of small birds. I set Prudenzia down so she could explore the courtyard, just as a painter's apprentice came out to meet us. He was a boy of no more than ten years of age, but he vowed to fetch men who could unload my trunks and crated paintings. When two burly men appeared, I admonished them to take particular care with the large box in which I'd crated my Susanna. I'd struggled with the decision to haul the huge painting with me to Genoa, but it seemed wise to have my best painter's sample with me. No one was going to hire me just because I was Orazio Gentileschi's daughter. Worse, the letter I carried from the dowager duchess would mean little this far from Florence, and in territory hostile to the Medicis (who are allied with France, not Spain).

The little painter's assistant, who told me to call him Mateo, said Papà was staying at a country villa outside Genoa. "The master, he tells me," Mateo said, "to stay here until you come, signora. And then I bring you to him." He bounced on his tiptoes when he described this important assignment. "We go now?"

"Not quite now," I told him, hoisting Prudenzia onto my hip and kissing her sweaty cheek. "I must bathe and change, and I cannot go anywhere until I find a nursemaid for my daughter." I certainly wasn't going to cart her out into the country after the already exhausting trip from Rome, not when this house looked so neat and clean.

"My *nonnina* is here," Mateo crowed. "She keeps house for the great painter and I am his assistant. He is teaching me to paint so I too can one day be a great man like my master."

I chuckled and resisted the impulse to tussle the boy's thick black hair. In less than three hours, Mateo had sorted my luggage into a large upstairs room. Meanwhile, his grandmother, a woman of middling age named Guilia, called up bathwater, fed the baby and me, then unpacked my trunks. Prudenzia, exhausted from the journey and with her belly full of bread and milk, was fast asleep on Guilia's bed by the time I'd dressed in clean clothes.

Mateo and I took a hired carriage north through the city along streets crowded with horsed men and people on foot, some dressed richly in linens and silk and others in the rough-spun cotton of peasants. In the failing light, the city's orange and yellow-gold buildings glowed like warm flames on a summer night. The air, cooled by the sea, stirred in a gentle breeze and I felt glad I had come to this place. We passed out of the city by climbing a steep hill past groves of olive and lemon trees. After the hill, our road turned back to run alongside the sea, and we traveled only a little further until we stopped in front of a magnificent country villa. I fought the urge to spring from the carriage and run away as fast as my legs would carry me. But then Mateo shouted our arrival, and before I'd climbed out of the carriage, Papà stood before me.

Though I'd meant to hold myself aloof, I allowed him to

pull me into a rib-cracking hug. He looked the same as ever, though his forehead was a little larger, his hair having retreated further back on his head. He still wore his mustache twirled into jaunty little points, a facial adornment that only enhanced his elfin appearance. My trepidation melted away at the sight of dear Papà.

"My darling daughter," he half-whispered into my ear. "You have grown into a woman. I have missed you so much."

"I missed you too, Papà," I said, and was surprised to find I meant it.

Papà introduced me to Marcantonio Doria, who owned the house. He was a fat little man, no taller than Papà, but draped in enough velvet and silk to cover a much larger man.

"Your papà will paint some frescoes in my gallery," he said. "I can't have that scoundrel Sauli outdoing me."

Signor Doria smiled at his pronouncement to show he meant no real insult, before leading Papà, Mateo, and me into his house. We dined on scallops over tiny noodles, roast partridge, and a host of salads and cheeses before we retired to the gallery to look over Papà's progress. He'd just sketched in walls to be painted, though he'd begun applying color in one spot.

"Your papà tells me you are talented, Signora Stiattesi," Doria said.

"Gentileschi," I said. "Signora Gentileschi."

Doria shared a look with Papà that told me they'd spoken of my errant husband, but he accepted my name change with no further discussion. I'd allowed Florentines to call me by my husband's name, though I'd never signed it to paintings. Instead, the first few years in Florence I used my Uncle Lomi's name before returning to Gentileschi. These days I used Gentileschi both on my painting signature and as my legal name.

"I do paint," I added, "but not generally frescoes. That is my papà's specialty."

Signor Doria looked relieved at this news, as if he feared he would be compelled to hire a woman out of politeness. We spoke of this and that, figures to be painted, and colors to be chosen, while I wondered what I was doing in this place. There wasn't anything here for me. And then I found out why Papà had ordered me to Signor Doria's house. The banker knew everyone in the art world, and he was willing to introduce me to them.

I met my first important Genoan painter only days later. I arrived at Signor Doria's house in the evening, as I had when I first met him, and was ushered into a fine sitting room. There sat a tiny, wizened woman. As I came in the door, she looked up, revealing eyes glazed with the milky whiteness of the blind.

"Sit, sit, little one," she said. Her voice was as small as she and rustled like dry fall leaves.

This could only be one person, and I hardly knew what to say. I was in the presence of one of the greatest female painters to ever live, a woman even more famous than Lavinia Fontana. "Signora Anguissola, it is my greatest honor to meet you. I am sure Signor Doria told you, but I am Artemisia Gentileschi and I too am a painter."

"You are a painter." She cackled and frowned. "Why must women understate their talents? My girl, I hear you are a very great artist. Signor Antoon van Dyck says your Susanna is transcendent. And you must call me Sofonisba, or you'll make me feel exceedingly old."

"My Susanna?" I'd unpacked the painting, of course, but I hadn't shown it to anyone yet.

She chuckled. "Your father's young assistant took Antoon to your rooms the other day—Antoon told me he stopped by looking for your father and that boy showed it to him. Antoon asked, you see? He was curious after seeing your *Judith Slaying Holofernes*. In Florence, you know."

I tried not to gape at the old lady. How could she be so blind and know so much about everyone? I'd heard of the great Dutch painter Antoon van Dyck, but I'd never met him, of course. "And he liked them, the Susanna and the Judith?"

"Liked them? He couldn't stop talking about them," she said. "You're going to have to be careful, my dear. Antoon is already a great admirer of yours and I hear he is a handsome fellow, though I also hear he is a redhead." She looked off to the left as if seeing something far, far away. "I never much cared for redheads. Too volatile, if you ask me. Not like my dear captain, who is blond. Blonds are the mildest of men . . ." Her voice drifted off and her chin fell to her chest. I was in the same room with Sofonisba Anguissola, and she'd just fallen asleep.

While I waited for her to wake, I thought about what I knew of this old lady. Like Lavinia Fontana, she'd been born into a wealthy family and was allowed by her indulgent father to learn to paint. At first she painted just for the family, and then, as her talent matured, for other rich families in Cremona. Like me, she'd never been formally trained. She painted mainly portraits, but her attention to detail, depth of color, and informal style made her famous before she was twenty-five. The King of Spain invited her to court, where she became the court's portraitist and a lady-in-waiting to the new Spanish queen. She married one of the king's courtiers, but after several years both the husband and the queen died, so Sofonisba left Spain. On the ship back to Cremona, she fell in love with the captain, a fellow with the same name as my papà. Luckily, Sofonisba and Orazio had enough money to ignore the gossips and lived happily in Genoa.

I was wondering when Sofonisba lost her eyesight and how she felt about that when her chin jerked up and she began talking as if she'd never been asleep.

"My Orazio is the kindest of husbands," she said. "I'd tell you to marry a kind man, my girl, but they're hard to find, and I hear you've had more than your share of man trouble."

"I regret to say you are not wrong, signora." Before she could get the wrong idea, I added, "I find an absent husband is my favorite kind."

"A woman can always get a man when she needs one, then send him away when she is done with him," she said, laughing. "Right, my dear?" I blushed, but didn't disagree. "Antoon tells me you paint the most marvelous scenes of defiant woman-hood." She shook her head. "I could never do that. I was afraid if I didn't paint what they wanted, I'd lose my place."

"They?" I knew what she meant, but I wanted to hear what she'd say.

"The rich. The powerful. The kings and queens and dukes

and princes. They want pretty pictures of themselves and their children—or they did. Antoon tells me that in Florence the Medicis like your bloody paintings of women lopping off heads."

I tried not to laugh. "They do and they don't." I told her about my Minerva, which was not only a portrait but also a work that significantly improved the subject's appearance (and erased a pair of nipples).

"Ooh, it is the same everywhere, I suppose," she said. "Still, I wish I dared to paint like you. I sometimes wonder if I had, if I could have changed their tastes. Isn't that an artist's job? Not just to reflect what people want, but to instruct on what is worthy."

"That is the age-old question, is it not?" I said, leaning forward and grasping her wrinkled hand. The bones under her skin felt no more substantial than the bones of a lark. "Signora, perhaps I can paint bloody scenes because you came before me. Without you and Signora Fontana, I think no one, not even my father, would have ever considered me a painter. And then there would be no defiant Judiths at all."

She smiled. "And perhaps you are painting the way for other talented women? Women not yet born. Who knows how many great female artists will come after us."

She nodded off again after that, and I took my leave of her. I would stay in Genoa for less than six months, but I visited Sofonisba once a week during that time. As old as she was when I met her, I heard she lived another twelve years after I left Genoa, dying in her nineties. I also heard her captain mourned her loss so fiercely that his friends feared he would join her in death. I don't know what happened to him, but I know that for the rest of my life I considered myself blessed that I had once called Sofonisba my friend.

While Papà painted frescoes at Doria's villa, I painted two pieces for Doria's friend Pietro Gentile, another rich Genoan banker. Gentile first asked me for a Lucretia. Intrigued as I was that he chose a female subject, I hesitated to undertake the project. Lucretia, you see, is a not an uncommon painterly subject. Her story goes that Rome was once ruled by the cruel Emperor Tarquin. Tarquin's sons were bragging about their wives and arguing about who was best, until one of the sons proposed a contest. They would all go home and see whose wife was engaged in the most virtuous activity. All the brothers' wives were dining in luxury or doing other thrilling (and thus unwomanly) things, but Lucretia was quietly spinning wool with her ladies. One of the brothers was so jealous of this that he came one day to rape her. When she refused his advances, he told her he would kill her and his slave, then put the slave's body in bed with her, shaming her before all of Rome. Unless, of course, she consented to sex with him. Lucretia submitted to the brother and the next day confessed to her husband, who absolved her because she'd been coerced. Nonetheless, Lucretia felt such shame at her adultery that she stabbed herself in the breast and died. Romans were so offended at the bad brother's behavior and inspired by virtuous Lucretia that they rebelled and drove out Emperor Tarquin.

I thought the story was silly. When a man rapes you, you don't kill yourself. You survive and go on with your life, or else he wins. Besides, I've never figured out how a woman's self-murder was an inspiration to rebellion. Lucretia didn't seem heroic to me, but lots of people disagree. I think she's Susanna in another guise, but weaker because she kills herself. And the church condemns suicide, which makes the story all the more incomprehensible to me. I guess being raped makes suicide acceptable. See? It's a dumb story.

It should come as no surprise that some painters portray Lucretia as complicit in her rape, as if she enjoyed it. Her suicide becomes more about guilt and less about virtue. I think Machiavelli wrote a story like that: Lucretia takes a lover with her husband's approval (because he is impotent and wanted a son), but she kills herself when she can't live with her sin.

I didn't paint my Lucretia like that at all. In my version, she's not particularly beautiful and she's clearly in anguish. I caught her in a moment of indecision, her breast bared, the knife poised, against a dark background that suggests she's aware the deed she contemplates is sinful. When I presented the finished painting to Signor Gentile, I expected him to be disappointed, or perhaps even angry. I was surprised when he declared the finished painting a masterpiece and paid me a bonus. I suspect the signor's wife had something to do with that, for she was happy to hang a painting of a seductress in her salon.

Pietro Gentile also asked me to paint a Cleopatra for him. Should you be unfamiliar with this theme, let me explain. Cleopatra paintings are nearly always no more than an excuse to display a naked woman holding a snake and call it respectable. On Gentile's insistence, I painted the most sensual, voluptuous Cleopatra I could manage. She lies semi-reclined in a rumbled bed, holding a serpent in one fist. The serpent coils around her hand, its head up and pointed at her lower body. The painting was so unsubtle, one could hardly call it metaphorical, but Signor Gentile could not have been more pleased. That the painting was entirely indecent bothered him not at all, and I needed the money. I had to hire a separate nurse for Prudenzia and I still had my husband's Florentine debts to pay off.

Papà had trouble understanding my need for independence. He believed in my talent and promoted my paintings to anyone who would listen, but he also wanted me to have a man who would take care of me. Papà couldn't seem to remember I was married to Pietro, and every time I reminded him, he pretended not to hear me. He brought many men to the house, some of them painters, none of them appropriate. For example, Giulio Cesare Procaccini, a Milanese Mannerist, was nice but as old as Papà. Domenico Fiasella was my age, but he'd been trained under Uncle Aurelio and I knew from gossip that the attractive young painter preferred the company of other young men. Not that it mattered. My husband may have been missing, but that didn't make me less married. As far as I was concerned, I'd told Sofonisba the truth: a missing husband was a good husband.

I met my favorite faux suitor in the fall of 1621, long after I'd heard so much about him from Sofonisba. Antoon van Dyck bore a physical resemblance to Papà, appearing more sprite than man, and shared with Papà a love of twirled and waxed mustaches. In Genoa, he went by Anthony instead of Antoon, but the little painter was from Antwerp, Belgium. His father made a fortune in the silk trade and spent another fortune making sure his son had the best painting masters. It was money well spent because the young artist had been a child prodigy, so talented that the great Flemish master Peter Paul Rubens had taken him under his wing. I'd never met Rubens, though I knew he'd been in Venice and Florence twenty years before and was greatly influenced by Titian and Michelangelo.

When I met Anthony, as I, being Italian, always called him, he bowed over my hand and kissed it with mocking formality. I caught the twinkle in his eye and giggled, setting the tone for our relationship for years to come. As supremely talented as he was, he did not take himself very seriously. He broadcast his sense of whimsy with his narrow pointy beard, which echoed the points in his mustaches and his love of ridiculously large lace-edged collars.

"They say you are a talented Caravaggisti," he said with a waggle of his eyebrows. "Your father even says you may, on occasion, surpass him."

I glanced at Papà, who blushed. He'd not seen any of my Judith paintings, and I considered those three by far my most Caravaggio-inspired works. Papà shrugged. "I hear things, my dear. And I have eyes in my head."

I waved Anthony to a chair, but Papà shook his head. "I want you to take him up to see the Susanna," he said.

I sighed. Papà was matchmaking again. The Susanna leaned against a wall in my bedroom. I liked to see it when I fell asleep because it reminded me that only I could protect myself from life's dangers.

"Oh, my goodness," Anthony gasped when he stood before the big painting. "Such lovely colors and ugly menace. Oh, dear." He stepped back, then stepped forward so far that his nose nearly touched the canvas. "I can feel her pain, her fear." He stepped back again. "Ooh, you little minx!"

"What?" I asked.

He glanced at me. "When I met him, your father went on and on about his talented daughter. I thought he was just another proud papà, overestimating his daughter's gifts. I'd never heard of a lady painter before—I mean, not just one of those flower-painting ladies, but a real artist." He looked at me again and shrugged.

"You didn't think women had it in them, did you?" I said as kindly as I could, seeing his confusion.

"I didn't. Not until just now."

I leaned against my bedroom doorway and folded my arms over my chest. "You want to know what I think?"

He stepped away from the Susannah and turned towards me, his eyes soft with kindness. "I think I shall always want to know what you think, Signora Gentileschi." He waggled his eyebrows again, breaking the spell.

I tried not to smile and failed. "I think there are as many talented women as there are men. Their talents never flower because women are not educated or trained. Worse, their creativity is drowned by housekeeping and baby-making. Even worse than that, we swim in a sea of ideas that tell us we are weak, stupid, illogical, and in all ways inferior to men. Many of us come to believe these ideas. It's a rare woman who doesn't believe she is inferior and has the circumstances to do something about it."

He peered at the Susanna again. "I thought I was a prodigy, but I, the great van Dyck, am humbled before this canvas. And your father is correct that you've never had a teacher, but for him?"

I gestured for Anthony to follow me back downstairs. If we stayed in my bedroom any longer, Papà would get ideas. "Papà was my first teacher," I said, "but every painting I've ever looked at taught me something. Every painter I see working teaches me something. The way I see the world, as a woman and as an artist, teaches me as well."

By the time we'd reached the parlor, where Papà waited, I knew one thing for sure. This funny little Flemish painter would surely be my friend.

In the spring of 1622, I left Genoa, fearing I'd do no more in the city than paint female suicides and bared breasts. And I couldn't be dependent on my matchmaking Papà. A woman who has to make her way in the world, especially one with a child depending on her, can't be overly fussy.

I also left because Anthony van Dyck had left Genoa for Sicily in March. He and I spent a good number of days that winter discussing art. Some of it was high-flown talk about the age-old argument of whether paintings should be idealized, light, and beautiful or realistic, dark, and even horrific. I tended toward the latter, as did Papà. Anthony contended that a smart painter, one who wanted to collect as many fees as possible, painted what the customer wanted. This led us to that other great favorite conversation of artists: whether artists could be true artists if they served another person's interests. I wanted to argue that art ought to come only from the artist, but I had bills and responsibilities and often painted subjects I didn't like. Perhaps only rich men's sons like Anthony van Dyck could afford to paint only to please themselves. When I ventured this argument to my friend, he laughed.

"What good is it to paint if you aren't painting for someone?" he countered. "If people do not see your work, why bother to paint it? Besides, my father's money is my father's money. I make my own money, and someday I shall be the richest painter in Europe. You wait and see." His mustache twitched when he said that, but I knew he was only half joking. If any man could get rich painting, it would be Anthony. I never wanted to be rich, or perhaps I dared not dream that large, but I did want to create work others found beautiful, disturbing, or both. And I wanted to support myself.

One day, not long after I'd watched Anthony's ship sail south to Sicily, I received a letter that told me it was time to leave Genoa. Venice called, and I answered.

Chapter Seven

THE REPUBLICS OF VENICE AND ROME, THE PAPAL STATES
1622

It is not difficult to get from Genoa to Venice. They are both northern cities, but on opposite sides of the Italian Peninsula, which sounds terrible until you look at a map. Luckily, the Po River runs all the way across the top of Italy from the western Alps to the Adriatic Sea on Italy's eastern coast. I hired a carriage to take my little family, my trunks, and my canvases from Genoa, over the tail end of the Apennines to Alessandria. There, I hired a barge and floated in Cleopatra-esque splendor to just south of Venice, though I took no deadly snakes with me.

Po River barges are not merely flat boats piled with crates and barrels of trade goods. Travel barges have small cabins, cooks onboard, and acceptable facilities for acts of cleanliness. I would spend my life traveling the Po Valley on a barge if I could figure out how to do it while raising my child and paying the bills. The valley's beauty almost made me wish I painted scenery. Almost.

The only problem with barge travel was my worry that

Prudenzia would fall into the river and drown. Five-year-olds are harder to keep track of than a litter of puppies, and Prudenzia could disappear faster than an eel that's slipped the hook. Having encountered this problem before, our ship's captain, Captain Russo, supplied me with a thin rope of silk affixed to a slim leather belt. We strapped Prudenzia into this belt each time she left our cabin and spent the rest of the voyage trying not to trip over her rope. The sailors, rather than being short-tempered with the chubby-legged girl who was everywhere, took to her like trained nannies—swarthy and sweaty nannies, but nannies nonetheless.

Because I had nothing to do, I let Captain Russo tell me stories of his city's past. The man was as enthusiastic about Venice as he was about storytelling. Unlike every other city on the Italian Peninsula, Venice has no roots in ancient Roman civilization. Rather, people fleeing the Romans built the city as a refuge. These rebellious people built their city on the hundreds of islands that filled the shallow bay between the mouths of the Po and Piave rivers. Thus, Venice is a city born from the water.

The key to Venetian history is right there on the map. I understood this when I saw the captain unroll his map of Northern Italy. While all other great Italian cities lie on the Mediterranean Sea or on rivers that flow to it, Venice faces the Adriatic Sea. It is the difference between the Christian and the Muslim worlds. For centuries, the Venetians have used their immense merchant fleet to trade with Ottomans, Greeks, Dalmatians, and even African nations.

Because the city comes into contact with people from so

many non-European, non-Christian nations, it is an exceptionally tolerant city. During Pope Paul V's reign, the city suffered under the Venetian Interdict because city officials refused to charge even the freest thinkers with heresy. The interdict held for two years, but because the the pope had no real power over Venice, the interdict served as little more than a cessation of diplomatic relations. This, according to Captain Russo, didn't bother Venetians one bit. This is not a city that cares about Rome.

The captain's stories of Venice made me happy I'd accepted invitation to visit the city. Don Giovanni was the illegitimate son of Cosimo I, and thus was the Grand Duke Cosimo's uncle, or at least had been until poor Cosimo died last year. Having no place in the Medici succession, the bastard Medici became a soldier of considerable note. He spent time in the Spanish army fighting the French, and then with the French army fighting the Spanish. Ten years ago or so, he returned to Florence as an ambassador for Spain. Despite Don Giovanni's heroism, Cosimo's mother, the dowager duchess, and Cosimo's wife, Maria (whose specialty was disapproving of things), hated him and that was a huge problem. With Cosimo dead, the dowager duchess and Maria had become co-regents of Florence and would be until Cosimo and Maria's ten-year-old son Ferdinando came of age.

How did Don Giovanni alienate the two most powerful women in Tuscany? He took the commoner Livia del Vernazza as a mistress and then, rather than installing her in a house of her own and discreetly visiting her, he moved her into his own home. Once he retired from the Army compounded his sin by marrying Bianca. The pair were not welcome in Florence, though Medici gossips whispered aplenty about Bianca's origins as a mattress-maker's daughter and her dubious first marriage.

The Medicis may not have approved of Don Giovanni's private life, but he was a respected man of science. He'd even designed the Chapel of the Princes at the San Lorenzo Basilica, the dome of which is considered a marvel of mathematics. I met Don Giovanni only once, when he came to court to testify in the Galileo controversy. In an effort to curry favor with the dowager duchess he took her side against Galileo. After the dowager duchess left the audience chamber, I teased him about his stance and he'd admitted that his official opinion on heliocentrism had more to do with political expediency than scientific inquiry. That was the only conversation we ever had; Don Giovanni left Florence not long after. I tell you this to explain that my new patron is a man of action and flexible morality, which made him, to my mind, an ideal patron. I hoped to sell him on several exciting ideas I had for paintings, and thus stretch my talents while getting paid.

We ended our journey not in Venice proper but in Murano, an island just north of Venice, where Don Giovanni kept his house. "Venice is famous for its glass, you know," Captain Russo explained. "A long time ago, there was a fire in one of the glassblowers' shops in town. It spread and burned many buildings. After that, the city fathers moved the glassblowers to Murano."

Murano was really seven islands packed together, separated by eight narrow canals. As our barge circled the island's eastern shore, I marveled at the city's gold-toned buildings, each seeming to rise from the sea like pagan gods. We turned into Canale San Giovanni and made our way to the center of town, passing under several arched stone bridges. We came to a stop in front of a most unusual palazzo. It rose three-and-a-half stories above the water, with a narrow balcony running across the front facade. It stood out with its frescoes adorning the exterior walls. Greek and Roman goddesses surrounded the upper-story windows, while paintings of Hercules and Neptune took up space to the left and right of the front door.

Captain Russo refrained from comment, but I could tell he disapproved of the building's excessive visual exuberance. I thought it was fun—why not paint murals on the exterior of your house? Before I knew it, the barge that had been my home for so many weeks floated away, its storytelling captain with it. I gave King Neptune a nod in acknowledgment of my safe travel by water and knocked on the narrow front door with one hand while holding Prudenzia's in the other.

A servant admitted us and set about disbursing our luggage. Prudenzia ran about the grand foyer like a child who'd not seen solid ground for weeks, laughing at the echo her feet made on the floor. Just as I caught her arm, I heard a woman's voice say, "Do not confine the little one for my sake. I do so love the sound of children in the house."

I looked up to see a pregnant woman stepping down the wide staircase that ran up the left side of the foyer. She descended slowly, her belly riding a step before her feet, her hair golden in the afternoon light. I saw why Don Giovanni had given up his position at the Medici court to marry this woman. Even pregnant, she was the most beautiful woman I had ever seen.

The lady held out her hand to me, but instead of allowing me to kiss it, she used it to pull me into a soft embrace. "You are the painter Signora Gentileschi, am I correct? I am Livia de Medici. And who is the little one?"

After introductions, we took Prudenzia to the nursery to join Livia's three-year-old son, Francesco, then Livia took me to my room. "My husband is in Padua," she explained on the way, "but I expect him home within the week. He is very pleased to have lured you away from Florence."

I shook my head. "I came from Genoa."

"Here," she said, pushing open the door to the room. A massive bed dressed with moss-green velvet curtains dominated the left-hand wall, while a desk and several chairs sat near a pair of doors that led to a small balcony. "My husband said you should have the best room." She drifted across the room to the balcony doors and opened them, letting in a sea-scented breeze. "He means to establish a dynasty here in Venice, and you are important to his plans." She laid her hand on her swollen belly and smiled fondly. "He has hired his family's best painter so she may create many great works for him. By the time his sons are grown, everyone will know the greatness of this branch of the family."

My heart raced at this news. I'd assumed Don Giovanni brought me here to paint one or two things for him, not to become his court painter. He appeared to be engaged in a personal battle against the powers in Tuscany, using me as his weapon. This would be either a dangerous post or an exciting new chapter in my artistic life—or both.

Livia left me with the promise that she'd have dinner sent up to me. "You must be exhausted. We shall dine together tomorrow and get to know each other. I miss the company of other women."

I woke the next morning to the sound of Prudenzia calling my name. "Mamma, Mamma, Mamma," she singsonged as she tugged on my blankets. "Come and see Francesco's kitty. It's orange and white and black, and its claws are ever so sharp."

I yawned, stretching my arms over my head, then curled one arm down around Prudenzia's waist and pulled her into bed with me.

"Mamma! No snuggling," she protested. "I want to show you the kitty."

I kissed my dark-eyed girl and nuzzled her soft curls. She had hair like mine, which meant it would spring from every net and braid, like a wild animal with a mind of its own.

After appreciating the calico kitten and Livia's son, Francesco, who was nearly as cute as the cat, I spent the rest of the day unpacking my trunks and canvases. Once again, I leaned the Susanna against the wall in my bedroom, though I put my unfinished paintings in a third-floor room designated for my studio. Livia poked her head into my room just after lunch, reminded me dinner was at eight, and left me alone again.

After a satisfying day—for what is more pleasant than establishing order over disorder?—I sponged myself off in a small washbasin in the water closet. I changed into my best dress, made of dark green wool with apricot-colored trim, and made my way to the dining room. There, a footman directed me to a small parlor after telling me the mistress of the house never used the dining room when her husband was not home.

Heartened not to be eating at a table large enough to seat thirty guests, I found my hostess in a room meant for family use. While we ate, we spoke of our children, as mothers nearly always do. I told her about Prudenzia's talent for drawing, even at her young age, and how I hoped to teach her to paint. Livia had big dreams for her son, who'd been born after they married and was thus a legitimate Medici, at least according to his parents and the law, if not to the dowager duchess. Having spent many hours with the dowager duchess and her daughter-in-law, Maria, I doubted the family would ever accept the son of a commoner as one of their own.

As servants cleared the table, Livia changed the subject. "I looked forward to your arrival, for I believe we have so much in common that we cannot help but be great friends."

I jerked back my head at her words. What did a Roman painter and a Florentine prostitute have in common? Or did she think my Roman scandal had turned me into a fallen woman not so different from her?

"Oh, I see I have upset you," she said. "I know the rumors of my past are quite salacious, but my story is not what you have heard. I suspect you might say the same of yourself."

I sighed. "Some bad men said many terrible things about me

in court, and worse was undoubtedly whispered in salons and over dinner tables."

She nodded. "I shall tell you my story and you may judge for yourself." She settled back in her chair and folded her hands over her belly. "Fifteen years ago, when I was only thirteen years old, my father married me to another mattress-maker, one Batista Granara. Granara had a large shop and no sons from his first marriage, and my father hoped to combine the two businesses. And Batista lusted after me, as men do. This was in Genoa, where my family has always lived. But Granara was old, and he drank too much and bathed too little, so I objected to the match."

"Much good that did you, I'm sure," I said. I'd had no choice about Tassi either, nor had my papà consulted me when he chose the rogue for me.

"Just so," Livia said with a vigorous nod. "He was a brute. A great, stinking brute. I was married to him for twenty-three long months and he never said a kind word to me. Instead, he beat me and abused me in all the ways a man can abuse a woman."

She paused to pick up her wine glass with an unsteady hand. It was clear that all these years later, the memories continued to frighten and shame her. I felt my stomach roll as my own memories flooded back.

"I would run home to my father when it got too bad, but every time he sent me back to Granara. So I made a plan: when my husband passed out from drink, I would rifle through his pockets and take any coins I found. He never noticed, or if he did, he assumed he'd spent the money while drunk. One day, when I thought I had enough money saved, I packed a valise and set out for Florence. My money ran out faster than I thought it would—I was only sixteen years old and sheltered from the ways of the world, so what did I know? I took a job in a *taverna*, but my looks did me no favors. Men would not leave me alone. Oh, how I used to wish I had been born a plain woman."

"Men don't abuse only beautiful women," I snorted. "Look at me." I swept my arm down my body.

"Bah. You speak as if you were a hag, but you are not, Artemisia. Your eyes are so large and expressive, and your hair is glorious."

"It's a rat's nest," I objected. I've always despaired of my thick, curly hair, with its tendency to frizz in hot weather.

"Even now, as your third decade approaches, you know nothing of men. They see your hair and imagine it unbound and trailing on their bodies," Livia said. She saw me blush and returned to her story. "I took a job in a house of the sort I'm sure you can imagine. With this face and this body, I could name my price. Giovanni found me shortly after my eighteenth birthday. He'd just turned forty and had grown tired of a life of dissipation and his loveless marriage. He set me up in a house and we lived as man and wife for many years, though his relatives hated me more than Satan. My lowly birth made marriage unthinkable, and yet after the birth of my first son he left the army, defied the dowager duchess and married me anyway. I admit he strayed from time to time, as men do, but he has ever been my protector.

"He sounds like a good man," I said. "My husband was not."

"But you had your painting to sustain you, body and soul. I have only my looks and I have worked hard to keep them, and equally hard to keep Giovanni ensnared. I envy your independence." She motioned to the bulge of her belly and said, "Though the children are some compensation, I suppose."

The next afternoon, Livia arranged for me to have a tour of Venice. She kept a private boat, a long, narrow thing with a striped awning across the back. She also had a man to maneuver it through the city's canals, like a carriage driver, but with a pole instead of a whip and reins. Venetians call these odd boats gondolas and the men who pilot them gondoliers, and the experience is delightful. A city full of boats is a city bereft of horses and the aromas and filth such creatures emit.

Given the advanced state of her pregnancy, it wasn't decent for Livia to appear in public. Still, we saw many sights from the gondola while sipping cool fruit drinks and nibbling a variety of small treats. We made our way south to Venice's Grand Canal, and from there floated past the Doge's Palace. The massive Gothic structure housed the government and the doge's apartments, and I found it as impressive as any building in Rome. Unlike the heredity of kingdoms and duchies of most of Europe, Venice is a republic, so its leader, the doge, was elected by the Venetian Council. We also saw Saint Mark's Basilica, though from afar because, like Saint Peter's in Rome, a huge piazza lies between it and the canal. By the end of the day, I began to see why Venetians believe their floating city is the greatest in the world. It has the grandeur of Rome, the bustle of Genoa, and the beauty of

Florence all wrapped up in the miracle of waterways and cool sea air. It was a city in which I might have lived for many years. That is, until disaster struck.

Livia and I were sharing a late lunch the next day when a booming series of knocks came at the front door, followed by the cries of someone in a great panic. The maid rushed out of the room to investigate while Livia and I exchanged perplexed looks.

Seconds later, the maid, Marina, rushed back into the room and stammered, "Come quick, signora. It is the master, home from Padua."

Livia stood and smoothed her skirt over her belly. "Calm yourself, girl," she said to the maid. "The master has come home many times, and never to this fuss."

"No, mistress," Marina half screeched. "Not like this. He is very sick."

Livia strode from the room, her face a mask of calm. I followed her to the entry hall, where we found two bulky men carrying Don Giovanni in. He was so pale that he looked dead, though he gasped for air as if his lungs were full of water.

"Follow me," Livia said, turning for the stairs.

I took charge of the removal of Don Giovanni's trunks from the gondola and sent the gondolier for the nearest physician. A stout man dressed in black robes arrived not thirty minutes later. I led him upstairs to the room Don Giovanni shared with Livia. As the doctor went inside, I took a chair in the hall and waited, but not for very long. Livia stepped out into the hall, her face as white as milk. "It is the plague," she whispered. "My husband has the plague."

In the next few hours, a great many things happened. A plague doctor arrived, sent for by the first doctor, who hustled away as soon as the plague specialist arrived. The plague doctor wore the strange beak-like mask of his profession. He assured Livia he was himself a plague survivor and that it was possible for her husband to survive. Next, a city official came to put the house under quarantine so no one but the plague doctor could come and go from the residence.

Livia and I got Prudenzia and Francesco out of the house before the quarantine. Lest you think badly of us, the evasion seemed perfectly sensible given the children hadn't yet seen Don Giovanni, nor breathed the air he breathed. To stay was to risk infection; any mother would have done the same. Marina took them to her mother's house and stayed there with them. We also sent the remaining servants away, except for the cook, who insisted he was too old and mean to die of the plague.

As soon as we got the children away, Lavinia and I undressed Don Giovanni, rolled him onto an old bed sheet, and applied damp towels to his skin. He was pinkish red with fever, except at his neck, armpits, and groin, which swelled with the plague's hallmark grayish-blue buboes. Every time we got a little water or broth in him, he would puke it right back up, making great retching sounds as he did. These were the only sounds he made, but for some nonsensical babbling brought on by delirium. Livia sent me away to rest sometime before midnight, and when I returned the next morning, the buboes had swollen to melon size and darkened to black. The plague's dreaded black spots had also appeared on Don Giovanni's body sometime in the night.

Livia refused to go to bed, so we kept on with the damp cloths and sips of water, though nothing we did helped.

By the end of that second day, Giovanni's hands and feet were black with necrosis and the buboes at his neck and groin had swelled to alarming proportions. The plague doctor returned, his beak mask in place, and applied dozens of leeches to the buboes. The leaches grew fat with blood, but the swelling refused to recede. When the leaches failed, the plague doctor retrieved a fat frog from a basket he carried with him and sat the frog on Don Giovanni's swollen neck. That didn't help either. I watched as the doctor returned the frog to the basket and next retrieved from it a little garden snake, an onion, and a knife. With no warning, he struck off the snake's head, hacked its still-writhing body into bits, and mixed it with chopped onion. I had to go to the window to take some deep breaths to keep my puke from joining the mess in the room. When I turned back from the window, the doctor had applied the bloody snake poultice to the buboes. As far as I could tell, the remedy did little but add to the room's already considerable stink.

That evening, Don Giovanni had the first of several seizures, in between which he vomited great quantities of blood and lost control of his bowels. The plague doctor declared the patient a lost cause and left us, saying he would send for a priest on the morrow. Just before dawn of the third day, Don Giovanni's anguish ended when God released him from suffering. Livia and I stood over his body as his breathing slowed and stopped, both of us too tired to do more than watch.

Livia's travails did not end with the death of her husband.

Ten days after Don Giovanni died, there came another pounding knock at the door. It turned out to be envoys of the dowager duchess, armed with lawyers and writs of annulment. In one fell swoop, Livia lost her widow's rights to her husband's considerable fortune and her sons were declared illegitimate.

Though I volunteered to stay with her, Livia de Medici bade me leave Venice. "I can't beat these people, and if you stay, they'll crush you as well."

As much as I hated to, I had to agree. As co-regents the dowager duchess of Tuscany and her daughter-in-law had control of the duchy and with it gained immense power. Neither woman would rest until they'd removed Livia from the family. If they had to take a common painter down to do it, they would and not blink an eye, no matter how many of my paintings hung in their private collections.

Prudenzia and I left Venice the next day. We took a barge back to Genoa, though the trip was much slower because we were traveling upriver. Along the way, I had plenty of time to think about what I should do next. If I stayed in Genoa, I'd end up back under my father's control, and I didn't want that. There was only one place I could go: back to Rome.

Inexplicably, on my return from Genoa and Venice, I became the toast of Rome, the same city that had seen my greatest disgrace and judged me a harlot. Or perhaps this was not inexplicable. While I was in Venice, the news of my success in Genoa came to Rome. More accurately, my dear friend Anthony van Dyck came to Rome, on his way home from Sicily. He arrived in the papal city not long after I left Venice, and he sang my praises to anyone who would listen.

Anthony particularly caught the ear of two cardinals, both rich men with more interest in worldly display than pious poverty. Most people said the twenty-six-year-old Francesco Barberini was only a cardinal because he was the new pope's favorite nephew. Cardinal Maffeo Barberini, the previous pope's ambassador to France, assumed the pontificate in the summer of 1623 as Pope Urban VIII, in great part because the Borghese faction threw their support behind him. He made his art-loving nephew a cardinal. Cardinal Ludovico Ludovisi, also in his twenties, had come to his cardinalship in much the same way, except his uncle was the previous (now dead) Pope Gregory. Both young men had few duties and family money aplenty. And they belonged to competing factions within the papacy, so what one had, the other had to have too. Lucky me.

After visiting my studio, Cardinal Barberini asked me to paint a Susanna for him, though he wanted a more lascivious one. The young cardinal wanted no real show of resistance from Susanna. Worse, he wanted the elders painted less as dangerous predators and more as men innocently intrigued by Susanna's nudity. I agreed, thinking I could hold my nose and paint the thing. I also thought, once I'd established a relationship with the cardinal with this first painting, I could guide the young man to make less repugnant choices in the future. I sketched the Susanna and painted a study, but each day it was harder to walk into my studio and work on it. I hired my first painter's assistant, Domenico Gargiulo, a young man trained in Naples who excelled at backgrounds and architectural painting, and had him finish for me. Domenico would be with me for years and become like a son to me, so this repugnant Susanna did that much for me. When it was finished, this Susanna wasn't a painting I liked much, but the young cardinal seemed too entranced by the naked woman to notice the painting lacked my signature style.

I painted both cardinals a Mary Magdalene, each nearly identical to the other. I liked these paintings a great deal more because I portrayed the much-maligned Magdalene not as a temptress nor a saint, but as a real woman. Because everyone of importance in Rome belonged to one of the two familial factions, everyone saw one or the other, further cementing my reputation as a painter worth hiring. People seemed to like my use of mustard yellow-gold in the Marys' dresses, so much so that the color became known as "Gentileschi gold." Everyone who commissioned a painting from me in those years asked for Gentileschi gold; it became, along with my tenebrist play of dark and light, my artistic signature.

I also found myself a former Genoese patron, the banker Vincenzo Giustiniani. He'd made so much money that he retired to Rome and became a full-time art collector. Caravaggio had further fallen out of favor since I'd moved to Florence ten years earlier, but Signor Giustiniani remained a fervent defender of naturalism and tenebrism. I painted a lovely *Esther before Ahasuerus* for him, the swooning Esther glowing in a shaft of light and wearing Gentileschi gold, while an effete Ahasuerus leans out of the dark from his throne. Rather than painting

Esther as delicate and afraid, I painted her as a sturdy woman whose swoon nearly undid her ladies' ability to support her. I first painted a growling dog at Ahasuerus's feet and a dwarf capering in the background—people loved dogs and dwarves—but I decided to remove both, preferring the empty divide between the women and the king. My patron liked the painting so much that he ordered several more on similar themes.

In the spring of 1625, Signor Giustiniani traveled to Florence, where he saw my *Judith Slaying Holofernes* and *Judith and Her Maidservant*. Giustiniani returned to Rome mad with the idea of having his own Judith, but he left the details to me. I thought back to Simon Vouet's *The Temptation of Saint Francis*, which I had seen in Genoa. Vouet was a French painter who painted for the wealthy Doria family. He'd painted the woman who tempted Francis on a heroic scale, with limbs so thick they were Michelangelo-like, yet she'd still been an attractive figure. I took this idea and combined it with the current fad for candlelit scenes. My favorite candlelit painting was a Judith painted by my father's old friend Carlo Saraceni. I didn't care for his juxtaposition of a beautiful Judith with her crone-like maidservant, but he'd done a masterful job with the stark shadows that would result from a single candle in an otherwise dark space.

So I sketched and sketched and came up with something I liked. I chose the moment just after Judith beheaded Holofernes. The maidservant I painted as a woman in the prime of her life (as I always did), caught in the act of wrapping the decapitated head in a sheet. Judith holds the sword in one hand but raises the other, looking left as if she hears danger. I put the candle on a table to Judith's left so the strongest light fell on the women's faces. Both are plainly dressed, but I had great fun painting folds in their sleeves, headdresses, and the bed curtain in the rich detail usually reserved for royal costumes. Plus, I used my signature yellow-gold for Judith's dress. It would not be immodest of me to say—because others already have—that my 1625 *Judith and Her Maidservant* is one of my best paintings. Sometimes I like it even more than my second *Judith Slaying Holofernes*—the one with great gouts of blood spraying from Holofernes's neck.

Thus, my Roman years were tremendously busy. I had my choice of patrons and was so busy with paintings that I never had to paint a fresco, nor a portrait. No, wait—that's not entirely true. I painted one portrait, of my old Genoan patron Pietro Gentile. He wanted something in the style of van Dyck, who specialized in full-length portraits. Gentile came to Rome for a month in early 1622 and stood for his portrait for five days running. Though he was a merchant, he wore the uniform of the gonfalonier, an independent military order that protected the small cities north of Genoa. Gentile is a funny little man and not one bit imposing or martial, but he has a natural dignity that I emphasized with his posture and facial expression. The portrait made me smile every time I worked on it.

I might have stayed in Rome for the rest of my life if I could have, but once again circumstances dictated I leave the life I'd made and begin again somewhere else. It started with the reappearance of my husband, Pietro Stiattesi. That rat. On my daughter's twelfth name day, he walked into my house as if he owned it, kissed his daughter, and asked when dinner would be served.

This, after we'd not seen of him for nearly ten years, yet he acted like he'd been gone for only a short time. He'd grown fat and had the bulbous nose of a committed drunkard, and he had the poor manners of a man who'd been living rough. But he was my husband, and everything I owned was legally his. Having no legal choice in the matter, I let him move into our cozy little house in Santa Sassia, though I drew the line at resuming marital rights. Pietro moved his clothes into my room and so I vacated that chamber. Instead, I slept in Prudenzia's room. We locked the door each night, and a good thing too, for on more than one occasion Pietro drank too much and came scratching at the door, demanding I resume marital relations. I ignored his drunken fits of temper and, as much as I could, his presence in my house.

I was also careful to hide my florins under a floorboard in the kitchen, where he could not find them. And I took measures to prevent my husband from once again driving me into debt. The morning after he reappeared, Prudenzia and I visited every tavern and art supply shop in Naples and told the shopkeepers to allow Pietro no credit, warning them he always reneged on his debts. Then I settled in and waited for the inevitable scene that would result when he discovered he could neither drink nor pretend to paint with my florins. It didn't take long. He raged and threw my best plates against the wall, but it did him no good. Pietro Stiattesi had the right to sleep in my bed, break my plates and disturb the peace of my household, but he couldn't do anything about men who would not allow him credit.

It all came to head one warm summer night. A group of young bravos, pages, and assistants in the household of Cardinal Barberini had taken to appearing outside my bedroom window on Saturday nights. Well lubricated by wine, they would serenade me with romantic songs until I threw them each a kiss from my window. There wasn't a bit of harm in it—they were boys playing at romance and having a great deal of fun besides. Pietro was home one of those nights when they came to sing. He charged out of the house in his nightshirt and accosted the boys in the street. Hearing the melee, I pulled on my robe and made my way to my bedroom window to see what was happening.

Pietro stood inches from the tallest lad and yelled, "That is my wife, you scoundrel!" He made a ridiculous sight in his nightshirt, his hairy legs bare to the night air.

"No you are not! Everyone knows Signora Gentileschi has no husband," the boy laughed.

Pietro grabbed the boy and roared, "She may be a whore, but she is my wife, and her name is Stiattesi."

"Filthy wormhead," one boy yelled. I smiled at the ridiculous insult.

Another cried, "You shouldn't be talking about a good woman, you devil!"

Pietro called the boys rogues and pimps, and once again insisted that I, his wife, was a whore. Lots of yelling ensued and then the shoving began. "She is a whore! A filthy whore!" Pietro continued yelling.

I sighed and shook my head. Would men never cease to use that word to describe women they could not control?

Finally, having had enough insults, one of the older boys launched himself at Pietro. Seconds later, my husband was rolling in the dirt with four boys half his size. The noise of the fight ensured everyone on the street opened their shutters and saw it all—including more than anyone wanted to see of a pant-less Pietro wearing a too-short night shirt.

Appearing at my shoulder, Prudenzia too saw her papà brawling in the street, half naked, dirty, and enraged. I told her to go back to bed, but at twelve years old and on the cusp of womanhood, my Prudenzia very much wanted to watch her father's disgrace. Pietro had not endeared himself to her during his recent weeks in our house. Nonetheless, no virginal girl ought to see such things as Pietro bared this night and so I insisted she leave the window.

After several minutes of this excruciating public display, the condottieri arrived and broke up the fight. The papal guards weren't likely to arrest members of a cardinal's household; instead they sent the boys on their way with stern words of warning. Pietro was not so lucky. They took my loutish husband into custody for public brawling and nakedness.

I admit I did not rush down to the jail to get my husband out. Rather, I left Pietro there for two days. When I visited him, I found him in a dank cell, squatting in filthy hay, surrounded by thieves and murderers. He threw himself at the bars and begged me to get him out. The rank smell of excrement rose from him as he moved. "Please, please, get me out," he whined. "I will reform. You must help me."

"I will help you," I said, "but only with conditions."

He reached through the bars and I stepped back, out of range. "Anything," he begged. "I'll do anything you say. Just get me out of here."

One of the larger men in the cell laughed. "Let him rot, mistress. He'll make a fine, soft prison wife." The other men made raucous sounds of amusement.

"Please, wife," Pietro pleaded. "Anything."

"Anything? How about this? You shall move out of my house and never come back. Never. You will cease your claims to my person, my income, and my daughter."

"But, Artemisia, I need you." He pressed his face against the bars and—I swear this is true—batted his eyelashes at me. Because he could not help himself, he added, "You are my wife and you must take care of me."

I turned to walk away, careful to keep my skirts above the filthy stones of the jail floor. The men in the cell jeered and laughed.

"I'll do it!" I heard him cry from behind me. "I'll leave you. I'll leave Rome the minute I get out of here." I nodded without turning back.

Pietro was out of jail before dinnertime, and he came home to find his few things crated and standing near the front door.

For a few days, I thought I'd won. But, alas, Pietro didn't make my life that easy. He didn't leave Rome either. He began appearing on the street outside my house, sloppily drunk and rank with wine. Sometimes he yelled insults and threw rocks at the windows, while other times he curled up against my front door and begged me to let him in. I kept the doors locked and the ground-floor windows shuttered, never knowing when he'd appear or in what condition.

Despite my warnings, shopkeepers began to apply to me for repayment of Pietro's debts. After several weeks under siege, Prudenzia's and my nerves were shot. We both had trouble sleeping, and sometimes my daughter wept for hours, unable to stop herself. By the end of the year, I'd had enough. If I could make my way in Florence, Genoa, and Rome, I could do it in yet another city, somewhere far away from Rome and Pietro. So, once again, I packed my household goods, crated up my favorite paintings, and prepared to start over.

Chapter Eight

THE KINGDOM OF NAPLES
DECEMBER 1631

I stood at my studio window and watched the mountain belch smoke and steam. *Why had I come to Naples?* I thought. *Papà was painting for the English king in London—why hadn't I gone there instead? London didn't have even one volcano.*

I admit to having a native Roman's prejudice about the cities on the southern Italian Peninsula, but a city on the edge of a volcano is madness no matter where you're from. The peasants who lived on the mountain's slopes had reported the mountain grumbled and sighed like a grumpy old man. The more superstitious among them believed devils were at work beneath the surface. Devils, five miles from the city walls!

Mount Vesuvius rises abruptly from the coast and looms over the city with immense physicality, even when it's asleep, as it was when Prudenzia, Domenico, and I first arrived in Naples. The city saw its first fumes from the mountain's mouth back in early summer. By the time the leaves fell from the trees, the ground was shaking every few days. The rumbly, rolling shakes sometimes knocked over pots of paint, and it disconcerted the three of us every time. I know Galileo says the Earth moves, but from my perspective it stays still, and that's the way I like it.

The smoke, like the earthquakes, was also intermittent, but white steam billowed from the mountain's summit night and day. Neapolitans took a casual approach to this, going about their business as if it were normal. Given Mount Vesuvius's history, this seemed foolish to me, but they say familiarity breeds contempt and that seemed to be the case here. While the mountain was famous for the first-century eruption that buried Pompeii and several other cities, it had erupted in nearly every century since. Vesuvius had not, though, erupted since 1500, and that one was hardly worth recording. As a consequence, Neapolitans had grown complacent about their smoking mountain. They regarded it as something like a house cat, friendly and familiar, but capable of swift violence that could leave you bleeding and wondering what you did wrong.

Prudenzia and Domenico and I were not native Neapolitans. We lived in a constant state of near panic and spent far too much time looking at the mountain from out our east-facing windows. Dear Domenico, my assistant who came with us from Rome, put on a brave face so he wouldn't frighten Prudenzia, whom he regarded as a little sister. He needn't have bothered, though. At fourteen, Prudenzia made up her own mind and she was too smart to be fooled by Domenico's facade of masculine nonchalance. To be fair, his familiarity with Naples's famous volcano might also inform Domenico's attitude with the mountain. Neopolitans have always lived on the shoulders of a rumbling and smoking mountain and they take its threats with a nonchalance that astounds those of us who expect our mountains to be still and quiet. He liked to take long walks on the mountain slopes and took the large trees he found there as evidence that the mountain was unlikely to erupt just because we'd moved to Naples.

Domenico's position doesn't seem logical to me, but then again, I know little of life in the country. I have never been one for nature walks, and even if I were, I am too busy with my work and teaching Prudenzia to paint. She had some talent, but not my drive to create. I know I should have been on the lookout for a husband for her, but I loved her company too much. It was a good city for my daughter, being far away from her drunken father and full of rich Spaniards who would buy the paintings of even a girl apprentice.

That's why we came here, of all places. The Count of Monterey, Manuel Zuniga, had seen several of my paintings when Spain's ambassador came to Rome. Now he was the Viceroy of Naples and he couldn't buy too many paintings. His letter inviting me to Naples came just before my husband's arrest, and at first I'd dismissed the offer. What kind of fool would leave Rome for the backwaters of the southern peninsula? But then Pietro made it impossible to live in Rome, and Naples started to look like a good place to start over.

Naples lies on the west coast of the Italian Peninsula, facing the Tyrrhenian Sea, the bit that lies between the triangle made by Sardinia, Sicily, and the mainland. The Kingdom of Aragon has controlled Naples since the time of those famous monarchs, King Ferdinand and Queen Isabella, which makes Naples a Spanish city. Most people say Naples is the largest city in Europe, though the French contend Paris has that honor. The French say a lot of things, and I am not one to confuse volubility with veracity. The Spanish viceroy's 1630 census counted the city at just over 300,000 souls, or three times the size of Rome.

The grandeur in Naples was paid for by taxing the people, many of whom could ill afford to fund Spain's desire for an Italian stronghold. This makes the native Neapolitans cranky about Spanish rule. For example, Spain had once tried to impose the Inquisition on Naples, but Neapolitans, having none of it, rioted to stop it. Sadly, the violence the Inquisitors brought with it stayed. Sentences for even minor crimes such as petty theft included torture and beheading and the people liked this no more than they liked high taxes. Pope Paul V called Naples "a seminary of criminal and sad people." He wasn't wrong. It is a crowded city where poor, unhappy lives are trampled under the heels of the rich and powerful. But this describes all cities, does it not? And for all Naples's improvements and rebellious feelings, no one can do anything about the smoking behemoth that broods over the city.

I guess what I'm saying is that I didn't particularly like Naples. I consoled myself with the fact that there was a high demand for my work here. Unlike Rome, Naples liked Caravaggisti naturalism. Caravaggio himself had once lived in Naples, though only for a few years some twenty years before. Nonetheless, he'd turned most of the rich Neapolitans into Caravaggistis. Not that the city had no idealized, Mannerist paintings. Ten years before, Simon Vouet, who straddled the divide between the two schools, left two massive and gorgeous altar paintings that continued to feed the city's taste for idealism. The viceroy hired me to paint a similar altar piece, this one for the San Giorgio de Genovesi, the church in Naples favored by expatriate Genoese. I painted an *Annunciation*, but with all the dark shadows that mark my work. My Virgin appeared more humble and pious than the women I generally paint, but to balance her my Angel Gabriel was none too authoritative either. Everyone who saw the completed painting said it was a masterpiece, but I know otherwise. It was a nice painting, and nice paintings are never great.

I also painted a lovely *Saint Sebastian* for Giovanni d'Affilito, one of the Neapolitan barons happy to live under Spanish domination, as long as it kept money in their coffers. I continued to paint for Cardinal Barberini in Rome, and the dowager duchess's grandson Ferdinand, the current Grand Duke of Tuscany. I'd also been corresponding with Charles, the Duke of Guise. The duke was in Florence, hiding from the King of France's Cardinal Richelieu, who sounds like an awful man, even for a cardinal. Charles may have been less than astute (otherwise, why oppose the all-powerful Richelieu?), but I was happy to sell him a painting. I could say much the same for the Duke of Modena, who wanted a portrait but settled for a large *David with the Head of Goliath*.

The most important painting of my first year in Naples was the one I worked on while the mountain belched outside my window. Cassiano dal Pozzo, Cardinal Barberini's secretary, sent me a letter asking for a self-portrait. The cardinal

173

collected paintings and dal Pozzo hoped to surprise the cardinal (and no doubt curry favor) with a self-portrait from me. Though I have long refused commissions for portraits, the idea of a self-portrait excited me. I hadn't done one for years, and never one I'd labeled as such. All my others had been paintings of other figures, such as Saint Catherine, in which I used myself as the model.

I determined I would use the painting to make a statement. All my life I've been an oddity, the scandalous woman painter, the beautiful painter—all that nonsense that emphasizes the female me, not the artist me. And my whole life I've painted the stories of strong women, heroines who stood in the foreground. I decided to paint myself as Pittura, the female allegorical figure who represents painting. Artists often portray Pittura as winged and posed on fluffy clouds, like a painting angel. On the other hand, male painters generally paint themselves as highborn gentlemen who just happen to paint. I decided to combine those imageries, then resist them both. I depicted myself painting, my right arm raised, paintbrush poised before the canvas. My other arm rested on a table, holding a palette. I reach for greatness but ground myself in the real, so I suspended a mask pendant on a gold chain around my neck to suggest the art of imitation, but I wore one of my everyday work dresses, sleeves pushed up, to demonstrate that art is hard work. To emphasize that, I painted myself facing the canvas my figure was working on, rather than facing the viewer. I wore a look of intense concentration and my hair was coming loose from its confines, as it does after a long day before the easel. Should anyone miss my point, I called the work *Self-Portrait as the Allegory of Painting*.

I have to admit, I liked that self-portrait so much that I didn't send it on to Rome. Instead, I propped it against the wall and in between the other paintings worked on a copy. I'd send the copy to the cardinal, who would never know I kept the original. My thought was to use the self-portrait much as I'd used the Susanna in the first half of my career, as a demonstration piece for patrons who needed convincing. And because my self-portrait was half the size of the Susanna, it would be easier to haul around.

I was putting another coat of dark green on the canvas when Prudenzia came into the studio.

"Light's failing, Mamma," she said, after kissing me on the cheek. I smiled at my girl, who wasn't a girl anymore. She wandered over to the window and leaned out, looking at the smoke that filled the air. "It seems worse, doesn't it?"

"It does. What do the people in the market say?" I'd sent her out to buy bread because we needed it for dinner, and because I wanted to know what the common folk said about the mountain.

"Oh, there's some talk, but no one seems worried. Domenico even went out drinking." She turned away from the window and leaned her back against it. "So maybe it's nothing."

"Let's hope so," I said. I looked at the failing light behind my daughter and decided I was done for the day. As I cleaned my brush, we talked about dinner, both of us pretending the smoking mountain outside our windows didn't scare us. We had some relief when it was dark, because we couldn't see the mountain, which made it easier to pretend it wasn't groaning and moaning over the city's shoulders.

It was still dark when the first booms echoed through the air. I pushed back the blankets, kicking against my nightshirt in my hurry to be out of bed. I pulled on my thick wool robe and some slippers against the December cold and met Prudenzia in the hall.

"Is it the mountain?" Prudenzia whispered, her voice thin with anxiety. "Something awful has happened."

"I fear you are correct, my dear." Her feet were bare, so I sent her back for her slippers. I headed up to my studio, which had the coveted east-facing window meant to catch the morning light, but was also good for viewing Mount Vesuvius.

Another thunderous boom came, so loud that the glass in the window shattered with a great crack as I crossed my studio space. I caught up a blanket I kept on the studio's little couch and threw it on the floor to cover the glass. Prudenzia appeared behind me as I stepped up to the window. A great ball of glowing red appeared suspended in the night sky. It was the mountaintop, or what was left of it. Another boom came, shattering the night. A plume of red shot up into the night sky, then fell to earth like a shower of falling stars. Prudenzia leaned into me and I pulled her close, the two of us shivering as much from fright as the cold air. Under our feet, the earth shivered too.

The earth shook every five or ten minutes for the next few

hours. Dawn revealed a column of smoke and ash that reached up to the heavens. "It looks like a colossal pine tree," I said.

"The western flank of the mountaintop is gone," Prudenzia said, pointing out the window. "And look at all the ash." She lowered her finger to point at the surrounding rooftops.

But the ash wasn't just on the rooftops. The air was thick with it, falling like dirty snow on Naples. We watched the ash float downward as the tree-shaped part of the smoke plume broadened and spread east. Then, as if matters weren't bad enough, it began to rain, first a drizzle and then a committed downpour. Dirty water sluiced off the roofs and ran down the street, while above us the mountain continued belching smoke.

Hunger drove us down to the kitchen, where we found yesterday's bread, some hard cheese, and a bowl of olives for breakfast. I was thankful I could afford to keep a larder full of flour, millet, and dried pasta and fruits, but I was in no mood to cook. Then again, I never was. A young woman named Chiara, not much older than Prudenzia, came each day to cook and clean for us, but I didn't expect her today. She had a half dozen younger siblings and a father who worked as a blacksmith, and her mother had died in childbirth. Chiara would be caring for her sisters and brothers this awful day.

I checked Domenico's room, thinking he might be hungry, but he wasn't there. I hadn't really expected him to be—no one could have slept through dawn's eruptions. He often stayed with friends, so I tried not to worry about him. We listened to the rain lash against the house as we ate and tried to convince ourselves everything would be all right.

After we ate, I sent Prudenzia to her room to dress in her warmest clothes. I took myself to my studio and lit a small coal brazier I kept for those few days when it grew cold enough to require it. On any other day, I would have closed the shutters on the broken window to keep out the cold air, but I knew we would want the view. The earth continued to shudder and roll as if it meant to shake Naples into the sea. As I swept up the broken glass, another boom reverberated through the city. I dropped the broom and rushed to the window. Once more, a plume of smoke and ash shot into the sky. The eruption seemed to go on and on, though it couldn't have been any longer than thirty seconds. On the mountain's lower slopes, a great brown gash appeared and began to slide. Soon, a river of what I assumed was mud began snaking its way down the mountain.

Again Prudenzia appeared behind me, holding my winter coat. I shrugged it over my shoulders as we watched.

"What about all those poor people who live out there?" Prudenzia asked.

I knew she meant the farmers and peasantry who lived outside the city walls, on the slopes of the mountain. I shook my head and shrugged. "And Torre del Greco, where the dukes have their summer palazzos?" I said. What I didn't ask was, "What about Naples and what about us?"

The mountain exploded again not long before noon. Smoke and ash shot out of the mountaintop while stones big enough to see from our vantage point rained down on the mountain slopes. Several rivers of mud and ash had appeared during the morning, each moving with sluggish relentlessness toward the lower slopes.

We later heard that several men, thinking the morning eruptions would be the only ones, hiked up the mountain to look into the crater. They died in a rain of fire and ash. Domenico arrived home in between the two midday eruptions to tell us the viceroy and Archbishop Boncompagno had ordered the city gates open. Commoners and the rich alike had streamed into the city from the countryside, most with nothing more than what they could carry on their backs.

The dark cloud spread all afternoon, bringing with it more falling ash. When the rain stopped, the air turned into dirty steam. Prudenzia and I emulated the people we saw in the streets below us and covered our mouths and noses with damp cotton cloth. We rinsed them when we could, as they quickly became encrusted with ash.

If this sounds like hell on earth to you, you would not be far off. The only good thing about the day is that the city opened its doors and arms to the increasing number of refugees. Town criers went through the streets, calling out the names of churches that had room for people, and everyone who had room opened their doors to strangers. Prudenzia spied an old woman on the street towing two small children in a dog cart and rushed down to bring them into our kitchen. The woman, who told us her name was Marianella, had come from Torre del Greco, where she worked as a cook for one of the dukes.

"Everyone's dead," she told us. Her voice was so hoarse,

I could barely hear her. She coughed up a great gob of black spittle before speaking again, gesturing to the children with her, "I found these two wandering in the streets. I don't know who they belong to."

I looked at the two children. They were maybe three or four years old and looked as if they might be brothers, though they were so dirty and red-eyed, it was difficult to be sure.

Marianella patted the closest boy to her on the head. "The poor dears haven't said a word all day, but that's just fine. You don't worry, little ones, you're safe now."

Between the three of us, we warmed up some water and made a gruel from dried bread, old cheese, and hot water. I also had a bag of dried apricots from the summer and spilled them on the table. The children picked at their food, so we put them to bed in Domenico's room, while he volunteered to sleep on the little couch in the studio. "If I ever go to sleep," he said.

I knew what he meant. I felt like an eighty-year-old woman, more from the stress of the day than from exertion. If I laid down for even a moment, it seemed as if the mountain would explode again and kill us all in our beds. Having seen plenty of the carnage, Marianella retired to Domenico's room with the children, while the three of us went upstairs to look out the window again. By now there was a thick stream of glowing magma cascading down the mountainside. Steam rose here and there all over the mountain where the hot slurry met streams and ponds.

Domenico and I ventured out before dark in search of news,

leaving Prudenzia with Marianella and the boys. We pushed our way through the crowds to the market but found nothing open, though we hadn't expected to. The streets were full of people; some milled about in the squares with blank looks on their faces, others wept, and a few were reduced to hysterical yelling from atop the low walls that surrounded the nicer houses. More than one man called for Saint Gennaro, the city's patron saint, to save us all. Others spoke of displeasing God or wondered when he would step in to save us. The earth's continued rumbling and the mountain's belching punctuated their words. As I listened, I spared a moment to be thankful the mountain hadn't erupted since midday.

We saw the archbishop ride by on his dappled mare, her head low in exhaustion. Later we heard that he fell off his horse unconscious, unable to breathe Naples's noxious air. Viceroy Zuniga stepped into the breach left by the archbishop, as did Giovanni Manse, Marchese of Villa, one of the city's most powerful men. I didn't see either man that day, but given the crush of humanity, I could have walked right by them and not noticed.

Domenico pushed our way upstream against the tide of refugees coming in through Porta Nola, the city's eastern gate. There we heard news from the people just arriving from the countryside. They spoke of choking on air so filthy, it made Naples seem like heaven. Trees and fields were on fire, they said, and they had seen lava fields a hundred feet wide and miles long.

Domenico hopped up on a wall and pulled me up alongside him. Together we watched the unstoppable flood of humanity into the already crowded city. "This will either be Naples's finest hour, or something awful will happen," he said. He waved out over the crowd. "There will not be enough beds and tonight will be cold. The food will run out unless the rich share. Does that seem likely? How many people will die because they came to the city?"

He had a good point. However melodramatic, the volcano might be the least of Naples's problems in the coming days. We hopped down from the wall and made our way home, feeling as downtrodden and afraid as the refugees.

The night brought several more eruptions, but each was smaller and less noisy than the ones earlier in the day. Domenico and I watched out the window most of the night, both unable to sleep. Prudenzia watched with us for an hour or two but staggered off to bed well before midnight. The earth continued trembling, the mountain belched and moaned, and the night sky glowed with reflected fire.

"I will paint this," Domenico told me. "The crowds, the fire, the darkness—all of it."

I turned to look at my assistant. He'd been with me for several years and I loved him like a little brother. Like Agostino Tassi, Domenico was an exceptional architectural painter, though unlike Tassi, he was also good with landscapes (and not an abuser of young women). I set most of my paintings indoors, but when I had landscape or architectural backgrounds, I sketched them and had Domenico paint them in. "I couldn't," I said.

"You could. You're better at buildings and landscapes than you think."

"I don't mean that," I said, shaking my head. "It's the pain of it. I wouldn't want to relive it every day I was painting it. Judith and Esther and Susanna—all those women in the stories? They're not real. Or if they were, it was so long ago that they're not real anymore."

He looked out the window and nodded. "You paint ideas, images of moments that live in your head. I can't do that." He grinned at me. "Besides, I can't get people's faces right. They always look like corpses when I try."

I bumped his shoulder with mine. "Then a scene from today would be perfect for you. All those people, like ants boiling out of an anthill when you break it open—you paint the crowd, not individuals, and you'll have the sense of it."

He hauled a chair over to the window and pushed me down into it. "You keep watch. I'm going to sketch."

So we spent a companionable night together, me watching the horror from the window, he recreating it on paper from across the room. Before daybreak, he put his head on the table and fell asleep amid his parchment and charcoals.

Dawn didn't so much come as the night passed into day. The sky was dark with clouds and ash, and the morning light was an eerie purplish color. I dressed and went out to the street to see what I could learn. A passerby grabbed me by the arm and said, "Hurry, before we're too late."

I shook my elbow from his grasp and asked, "Late for what?"

He kept walking but shouted over his shoulder, "The miracle. Saint Gennaro's blood has liquefied."

I followed the man as he made his way toward the Naples Cathedral. Though the day, if one could call it that, was ominously black and the air still thick with ash, the streets were full of people. I fell in beside an older woman, who told me there'd been a procession in the night.

"The archbishop himself led it," she told me, "and all the lords of Naples too. We small folk came along, praying and such."

"Where did the procession go? And to what purpose?" I asked.

"Ah, we escorted Saint Gennaro from the church to the east gate, so he might watch over the city."

"Saint Gennaro is here?" I asked before I could help myself. My excuse was that I hadn't slept in two days, nor had I broken my night's fast. Saint Gennaro—or Januarius, as the Romans called him—died over a thousand years ago. They kept an ampule of his blood, as well as some of his bones, in the cathedral. That was about all I knew about him.

She frowned at me. "He is always here. Saint Gennaro protects Naples."

I refrained from pointing out that the saint didn't seem to be on the job right now.

When I arrived at Porta Nola, pushed along by the stream of humanity, I saw the life-sized wooden statue of the city's patron saint. They'd mounted it on the arch over the gate and dressed it in bishop's regalia, though the fabric was already dark with ash and smoke.

As I stood there, jostled by the crowd, the sun broke through the gloom. A shard of light shot down on the gate and illuminated the saint's statue. The crowd sighed, then began yelling about miracles and the like. I gathered from the talk that, sometime in the night, the archbishop announced the saint's dried blood had liquefied in its ampule. It did from time to a time, whenever the city needed a miracle.

I spared a moment of doubt about this so-called miracle but had the wisdom to keep my thoughts to myself; not only was the crowd in no mood for naysayers, but because no city needed a miracle more than Naples right now. Except perhaps Torre del Greco, that small town about three miles outside the city walls. Word on the street was that the volcano had buried the town, along with hundreds of its inhabitants, under a river of mud and ash.

As I turned to go home, a contingent of horsed men appeared. They rode through the mass of humanity and stopped at the open gate, under Saint Gennaro's statue. One man rose in his stirrups and called for quiet. When the crowd stilled, he announced there would be a second procession today, starting at noon bells, this one from Porta Capuana to the base of Mount Vesuvius. The archbishop would bring the miraculous blood and, with the viceroy, lead the people out to the mountain to pray for deliverance from our travail.

I knew from my short tenure in Naples that Porta Capuana,

like Porta Nola, faced the mountain. The road that ran from that gate went to one of the small villages on the mountain slopes, a village now deeply buried. I made my way home and shared the news with Prudenzia, Domenico, and Marianella, who'd made a breakfast of pasta and dried sausages while I was out.

"I've seen all the destruction and death I need to see," Marianella said as she spooned pasta into bowls for the still-mute boys. "And that's what this procession is about. If they just wanted to pray, they could kneel in the churches."

She wasn't wrong, but Prudenzia, Domenico, and I went anyway. Even if I didn't believe a long-dead saint would help Naples against a deadly mountain, it was something to do, and all of us wanted to be out of the house.

We arrived at the piazza well before noon to find a crush of people already milling. We were nowhere near the gate, but we could see it about two hundred yards away. The archbishop and his clergy stood atop one of the crenelated towers that flanked the gate. We waited in a light so dim, it seemed more like dusk than midday. Behind the gate, the mountain continued smoking. I couldn't see its rivers of mud from my place behind the city walls, but I knew they were there all the same.

As the noon bells tolled, the crowd quieted. When the clangor of the last bells had melted away, one of the archbishop's clerics rang a small handbell. All eyes turned toward the tower, where the archbishop faced the crowd and thrust a small clay pot, presumably the container for the miraculous blood, above his head. The crowd roared. The archbishop turned to face the mountain, the pot still high above him.

I swear on my dead mother's head that what I write here is true. The mountain went quiet and the dark cloud above it seemed to dip, as if in a bow. As thousands of us watched, a rift opened in the middle of the cloud, and within minutes the black miasma dispersed into the unseen wind. Beside me, I heard Prudenzia sob. I pulled her to me while on my left I heard Domenico murmur, "Hail Mary, full of grace . . ." Was it a miracle? I do not know, but it felt like one.

What happened next was anti-climactic. The archbishop came down from his tower and mounted his gray horse. I saw Viceroy Zuniga join the churchman with much solemnity. The two led the crowd out the gate and down the road to the base of the mountain. We followed along a good half mile behind the procession's head. The road was thick with black mud and charred rocks, but the crowd ignored the mess. We prayed and sang as we walked, and in our common brotherhood and sisterhood, we healed ourselves, if not our city.

The procession from Porta Capuana didn't solve all the city's ills. The mountain ceased its eruptions, but the sky remained ash-laden and dark for weeks. That winter, rains flooded the burned areas so that the people could not return home to the mountain. Naples was a city of refugees that winter, and as the months dragged on, the food ran short and disease ran rampant.

Before the city could starve, ships came from Pisa and Genoa with food and medicines. The city gradually cleaned up and the countryside buried its dead. In March, Viceroy Zuniga announced that three thousand souls had perished in the eruptions, but the small folk said it was at least twice that many. Surely, some dead were uncounted, buried in mud and lava, or burned in fires. But the city endured, as cities do.

Domenico did go on to paint the Mount Vesuvius eruption, and I thought it was the finest thing he ever did. As for Saint Gennaro—did his miraculous blood save the city? I only know what I saw that day, and I am no holy woman. I know the murderous mountain went back to sleep and never woke again in my lifetime.

Chapter Nine

My hands gripped the rail so hard, I felt my fingernails press into the salt-softened wood. We were going to hit that tiny boat down there. I held my breath as the rowboat in question slipped to our port side and safely past us. I'd heard that the English watermen who ferried Londoners up and down the river were as skilled with small boats as Venetian gondoliers, but now I believed it.

The *San Luigi* eased up the River Thames, pushed by the incoming tide and one carefully rigged sail. Our ship, a two-hundred-ton xebec frigate, was considerably smaller than many of the ships that clogged the Thames, especially the war brigs bristling with guns. The little ship arrived in one piece and at half the passage price of the larger ships, so I was more than satisfied with her.

I'd sailed from Naples only twenty-one days before, prompted by a set of letters delivered in person by my brother Francesco. He had appeared on my doorstep in Naples so much a stranger to me that it took me a second to realize who he was. My brother, who'd turned into a man in the years since I'd last seen him, had received a letter from Papà and another from King Charles. That had been well over a month before.

I pulled Papà's letter from my skirt pocket and examined it again, though I'd read it so many times that I'd memorized the words:

My darling girl,

I write in a rush, for your brother Francesco is to set out for Naples on the morning tide. The king wishes to collect both painting Gentileschis for his stockpile of pet artists. He has unlimited funds and a voracious appetite for paintings. Bring your best works with you, but do come at once. I find myself in need of assistance with my current project, a ceiling at one of the queen's estates. I would appreciate your presence more than you can know and look forward to painting with my daughter one last time.

Francesco awaits, so I must come to a close.

Do not hesitate. Take the first ship to England.

Your Papà,
Orazio Gentileschi

All in all, it was a mild letter, unless one knew my papà. He never admitted to needing help, nor had he ever shown any interest in sharing projects with me. He'd worked with many painters, including the rat Agostino Tassi, but never with me. And then there was that "one last time" at the end of the letter. I would be forty-five years of age this summer, which meant Papà was seventy-five. What was he thinking, taking on a ceiling at his age? They were hard enough to paint in a person's twenties or thirties. And not just any ceiling—if the ceiling was in a royal residence and important enough to hire a foreign painter, the project was bound to be huge and the stakes high.

The second letter, from the king, was even shorter. I had read it and looked at Francesco in astonishment. "He *commands* me? I am one of his subjects?"

My brother wiped the sweat from his forehead. Francesco was four years younger than me and quite handsome. He dressed in the English style, with velvet and fur much too warm for Naples, even in early spring, but he appeared like a prosperous merchant. "King Charles thinks he's appointed by God to rule England."

"England, yes, but not Naples."

"Ah, true," Francesco had said. "But he wants to make England great not through war—or not *only* through war—but by the arts. He believes having Orazio's famous painting daughter in England will reflect well on his rule and his country."

I shook my head. "Kings, they're worse than grand dukes or viceroys."

Francesco agreed but reminded me that this king had great rafts of money to spend on art. He hemmed and hawed, then got to the crux of his mission. "I fear this ceiling will kill Papà,"

Francesco had said, rubbing his brown curls. "I rarely regret my lack of talent. I am good at the business of art, and even artists must do business—but watching our father struggle to complete the Queen's House ceiling made me wish I were a better painter. I'm good for little more than clouds, so I'm no help. We need you, my sister."

The ship bumped against the wharf, bringing me out of my reverie. I put the letter back in my pocket and pulled my heavy wool cloak around me. Most of the trip had been pleasant, but after we rounded the Iberian Peninsula and sailed up the Spanish coast, the weather became increasingly frigid. Francesco had warned me that summer in London would be no warmer than winter in Naples. I hadn't believed him and felt like a fool when I packed my heaviest cloak, but now I was glad I had.

One of the sailors approached me. "Better gather your things, mistress. We'll be tied up and offloading in a jiffy," he said.

I looked around at the forest of naked ship masts that made up London's port. "Are we far from Greenwich?" I needed to ask directions from an Italian speaker before being thrown up against a host of English speakers.

The sailor removed his cap and scratched his head. "Mistress, we be in the Lower Pool now and Greenwich be just across the river a wee piece."

"The Lower Pool?"

"Ah, well, the port of London be divided into two parts, the Upper Pool and the Lower Pool, with the London Bridge in between. See, the *San Luigi*'s mass be too tall to sail under the London Bridge, like all the tall ships, so we're for the Lower Pool." He pointed across the wide river to the far side. "Greenwich is just over there and a bit downriver. You'll need a water taxi to the other side, then a carriage. Or you can take a carriage upriver to the London Bridge, cross over, and go down again. It's up to you, my lady."

I thanked the man, grateful he spoke both Italian and English. Only a few of the sailors on the *San Luigi* were bilingual and I'd used the shipboard time to learn a little English. Not much, but enough, I hoped, to get me to Papà. Francesco spoke English fluently, but he hadn't returned with me. King Charles desired Francesco to deliver invitations to a handful of other painters, including three Romans. So I left my household to Prudenzia's care and sailed to London alone. This had been easier said than done, because Naples was held by Spain. Spain and England were not friendly anymore, not after the current English king married the daughter of the French king (and his Medici wife, Marie). Or maybe that marriage was the result of political differences with Spain. I don't pay much attention to politics in my home country, let alone one on the far western side of Europe.

It took several hours before my crated paintings and trunks were taken off the ship and another hour to organize transport. Part of the problem was my difficulty with English, but also no one believed a woman as commonly dressed as myself had any business at the Queen's House. Eventually, I commandeered a carriage and a wagon to take me across the river by way of the London Bridge. Along the way, I noted that the streets of

London were nearly as crowded as Naples and twice as filthy—and cold. It drizzled off and on all afternoon while I shivered in my heaviest cloak, wishing I'd invested in something fur-lined.

By the time I arrived in Greenwich, it was well after sunset. Even as tired and hungry as I was, the beauty of the new place surprised me. The moon lit up a white marble edifice built on the symmetrical lines one found in Venetian palazzos. I would later learn the building was a perfect square, as was its central hall, where I'd be working for the next eighteen months. The gate porter directed us up the road a few hundred yards to the Old Palace, where, according to Francesco, Papà had rooms. I left the wagon in the Old Palace's rear courtyard and stumbled off to bed, not caring that the room was cold and the bed lumpy.

I awoke at midday to find my trunks and crated paintings had been delivered to the small sitting room adjoining my bedroom. Even better, some quiet maid had lit fires in both rooms, which went a fair way to driving out the English chill. So too did a large pot of tea and a tray of food, delivered by a maid with skin so white, she looked ghostly. Eating my breakfast, I reflected that the English complexion might also be the byproduct of a bland diet of cooked oats, soft-cooked eggs, and cold white bread. I'd eaten better than this in the post-volcano food shortages. In Italy, we fed oat mush to sick horses, not people. I was just finishing my dubious breakfast when Papà burst into my room.

"Darling girl," he cried, rushing over to pepper me with dry kisses.

I hugged Papà back and tried not to let shock show on my

face. Papà had never been a big man, but he'd always looked vital and bursting with energy. Now he was so thin, I could see the outlines of his bones under his dry skin, which sagged like it was too big for his body. His nose, which had never been a delicate, retiring organ, poked out from his face like a sharp beak, and his hair hung to his shoulders in strings of gray.

"Come, get dressed as quick as you can, and we shall go see the work," he said, beaming at me and rubbing his hands together.

"Slow down, Papà!" I said. "I only just arrived last night." Despite my protests, I rose and threw open my clothing trunk.

"No time to waste," he said as he left the room. "We have work to do."

A half hour later we were strolling up the gravel path between the Old and New Palaces. The Queen's House was no less lovely in the daylight.

"Isn't it marvelous?" Papà said, waving his hand at the white edifice. "Inigo Jones designed it. Have you heard of him?"

I shook my head no. Papà had been in England for over a decade and he'd forgotten how little English news reached the Italian Peninsula.

"Ah, well, I shall see to it that you meet him. Jones might as well be a Roman, so influenced is he by our classic architecture."

"I thought it looked Venetian," I said as I tucked Papà's hand into the crook of my arm.

"You have a good eye, my darling. Jones began this house for Charles's father, King James, who wanted it as a present for his Queen Anne. It was Queen Anne who taught Charles to love art so much. When Anne died, the work continued. Neither James nor Charles cares to use the old place. Too much Tudor history there, you see."

"Tudor history?" I had no idea what Papà was talking about.

He jocularly tugged at my arm. "I see I should have taught you more than painting. The English King Henry VIII, and his daughter Elizabeth, lived there. She was born there, or so I have heard."

"Really? I'm staying in the old queen's house?" I grinned. In Naples, I lived in a six-room row house, so I'd come up in the world, even if only temporarily.

Papà winked. "'Tis only fitting for my talented girl, who paints better than any queen ever has."

Now I knew Papà needed my help, and badly. He'd never been a doting parent, nor loose with compliments. We entered the house (even buildings big enough to qualify as palaces are called houses by the English) through a side door that stood under a columned portico. Before I knew it, I found myself in the building's great hall. It was a perfectly square space, tiled with a striking pattern of black-and-white marble squares. A dark stone balustrade lined the second-floor interior balcony, which circled the room. Windows on both stories filled the room with light, even on this less-than-sunny day.

I peered up at the ceiling. The central rondel, if nowhere near as large as the paintings in the Sistine Chapel, was a surprising fifteen feet across.

"It's *Peace Reigning Over the Arts*," Papà said, pride evident in his tone. "It was Queen Henrietta's idea. I had it and the others temporarily installed, knowing you'd arrive this week, but they're on canvas so we can take them down and work on them."

"Not frescoes?" I asked. That was one good thing. Painting on a platform with your head craned back is not fun.

"No," Papà said with glee. "Canvas."

"And Henrietta—who's that?"

"Oh, the queen doesn't like being referred to as Marie or Maria, because that's her mother's name," he explained, "though it's what Charles decreed she'd be called. She prefers her birth name, Henrietta. She's an interesting woman. You'll see when you meet her. No one takes her seriously, perhaps because the king does not, but she's no fool—no daughter of Marie de Medici was a featherhead. There's unrest in the realm, you see, on account of the queen being Catholic. She hopes this room might remind the more fervent Protestant courtiers that only in peace can we have all the things that make life good. The Duke of Buckingham, who brought me to this country, agreed, though unlike the queen, he is a Protestant."

Ah, the notorious Duke of Buckingham. He'd met Papà in France when he'd gone for the proxy wedding between Charles and Henrietta Marie, and he ended up one of Papà's greatest supporters. Still, rumor had it that the lowborn Buckingham had ended up a duke after he captured James I's heart. Protestant England was even more prudish about sexuality than Catholics, and it came as no surprise when parliament twice tried to unseat him from his ducal post. The army officer who murdered Buckingham a decade ago was still considered a hero by common Englishmen. I'd even heard sailors sing a sea shanty about the assassin's heroism. Papà lived at Buckingham's York House for years, until the duke's untimely death, after which he became court painter for King Charles.

I craned my neck toward the ceiling. Peace, identifiable by the olive branch she held aloft, sat on a cloud in the center of the circle. Victory presided over the outer circle, her foot on a cornucopia and arm upraised with a palm frond that looked suspiciously like a cavalry saber. "Are those Grammar, Logic, and Rhetoric to the left?" I asked. Muses of the lowest of the liberal arts, they were expected in this sort of thing.

He clapped me on the shoulder. "Exactly. Do you see Rhetoric's mirror? And there's the quadrivium to the right."

The quadrivium, or the four high liberal arts, include Mathematics, Geometry, Music, and Astronomy. The figures representing Mathematics and Astronomy were only outlined so far. "What are the others?" I asked.

"Ah, well, Queen Henrietta also wanted the seven liberal arts, plus Meditation to stand for religion and Agriculture to represent the more mechanical arts."

I scanned the ceiling. Carved wooden armatures divided the space into four corner squares, into which were set a smaller rondel, while four rectangular canvases centered on each of the walls.

Papà pointed to the long rectangle to the left. "There will be the Muses Euterpe and Polyhymnia. On that side," he said, shifting his finger to the right side of the room, "we'll have the Muses Clio and Thalia. On the far wall will be Erato and

Terpsichore, and here, just above me, Urania, Calliope, and Melpomene."

I nearly cried at the scope of the work not yet done. He'd begun Erato, Urania, and Thalia, but each painting was at best half done, and he had completed two of the four corner rondels. Almost as disturbing, he'd abandoned his Caravaggisti naturalism for an idealized style of luminous light, saturated colors, and porcelain skin, so I was going to have to paint that way too.

"You see it, don't you?" he asked. "The liberal arts in the center, the nine Muses along the walls, and personifications of the arts in the corners. I've left Pittura for you, knowing you've painted yourself as the allegory of painting. But isn't it grand? It shall be my masterpiece." He tore his eyes from the ceiling and looked at me. "*Our* masterpiece."

He'd left me a good deal more than Pittura, but it seemed mean-spirited to point that out. I'd come to London thinking I would help my father over the summer and sail for home before the winter storms. Standing in the Queen's House now, I knew it would be years, not months, before this wretched ceiling was done.

The canvases, once removed from the ceiling, were too large to move, so we painted in the Grand Salon. The Queen's House's magnificent windows lit the way on all but the gloomiest days. I've only experienced one other winter so dark and gloomy as that first summer in England, and that was in the months after Mount Vesuvius's December eruptions.

Papà and I worked day after day, week after week, on the canvases. I first finished the Mathematics figure in the central rondel, and when Papà wasn't paying attention, touched up the hands and feet of some other figures. That bit of work took only a few weeks, after which we had the fifteen-foot rondel reinstalled on the ceiling. This created the impression of forward movement on the project, though I continued to despair at the amount of work yet to be done.

Papà and I next undertook a shared painting on one of the side panels. Papà worked considerably slower than I, so while he painted Calliope, the Muse of epic poetry, I undertook Urania, the Muse of astronomy, and Melpomene, the Muse of song. Papà had painted most of Erato, the Muse of love poetry, before I arrived, but only some of Terpsichore, so I finished her. Before the summer ended, we'd completed the two largest side panels and the central rondel. That fall, we finished Clio and Thalia, with Papà taking Thalia, the Muse of comedy, and me the Muse of history, Clio.

Each month, Papà spent more days in bed. His feet and legs swelled terribly, causing him great pain when he stood all day. He would also get short of breath and dizzy, particularly if he worked from a ladder. He used a three-legged stool when possible, but painting large canvases does not allow much sitting. Some days the swelling was so bad, he returned to his rooms to spend the rest of the day with his feet elevated on a pile of pillows. The queen's physician visited Papà and declared he had dropsy. The physician applied leeches to Papà's swollen legs, but the treatment didn't seem to help. It reminded me of poor Don Giovanni's death, which in turn reminded me of his widow, Livia. I hadn't heard from her in the sixteen years since my sojourn in Venice. I feared she'd experienced the Medici taste for revenge, and I had no way to find her.

In October, Papà sketched Euterpe and Polyhymnia, and I painted most of them. Some days, Papà arrived in the afternoon and tried to do his part, but by then he'd become so weak that he wasn't much help. Francesco arrived from the continent that fall with wagonloads of paintings he'd bought for King Charles. Most were from minor painters in Pisa and Verona, but he also had several fine Vouets he'd picked up in Paris. When Francesco wasn't installing paintings in one of the king's dozen houses, he would work with us at the Queen's House. I remembered what he'd said and confined his brush to painting clouds or touching up woodwork.

I am proud to say that each month my grasp of English grew, though I found I was better at understanding people than I was at making myself understood. I had a maid at the Old Palace who practiced with me each morning and I made Papà speak English while we painted. While I didn't enjoy the work, I liked being with Papà. It was like the old days, before everything went bad in the shadow of Agostino Tassi.

At first, we spoke of only general things like the work, but as the months went on, we spoke more and more of the old days. He told me funny stories about Mamma and about when my brothers and I were small. Papà also had outlandish tales of his two years at the French court, painting for Marie de Medici. I discovered my papà had never forgiven himself for what he called "that Tassi mess." He didn't quite apologize for it, but I didn't need him to. He was my papà, and if he'd made mistakes—which he definitely did—he'd done his best. As a parent myself, I knew how hard it was to raise a child and not make some mistakes. He'd kept a roof over my head, fed me, and taught me to paint, and I owed him some forgiveness for all that.

We didn't paint in noble isolation either—not at all. People came and went; some of them were men finishing the interior spaces of the Queen's House and some were nobles, checking on our progress (and wasting our time with foolish talk). My dear friend Anthony van Dyck came by the Queen's House often, always with fabulous treats packed in a wicker basket. Like Papà, Anthony had been in London for years. He'd painted dozens of court portraits and acted as the king's procurer of artists. Anthony had also brought the great Peter Paul Rubens to London one year, as well as several other Dutch painters, much to King Charles's delight. Charles rewarded Anthony with knighthood and proclaimed him the King's Principal Painter.

"All I do is paint Stuarts," Anthony declared the first afternoon he visited. "I paint family scenes, just the children, the king and queen alone and together—it goes on and on. You'd think that family would get tired of standing for their portraits, but no, they do not."

I noted with envy that Anthony's English was as good as his Italian, and he was so familiar with London that he'd managed to find food worth eating. The exotic foodstuffs he brought for our lunches made for a welcome respite from the endless porridge and overcooked mutton at the Old Palace.

I swallowed a bit of smoked fish and shook my finger at Anthony. "You are much too good a painter to paint only portraits," I said.

"Bah," he said with a wave of his hand. "I'm much too good to starve. I've set up a large studio at my house in Blackfriars and hired many young painters. They do the backgrounds for me, so all I have to do is paint in the central figure. It is a fast way to work, and allows more time for my mistress and lunch with my Italian friends."

I sighed at this frivolity, but he laughed and gestured up at the ceiling. "Are you any better? At least my portraits are in my style."

Papà sputtered and argued at this, but Anthony made a fair point. If I were painting the queen's portrait, I might do it as an Artemisia painting, instead of working on this old-fashioned English idealist fluff.

Speaking of the queen, she came to visit us once, along with her mother, Marie. Queen Henrietta had her mother's long face and pale skin, but none of her mother's Medici beauty. She looked like a Hapsburg with her bulging eyes and a chin that slid away just under her lower lip.

The visit was planned down to the tiniest detail. There were a hundred rules about how we were to act and what we might say and not say, but it was still exciting. The royal retinue entered the Grand Salon. Anthony, who'd been standing by, took them straight up the stairs so they could see the ceiling from the second-floor balconies. After a time, the large group made its way downstairs again and deigned to speak with the painters, though they said little more than polite niceties before leaving en masse.

After the visit, Anthony said Henrietta wished to speak with me in her private chambers at Denmark House. I was to bring with me any paintings I had that she might enjoy.

That meeting was entirely different than her previous visit. I took my *Self-Portrait as Allegory of Painting*, as well as a Lucretia copy with me. Denmark House, once called Somerset House, was no mere house. It was a massive neo-classical palace in the middle of London, far larger than the new Queen's House. When I arrived, I was escorted to the queen's chambers, where I found her surrounded by a half-dozen spaniels, three ladies-in-waiting, a monkey, and two dwarves playing cards at a half-sized table in the corner. One of her ladies held a leash attached to the monkey, who shivered so badly that I wished someone would get him a little coat. The dwarves ignored me in favor of their game. When I unwrapped my self-portrait, the queen understood immediately what it meant.

"It is magnificent," she said in her French-accented English. "Sir van Dyck has spoken of your talent for strong female figures, but I thought he exaggerated." She winked at me. "I think he is a little in love with you, but I see he also tells me the truth."

I smiled at the queen, knowing she saw romance everywhere, in part because she had none in her own life. How could a woman whose greatest accomplishment was being born into a powerful family and marrying into another understand the respect one painter might have for another?

We also looked at the Lucretia, which she liked as well,

though her eyes strayed back to my self-portrait as we spoke of Lucretia's story. Seemingly unable to help herself, she asked, "Would you sell me these paintings for my private collection?"

I'd never be paid a cent for the ceiling work, so I'd hoped she'd ask that. I needed to send money home to my household in Naples and so I could sail back there shortly.

"I would sell my dearest paintings only to you, Your Highness, in honor of your great work on behalf of artists everywhere." I curtseyed to emphasize my ingratiating yet sincere point.

She clapped her hands together in glee, then waved the dwarves over to appraise her new paintings. One of the dwarves was built proportionally and stood less than two feet high. The other was a foot taller and had stubby, bowed legs and a large head.

"May I introduce Lord Minimus," the queen said, sweeping her hand toward the shorter dwarf.

He bowed his head at me and said, "Jeffrey Hudson at your service, madame." I smiled at the man, charmed by his dignified demeanor.

"And Royal Dwarf Richard Gibson," the queen said, gesturing to a second person. Before he said a word, she added, "Dwarf Gibson is a skilled painter in his own right."

One expects dwarves in a royal court to juggle and tell jokes, not engage in the higher arts. "What do you paint?" I asked, intrigued.

"Miniatures, my lady." He winked as he spoke, which made me laugh, that is until I saw his smile falter. I wanted to reach out and pat him on the head and stopped myself. What must it be like to be treated as a performing pet just because one was born small? I suspected it was a little like being a woman, perpetually under estimated and over looked. But worse, because there are so many women we can go un-noticed in the world, where as Signor Hudson and Gibson would be seen as oddities no matter where they went or what they did with their lives.

The queen retrieved a small case from a tabletop and opened it to reveal a double frame. She held it out to me. "Gibson is quite good. He painted the Prince of Wales and Princess Mary for me."

I examined the double portrait and agreed with the queen's assessment of the painter's talent. "I never got the hang of miniatures," I told him.

"The trick is to exaggerate the eyes, but only a little bit. And, of course, there are the tiny brushes, some no more than a hair."

We spoke of painting for a few minutes more before Queen Henrietta changed the subject. "I met dear Richard when he was presented to me in a pie," she said, gesturing to the smaller dwarf. My eyes widened and the queen laughed. "I see you're not familiar with the story. The Duke of Buckingham, God rest his soul, used to have the most extraordinary dinners and entertainments." She looked down at the dwarf. "When was it?"

"1626, my lady," he said stiffly.

The queen didn't notice Richard's discomfort. "Ah, yes. Well, it was happier times with many, many entertainments. The duke ordered a large pie to be delivered to my table. Before I cut into it, dear Richard broke through the top crust and nearly scared me to death. I can still remember how pastry stuck in his hair as he capered about for my amusement."

I looked down to see Richard frowning at this remembrance, so I steered the topic back to painting. We talked of art for another hour before the queen dismissed me. I left my first royal audience pleased and disturbed—pleased that I'd sold two paintings for more money than I'd ever before charged, but disturbed by the queen's treatment of her dwarves. I understood what it was like when people decided who you should be and shoved you into that mold, regardless of whether you fit. Though those men were dwarves, they were men first, yet the queen kept them like she kept her dogs and monkey. It seemed little more than slavery to me.

Papà lived through one last Christmas season. Together we attended one of the queen's famous holiday celebrations. This one featured the light opera *Luminalia* by her favorite musician, Sir William Davenant. Inigo Jones, who'd designed the Queen's House, organized the lighting and the queen herself performed, along with her many ladies-in-waiting.

The lights were so elaborate that Jones had designed a special building of timber and canvas for the performance. This kept the candle and lantern heat from damaging any of Rubens's paintings that adorned the Banqueting House at Whitehall Palace. In the play's final scene, the queen, playing the Queen of Brightness, descended from a second-floor balcony on a swing. She was bathed in lights so her jeweled gown sparkled like the sun. It was quite unlike anything I'd ever seen, and if it was not in the best taste, it was entertaining. Papà enjoyed it ever so much, though he spent the next two days in bed recovering from the exertions of the evening. Poor Papà, gone were the days when he could drink wine all night and still paint the next day.

Other than the queen's extravaganza, we passed the winter holidays quietly. Some days Papà joined me in the Grand Salon for a few hours of painting, but most days he stayed in bed. While his swollen legs gave him a good deal of trouble, by the new year his breathing had become his most urgent problem. The doctor listened to Papà's chest through a rolled-up tube of parchment and pronounced water in the lungs, caused by an excess of yellow bile. He bled Papà twice, but each time Papà could hardly breathe afterward. He would lay in bed, gasping like a fish pulled from the water. The third time the doctor came to bleed Papà I turned him away, which displeased the man, but I held firm. There seemed little sense in torturing Papà with bloodletting when it didn't make him feel better.

As January ran out its days, Papà ate but little and began to cough at the slightest exertion. Francesco and I took turns sitting with him, as did dear Anthony. In fact, on Papà's good days, a maid would dress him in his best robes and prop him in a chair. With charcoal, Anthony drew Papà's portrait on those days, showing Papà at his most dignified and wise. Papà kept the drawing near his bed until the very end, and when he died, Anthony copied it for printing. He sent me a copy several months later; it is one of my most treasured possessions. Indeed, it hangs above my writing table, where I may see it nearly every day.

By the first week of February, Papà's breathing had become so bad that we propped him up with many pillows and kept watch, lest he slip down and be unable to breath. I stayed with him for hours at a time, fearing he would pass into the great beyond if I left him for even a moment.

Once, in the middle of the night, he grasped my arm, waking me from a doze.

"What, Papà?" I asked. Was this the end?

"I am sorry, you know," he said, drawing a gasping breath. "I never said, but I did you a great wrong."

"I forgave you a long time ago, Papà." As I spoke the words, I knew they were true. I'd been angry with Papà for years and years. Even in Genoa, I'd still been mad at him for allowing Tassi to do what he did to me. But sometime in the last ten years or so, that anger had melted away, though how or exactly when it left, I did not know.

"It was wrong of me," he gasped. "I'm going to hell for it."

"No, Papà," I said with a small smile, "you are not. God forgives greater transgressions than yours."

His fingers dug into my arm. "Do you think so?"

"I do." Tears spilled from my eyes. "I will see you in heaven one day, I know it."

"How do you know?" Papà's tone was both bleak and hopeful.

"Because, Papà, it wouldn't be heaven if I were there without you." Whatever I was, it was because Papà had taught me to paint. He'd made mistakes, but we all do. And here we were, together at the very end.

Papà died two days later. King Charles commanded he be buried at Queen Henrietta's Chapel at Somerset House, where all the important English Catholics were buried. I didn't go to the funeral because the English thought it unseemly for women to attend such functions, but it didn't matter. I walked to the church later, when the crowds had gone, and laid a wreath of bay leaves at Papà's grave. The building had the same barrel-vaulted ceiling as the Sistine Chapel and nearly as many paintings and sculptures. It was as good a place as any to leave my papà behind.

Not that I could have taken his body back to Rome even if I wanted to. As I wrote at the opening of this journal, I found myself in the untenable position of being trapped in England by two monarchs who would neither pay me nor release me from service even when it became clear we were at war. I fear I would still be on that dreary isle, forced to paint for spoiled royalty who treated humans like toys, if it were not for English Protestants, who could no longer tolerate Catholic monarchs. The Queen sought refuge in the Netherlands with the Prince of Orange, to whom she had betrothed her nine-year-old daughter Mary. That poor child. As bad as my Papà may have been, he would have never done such a thing to me, not at that age, but queens and kings use their children as pawns in seemingly endless games of power and think nothing of it. Of that time of my life I wish to write little more. Suffice it to say I was lucky to escape before Henrietta returned to England the following spring.

A few years later, word of King Charles' execution came to Naples. I was in my studio when my daughter brought me the news and try though I might, I could muster no tears for the headless king. He never did pay for my *Self Portrait*, nor did he return it to me. Would that all art patrons who refuse to honor their debts suffer a similar fate. I hear Henrietta lives in a luxurious Parisian convent these days, while my *Self Portrait* most surely hangs in some rich Englishman's house as spoils of war. There is little justice in the world for those of us who must pay our own way.

Chapter Ten

THE KINGDOM OF NAPLES
1641–1647

I knocked on Prudenzia's door. "May I come in?" I called. From inside the bedroom came a muffled sound I took to mean yes.

I opened the door to find my grown daughter still in bed. Again. Her grief was understandable, I suppose. I'd never grieved a husband's passing, but I knew some women did, women with better husbands than mine. Luckily, my daughter had been one of those women. She'd been a widow for less than a month, which is also about how long it had been since she'd eaten an entire meal or left the house.

People die, I know, but I hadn't expected Prudenzia to be widowed so young. Six years ago I arranged a marriage between my then eighteen-year-old daughter to Priore Figino, the son of a wealthy merchant. I'd sold a small painting to his father, Nardo Figino, and saw the way my daughter looked at his son. The marriage had been difficult to arrange, though the young people very much desired it. Papà Figino aimed higher for his son than the daughter of a lady painter, which is fair. He hoped to use his son to launch the family from the merchant class to more elite status. The sizable dowry I put together by selling a house left to me by Uncle Aurelio helped solve the problem. To Priore's delight, Prudenzia became Signora Figino. The young couple lived first at the Figino family palazzo and then, after I left for England, at my house near the Naples waterfront.

Prudenzia painted a little, mostly helping Domenico with his commissions. While I was gone, the two of them added two painters to my workshop. The first was a talented fellow named Bernardo Cavallino. Bernardo came from Massimo Stanzione's workshop, but he'd fallen out of favor with his master and been put out of Stanzione's house. Prudenzia said Bernardo had nearly starved to death on the streets before she found him and took him in. Bernardo proved to be one of those men who genuinely liked and admired strong women, so much so that he lived with me and Prudenzia as a member of our family.

I wasn't surprised Stanzione and Bernardo ended up at odds. When I first moved to Naples, Stanzione spent nearly every afternoon at my studio learning techniques of Caravaggism. He'd learned much from me about the use of light and dark, as well as how to mix and successfully apply strong colors. Unfortunately, he never enjoyed my images of strong women. Stanzione's *Judith with the Head of Holofernes*, for example, was of the "Judith as a temptress" type. Stanzione also had a long-standing feud with the Naples Cabal, a group of cranky old painters who tried to control the city's art scene. I'd managed to stay out of their way, but Stanzione wasn't the sort of man to play nice with men he didn't like.

The second painter to join our little studio reminded me of Domenico in his younger years. Viviano Codazzi specialized in architectural painting. I thought he had the talent for human figures, but not the confidence to paint people. Whenever his paintings had people, they were small, distant figures and often either Domenico or Prudenzia painted them in. Viviano worked with us during the day, but he lived with his wife, Candida, who was pregnant with their first child, in a small apartment several blocks away.

Anyway, I digress. While I was away, Prudenzia and her husband, Priore, created a happy household. He worked at his father's waterfront warehouse each day while his wife and her collection of talented young painters created a mini workshop. They pumped out the sort of paintings middling merchants might afford, and they made a fair bit of money doing it. Then, not long after I returned home to Naples, Priore sickened and died. The doctor said he had the plague, but I didn't think so. I'd seen the plague, and Priore had suffered none of its grim symptoms. It mattered not—poor Priore was just as dead as if he'd been covered in swollen buboes and black spots.

Prudenzia grieved with all the energy of a young woman who'd genuinely loved her husband. It would have helped if they'd ever had children, but sadly my daughter had the same problem with babies I'd had. She carried two daughters to term and both died soon after their birth. She'd sent me many sad letters about her babies. Her grief for Priore was tangled in her belief that she'd failed in her wifely duty—which is ridiculous, but humans are rarely logical in matters of love and grief.

This morning, I decided Prudenzia had lain in bed long enough. I pulled the covers to the side, grabbed my daughter's arm, and hauled her from the bed. She came to her feet sluggishly, as if still half asleep. "Today you will eat something, then you will wash and dress in clean clothes. After that, we will walk to the market," I said, shaking her arm. "Do you hear me?"

"Yes, Mamma," she murmured, though she barely opened her eyes.

I pushed her downstairs and fed her a bowl of buttered polenta like she was a child, all the while feeling like a rotten mother. Had I sheltered her too much? Should I have arranged a marriage with someone she might have loved less?

The boys, as I called our two new painters, came into the kitchen and greeted Prudenzia as if she were their sister. Viviano insisted he needed her help with his latest painting. Bernardo complained that he'd been mixing his colors and they weren't as good as when she did it. Marianella, who had stayed with us after the eruption (though we'd found the two boys' father and returned them), heated water for a bath and together we washed Prudenzia head to toe, then stuffed her into a clean gown. I made her go with Marianella to the market, though the two were not gone long. Prudenzia saw some octopus at the fishmonger's shop, burst into tears, and insisted they go home. Octopus tentacles in ink sauce had been Priore's favorite meal.

Still, she'd eaten, bathed, and left the house, so it was a step in the right direction. We kept at it, and every day got a bit better.

As Prudenzia grew more lively, so too did my commission. While I had not enjoyed King Charles and Queen Henrietta's court one bit, my association with the English monarchs did much to enhance the value of my work. The Dukes of Parma and Modena sought my paintings, as did the archbishop of Naples. For the archbishop I painted a ten-foot-tall image of Saint Januarius as he was thrown into a bear pit by his enemies. The bears were said to have licked the man's feet instead of killing him, making the city's patron saint story sort of fun. Thus, I undertook my first and only painting of a bear. I would not say it was my most successful painting, but the archbishop liked it well enough to hang it in the cathedral's front vestibule.

Anthony van Dyck found me my best patron when he gave my name to Don Antonio Ruffo, one of the greatest art collectors ever to live. Though Don Ruffo lived in Messina, on the island of Sicily, he carried out a lively correspondence with dozens of artists. He bought as many paintings as King Charles had, with one huge difference: Don Ruffo paid, and he paid on time. The first work I did for Don Ruffo set the pattern for those years. He asked for a Bathsheba painting, but he wanted it in the modern style. You see, I'd spent my life painting one, two, or three figures close up so I didn't have to worry about perspective or landscape. But since I'd been to England, the style had changed. Patrons preferred large canvasses with figures in the foreground and substantial landscapes or architecture features in the background. This necessitated a mastery of perspective, which I'd never learned because my teacher had been the rat Agostino Tassi.

Luckily, two of the painters in my household excelled at backgrounds and had the time and inclination to collaborate with me. Not Domenico, of course, who had his own commissions these days. His painting of the Vesuvius eruption made him famous and brought him to the notice of Neapolitans with money to spend. Nor was Bernardo much help in my work. He specialized in old-style religious paintings, for which the church had a nearly boundless appetite. But young Viviano proved to be the perfect partner for my larger, more background-intensive paintings, as did Prudenzia.

For Don Ruffo's first commission, I sketched a study that put Bathsheba in the foreground, one maid behind her, scrubbing her back, and the other at her feet, washing her legs. Bathsheba combs her hair, her breasts exposed, while on the balcony of a house in the background the distant figure of David watches her. If this sounds like another one of those Biblical stories that allows men to hang pictures of naked women in their homes, you'd be right.

But, as always, I put my interpretation on the painting, turning Bathsheba from sexual temptress into a gracefully innocent woman. My David looms behind and above Bathsheba, much like the elders in my Susanna painting, but he does so from far away, as a shadowy figure. I liked the metaphor a lot, for such is the way with male power, which is rarely obvious. Viviano painted the background and did such an exemplary job that we vowed to work together on many more paintings. Don Ruffo liked the Bathsheba so much that he bragged about it to other art collectors. They soon wrote asking me for their own version of the piece, so I painted several, altering them slightly so each was unique but not strikingly different from the original.

Lest you think poorly of me, let me be clear: I had a large household to feed, including two servants, three male painters, and one daughter. And Viviano's family became larger each year, though his ability to manage his money did not. Thus, at any given time, I was supporting at least ten people. A woman with many dependents does not turn down a commission because the patron wants an image she's already painted. Also, Don Ruffo paid more for paintings with more figures in them, so I was only too glad to crowd people into paintings. No topic lent itself better to that technique than Bathsheba.

Bernardo and I also painted a *Triumph of Galatea* for Don Ruffo. I mention the painting because it was such fun to do. Years and years ago, I saw Rafael's *Galatea* in Rome—it is an exuberant painting full of naked nymphs, satyrs, and angels, in the middle of which the goddess Galatea rides a giant scallop shell pulled by dolphins (who were also naked). Bernardo and I painted something like that, only we left out the angels and kept the satyrs waist-deep in the water to preserve their masculine modesty. Also, we put our Galatea on a chipped crab shell instead of an elegant scallop shell, and Prudenzia painted such corpulent dolphins that it was difficult to believe they could pull the gloriously naked goddess anywhere, so we giggled our way through that painting. In the evenings, we would open a bottle of wine, get tipsy, and dream up more and more ridiculous ideas for Galatea. It was a silly painting masquerading as a serious piece of art, but it had half a dozen figures and made us enough to pay two year's rent.

I also painted one more *Judith and Her Maidservant* during these years, in part to keep me busy while the boys painted backgrounds on my other works, and partly because Don Ruffo wanted one of his own. I took my inspiration for the painting from my earlier Judiths, but moved the scene back a little to show more of the room and the table. I put Agostino Tassi's face on Holofernes's head again, having heard from friends in Rome that he'd died in the spring of 1644. This time I painted it with little rancor in my heart. To know one's tormentor is rotting in the grave while you still live is a great balm to the soul.

However smoothly and harmoniously my household ran in those years, it was not reflected in the surrounding city. Naples had never really recovered from the volcanic disaster of 1631. Every year the city grew more crowded and its inhabitants poorer and more discontented. Poverty caused people to forget the miracle of Saint Gennaro and remember only the tragedy of the eruption. Viceroy Zuniga, who'd held the city together during the disaster, died while I was in England. His replacement was a foolish man named Guzman who ignored the commoner's complaints, many of which were exceedingly real. He'd gotten the job not through any demonstration of competence in governance, but because he was the son-in-law to one of the Spanish king's favorite dukes.

Guzman died in 1644, leaving Naples as a city on the

edge. The next viceroy came to us from Sicily and was no more competent than the man he'd replaced. He too died soon after assuming the role, having misruled Naples for less than two years. The homeless and the poor choked the streets, their begging bowls always empty, competing for the city's scraps with packs of mangy dogs and hordes of feral cats.

The Duke of Aros, lately of Valencia, had the viceregal post next. He took a livelier interest in Naples, but of the type that made the situation worse. From what I gathered, this latest viceroy thought poverty and suffering were problems one solved by raising taxes and hanging anyone who stepped out of line. Naturally, this technique only increased the city's discontent.

A poor harvest and a cold winter created suffering such as I'd never seen before, not even in London (a city famous for its callous treatment of the poor). Any fool could see that something terrible was about to happen, but Naples's ruling class carried on as if nothing were wrong. The viceroy made matters worse when he had paupers thrown into workhouses, where they were treated as little more than slaves. Anyone caught stealing food was hanged the very day they were arrested and beggars were gathered up, whipped, and tossed outside the city walls.

Summer's early harvests brought some relief to the city—that is, until the fool of a viceroy declared an additional tax on fruit. Apricots, plums, peaches, oranges, pomegranates, melons, figs, and more grow plentifully in the countryside around the city, making them a favorite inexpensive food for the poor. Thus, a tax on fruit enraged the peasantry to their breaking point.

The first Monday in July of 1647, representatives of the

viceroy announced the new tax on the goods in the city market. A young fishmonger named Tommaso Aniello took the lead in the ensuing riot, and before the day was out he'd become the leader of the nine-day revolution. The people called him Masaniello, the latest hero of Naples.

Here's what I learned: Revolutions, even short, unsuccessful ones, are more interesting to read about than they are to live through. On that first day, the mob in the market hanged the viceroy's representative, the one who'd announced the new tax. I later heard rumors that the crowd also cannibalized the man's body, but I don't believe it. The city's ruling class said many things about the revolt and much of it was untrue.

By the second day of the revolt, roaming mobs of commoners had ransacked the city's armories and opened the jails. Domenico armed himself with a pike and stood guard on the street in front of our house. Sometime in the afternoon, a mob came to the house and demanded admittance, saying all the food we had would be theirs. Domenico held them off for a time with his pike and sheer stubbornness. Once the howling mob surrounded Domenico, I ran down to the kitchen and ordered Marianella to gather all the dried food and nuts we had into a basket. We took it outside and handed the food to the crowd. That settled them down considerably. The sight of me and Marianella in our everyday clothes, mine splotched with paint and smelling of turpentine, reminded the crowd we had more in common with them than the nobility.

On the thirteenth of July, Masaniello presented the viceroy with a list of demands. The two men met and signed an agreement to pardon the leaders of the revolt, void the fruit tax, lessen other taxes, and grant common citizens some rights of governance. That would have been fine, but later that day Masaniello went insane (so people said). He put on a gold chain like the viceroy wore and began making outlandish demands. People said he insisted he could fly because he was an angel come to earth. Later they said he'd been poisoned while in the viceroy's palace, but at the time it seemed as if Masaniello had turned on the people. Popular sentiment turned against him, mob violence increased, and the dead became so numerous that people began piling bodies outside the city's churches.

The city awoke the morning of July 17 to find Masaniello's head on a pike at Porta San Gennaro, one of the city gates. Rumors circulated again, some blaming Masaniello's followers for their leader's demise, others blaming the viceroy. By that evening, Masaniello's reputation had transformed from a villain into a peasant martyr. To make matters worse, rumors about the viceroy further inflamed the crowd. It was said that he'd gotten drunk and danced at the news of Masaniello's death. As a result, the peasant leader was given a procession every bit as magnificent as those that followed the Mount Vesuvius eruption. This time there was no miracle to stop Naples's tide of death.

By the end of August, Neopolitans had settled into an uneasy truce with the viceroy's government. Then John of Austria, the Spanish king's bastard son, arrived at Naples with a fleet of Spanish warships. They bombarded the city, or tried to. Few of their cannonballs breached the city's immense walls. This evidence of Spanish treachery proved too much for Neapolitans, commoners, and the merchant class alike, and the city once again descended into chaos.

The cannon fire proved too much for poor Viviano to bear, given how close he lived to the city walls, so with my permission he moved his family into my house. He spent his days alternating between tears and paralyzed fear, though he could lose himself in a painting for several hours if no one spoke to him. Candida, a stouthearted woman, kept their sons busy and worked hard to keep our household functioning in the midst of an increasingly violent revolution.

Just when I thought matters could not get worse, a gunsmith named Gennaro Annese led the crowds in yet another riot. As the second wave of violence rolled through the city, we cowered in my house, hoping to escape notice. We hoped in vain. I was in bed one night, awake because of the noise on the streets, when a tremendous pounding came at the door. Fearing the worst, I pulled on my robe and jerked my bedroom shutters open to get a better look. A mob—there was no other word for it— stood outside my door, torches in some hands, cudgels in others.

"What do you want?" I yelled down to them. I'd never replaced the windows that had broken in the eruption, glass being too expensive after 1631, so I could yell out the window like a common fishwife.

"Open up," one ruffian hollered.

I peered down at the man and yelled back, "I know you. You're the baker from down the street."

Franco, the baker, threw back his head and roared, "Not anymore. Not since your sort ruined everything."

"My sort?" My voice rose to a screech. "My sort!" I waved my hand out the window. "Does this look like the house of a rich woman?"

"You consort with 'em," another man yelled.

Prudenzia pushed in next to me and chimed in. "We all consort with the rich, Guilio!" she yelled, picking out faces she recognized from the crowd. "Don't you sell boots to the rich men? And saddles? And you, Franco—what about you?"

The baker waved his torch but had the good sense to look ashamed. "Well, I have to sell my wares to them that have the coin, don't I?"

I pushed Prudenzia behind me. If there was going to be violence, I didn't want them focused on my daughter. "It's the same with the painters in this house," I yelled down. "Who would you have me sell my paintings to, a fishmonger?" This allusion to Masaniello caused a ripple of unease in the crowd. Life had become so difficult in Naples that Masaniello had ceased being a holy martyr to the cause. His name once again provoked only bad feelings.

Then two things happened: behind us, a large thump reverberated in the hall, and below, the front door of my house opened. I ignored the thump and looked down to see Domenico stepping out, the pike—which we now kept in the kitchen—in his hand. He stepped up to Franco and in a commanding voice said, "Go from this place now. In the morning, my mistress will open the house to those who need a meal."

I almost yelled down "I will not," but I realized Domenico had a good idea. We'd been feeding friends and neighbors already, but no one knew it. If we fed some of these people, we'd get public credit for it.

Domenico looked up at me for confirmation, and I nodded. He turned and stared at the baker. Franco shrugged and made a small bow toward my window before leading the crowd away.

Once I'd closed the shutters against the chill night air, I hugged Prudenzia with all my strength.

"Did you hear that noise in the hall?" she asked.

We opened my bedroom door to find Candida crouched in the hall over a bundle of clothing. "It's Viviano," she said, looking up at me with a half smile on her face. "He's fainted."

We got our fallen comrade to his feet and off to bed, no worse for wear but for a small bump where his forehead had hit the wall. I didn't know which man to admire more—Domenico for braving the crowd's wrath, or Viviano, who disliked violence so intensely that he could not face it. It would be easy to call Viviano a coward, but if Naples had more Vivianos, we wouldn't be in this fix.

After that night, Domenico gathered several like-minded men and took to the streets in defense of Naples. What violence he did there, I do not know, but people later told me he killed many Spanish interlopers.

In early October, Spanish officials, including the viceroy, fled Naples with the Spanish army. On October 22, 1647, leaders of the revolt declared the Most Serene Republic of the Kingdom of Naples. While this had a lovely ring to it, in truth, the republic was never more than a straw man. The Spanish fleet continued to occupy the Bay of Naples, so no ships could pass through. This strangled trade in the city, which further desta-bilized the economy. And the Spanish army might have left the city, but it did not leave the Kingdom of Naples. The army battened down the countryside so no traffic moved in and out of the city from the roads.

Essentially, Naples was a city under siege that winter, and like all besieged cities, we soon ran out of food. The city's dog, cat, and rat population gradually disappeared, and by spring the republic was as unpopular as the viceroy had ever been. The revolutionaries, mindful that they didn't have the resources to save Naples, offered the city to Henry, Duke of Guise, a Frenchman and natural enemy of the Spanish. The duke arrived mid-winter and took control of the city, but the Spanish continued to control the harbor. Then, in April, a French armada lost a battle to the Spanish ships. By midsummer, Henry had fled north to Rome.

Candida, Marianella, Prudenzia, and I did what we could to help the poorest in Naples. I had more money than some people because, every once in a while, a letter arrived for me with money in it. Knowing of the trouble in Naples, patrons paid me for paintings as yet unpainted and friends such as Anthony van Dyck sent what they could to help. We used the money to buy food, when it was available, which Candida and Marianella made into great pots of soup and stew. We fed people from the kitchen door every day—or every day we had enough food. Some weeks, we were as hungry as everyone else in the city.

If this sounds confusing and horrible, it's because it was. The eruption of Mount Vesuvius had been more dramatic, but that crisis lasted only a few days. The city's flirtation with rebellion and independence from Spain lasted nearly twelve months. While the powerful and the drunk with power (often the same people), played political and military games, the people of Naples suffered unimaginably. The poor are not stupid (or no stupider than everyone else) and they soon figured out it didn't matter who controlled Naples. They were going to starve and die either way. In August, with the French gone and the Spanish literally at the gates, common Neapolitans rose up against Annese and his fellow revolutionaries. They beheaded Annese in the Piazza del Mercato one day and invited the Spanish back into the city the next.

Viviano and Candida began packing while Annese's head was still on a pike in the piazza. I couldn't blame them. Naples has always been a difficult city, but the failed revolution caused as many deaths as Mount Vesuvius's reign of terror sixteen years before. I didn't have the heart to leave Naples, but I could certainly see why Viviano would want to. The city was no place to raise small children, nor was it a city for the faint of heart.

Domenico, on the other hand, became a sort of folk hero after the revolution. He and his men saved many families from Spanish violence, and if they did violence themselves, they did it to keep Neapolitans safe. The people who live in Naples are different from people in other places. I think it comes from living on the edge of a mountain that explodes from time to time. Whatever it is, Domenico showed himself a true Neapolitan and the city never forgot.

～

The Christmas after the revolution, Prudenzia came to me with the news that she would be married again. Lest you be shocked at this, remember Prudenzia was thirty-two that year and no virgin girl. I did not keep her sequestered in the house, nor expect her suitors to approach me before her. As far as I was concerned, she had every right to decide whom she married and when.

I'd just finished painting for the day and poured myself a glass of wine when she came bounding into my studio with the news.

"He's wonderful, Mamma," she said. "And he wants to marry me, even though I'm a commoner and too old to have babies."

"Well, for one thing, you are not too old," I said. "Lots of women have babies at your age. And there's nothing common about you, my dear."

She glowed with pleasure. "We'll see, but he doesn't care about any of it. He said so. And he's so handsome—and rich!"

"You rotten girl!" I grinned to show I was only teasing. "Where did you meet this paragon of manhood?"

She smiled. "At church. We go to the same mass. At first we just looked at each other, then we started to talk a little after the service. He goes there to pray for his dead wife's soul. When I told him about my poor husband and how he died before we could grow old together, why, Tristan understood right away. He's so kind and he knows so much. Did I tell you how handsome he is?"

"That's his name?" I poured my daughter a glass of wine and handed it to her. "Tristan what?"

"Tristan de Lara. He's a Knight of Saint James of the Sword."

I felt my heart pinch for a moment, but I ignored it. What if this man took my daughter away from me? "So he's Spanish?" I asked.

The Knights of Saint James was a military order of Spanish nobles. To become one, you had to prove noble birth back four generations, and if even one person in your family tree had ever been a tradesman or merchant, well, then you couldn't be a Knight of Saint James.

She swallowed her wine and laughed. "Well, yes, didn't I say that? Maybe I didn't. But it's all right. I know what you're thinking, but he's not going back to Spain. His family came here two generations ago and he considers himself a Neapolitan."

"He does, does he?" He could consider himself a local all he wanted, but there was still a lot of anti-Spanish sentiment on the streets of Naples.

"He has huge holdings in Sardinia and Sicily, but he lives in a palazzo here in town, over by the Old Castle." Her eyes shined while she talked. I hadn't seen my sweet girl this excited for years, maybe not since her marriage to Priore.

"He wants to meet you," Prudenzia said. "He's all agog that I'm your daughter. He's seen your paintings, here at the vice-regal palace and in Florence. Tristan thinks he's lucky to get the daughter of Artemisia Gentileschi."

I laughed at her excitement. "Well, I don't know about that, but I do know he's lucky to be getting you."

We talked into the night, and the more Prudenzia spoke, the happier I became. Prudenzia wasn't a girl in the flush of her first love, but a mature woman. If she loved this man, then I could be sure he deserved it. I thought of the men I'd loved in my life and how I'd moved on from every one of them. Papà thought he knew what was best for me, Agostino had tried to own me, and Pietro had used me. Only my dear Maringhi had understood my need for independence, and he'd been dead for years.

Prudenzia had once asked me if I ever got lonely. "Lonely? Do five people live in this house with me?" I rebutted. "How could I get lonely when I can't get a minute to myself?"

She insisted I'd misunderstood, but I hadn't. I didn't get lonely. But Prudenzia did, which is why she'd asked the question. And now she would have a family of her own and a chance at happiness. What mother would ask for more?

Epilogue

THE KINGDOM OF NAPLES
DECEMBER 1656

I must begin with these terrible words: Mamma is dead. I, Prudenzia Lomi Gentileschi de Lara, look upon these words and still cannot believe it. Mamma has been gone since August. She was a force of nature, an imminently practical woman who took care of her people, while never expecting anything for herself. I don't mean Mamma was a saint or a martyr—I said she was a practical woman, and I meant it—but she was a woman who knew how to work hard and take care of herself and those around her, and she never, ever whined about life's tragedies. She seemed too solid and real to ever die, but she is dead and I have determined to finish her book.

Mamma came back from England with the beginnings of this manuscript. She would add to it from time to time, but it was always last on her list of things to do. Mamma always painted first. She didn't bathe, eat, read, write, or even talk much until she was done painting for the day. Paint dries slowly and must be applied in layers, and on days when no more could be done to a painting, she would write. But she wrote letters first, not this manuscript.

Mamma kept up the most astounding circle of friends by the simple expedient of a lifelong habit of letter writing. I don't think she ever made a friend she walked away from—not even Signor Galileo when the rest of the world called him a heretic. Mamma left Florence in 1621 (or 1622—it's hard to keep track of my mother's whereabouts), well before the great scientist fell out of favor with the church. When the Inquisition found Signor Galileo guilty of heresy ten years later, Mamma wrote him while he was in prison, and continued to write him throughout his lifetime of house arrest. You can imagine how dangerous this was, to be the acknowledged friend of a heretic, but Mamma didn't care. Signor Galileo was her friend, and that was that.

She also wrote hundreds of letters to patrons. She negotiated commissions, harassed them for payment (rich men have a nearly universal dislike of paying for goods), and flattered their taste while shaping it to her own. Then, if she had any time once the business of painting had been taken care of, she'd take care of the people around her. She mentored other painters, including myself, helped Marianella feed the poor who came to her kitchen door, and all the thousands of other domestic tasks that make up the running of a household. Then, and only then, when all her other tasks were complete, would she sit down with this manuscript.

If you think the idea of a writing woman unnatural, you are not alone. My whole life my mamma wrote and wrote, though she told me she'd been illiterate until after she'd had her first two babies—the ones who died before I was born. According to Mamma, it was Signor Galileo who taught her to write, and I will admit here I never believed her. The infamous Galileo and my mother—how could it be? Now that I've read her manuscript, I know the truth of it. Most women can neither read nor write, but Mamma taught me when I was only a little girl. She said it was the best way for a woman to protect herself. I used to think she was right, but then the plague took her and now I'm not so sure. What good is writing against the horror of death?

When I first went through my mamma's things, I bundled the papers that make up this story into a box, took it home, and shoved it in a closet. But the box would not lay itself to rest. Instead, it preyed on my mind each night as I laid next to my dear husband, Tristan (for whom sleep has never been a stranger). Mamma had been gone for less than a month when I yielded to her manuscript's demands. It took me less than a day and a night to read these pages, so taken was I with her tale. And when I discovered her writing left off with my impending marriage over seven years ago, I felt like a child hearing a story cut off before it was done—which is ridiculous, because I was there for the last years of Mamma's life and I know how it ended. Her writing has taught me that I knew only my mamma's story, but not the story of a woman who was a painter, mentor, and friend. Her story deserves an ending, however imperfect. It is in that spirit that I take up my pen and finish the story of Artemisia Gentileschi.

The plague came to Naples in January of 1656. At first, only a few people recognized it as such, though the pestilence had been in Sardinia the previous year. A doctor at the Annunziata Hospital near the Cathedral of Naples first diagnosed the plague in a sailor recently off a ship from Sardinia. Dr. Bossutto tried to warn city officials, but no one listened. One case of the plague hardly seemed worth noticing, but then more cases appeared in February. The good doctor tried again and again to get the city officials to declare a quarantine, but no one would listen. In early March, the viceroy, a fool named Garcia, solved the problem by getting rid of Dr. Bossutto. No one knows what happened to the poor man, though rumor has it the viceroy gifted him to the dungeons at the Old Castle, where he died of thirst and starvation when the plague killed all the jailors.

Of course, the plague didn't go away just because the viceroy wished it to. While city officials pretended everything was fine, the disease spread through the city. By March, all the hospitals were full, and by April, we began seeing bodies in the streets. That's when Tristan tried to take Mamma and me to his country estate outside the city walls, but Mamma wouldn't go.

"But Naples is my city, and I will not abandon her," Mamma declared.

She meant that she would not abandon her friends. Besides, Mamma said she'd once nursed a man with the plague in Venice and had not gotten sick then, so she'd be perfectly safe.

Tristan was about to move our household to his country estate when Bernardo fell ill. Though I was frightened for our daughter, who was in the country with Tristan's mother, I could not leave the man who'd been like a brother to me. Mamma and I nursed first Bernardo and then Marianella a few days later. I don't know how old Marianella was—she always insisted she didn't know her age—but she'd been old when she'd joined the household twenty-five years ago, when Mount Vesuvius killed so many people. She didn't last long enough to get the buboes. Her lungs filled up with phlegm and she couldn't cough it out. She died less than forty hours after she first fell sick. We wrapped her in a clean tablecloth, said a prayer over her corpse, and buried her in the garden behind the house, because by that time there were too many bodies for the undertakers and priests to manage.

Bernardo, who has always been hale and hearty, fought the disease for over two weeks, while Mamma, Domenico, and I nursed him. The buboes at his neck, armpits, and groin became so swollen and painful that when we laid cool cloths upon them, he would scream in agony. Then, one morning in the third week of his suffering, Bernardo's fever broke and his buboes began to subside.

In May, about the time we knew Bernardo would live, the viceroy declared the city plague-stricken and called for a quarantine. I curse the man here in writing, and I hope there is a special circle in hell for him and men like him. He kept the city open because to do so was to keep commerce flowing. But every ship that entered the city's harbor brought more plague, and every ship that left the harbor took the plague with it.

Before the year was out, the plague had taken a quarter of Genoa, a third of Venice, and half the population of Barletta. Pope Alexander closed Rome early in the crisis and Grand Duke

Ferdinand closed Florence, thereby saving their cities from the worst, but Naples had no such protector. Rather, we had a greedy viceroy and a flock of moronic dukes who thought they could pretend the crisis away. As if having a volcano on the city's slopes wasn't bad enough.

As a consequence, Naples suffered the pestilence more acutely than any other city. One day in late May, Domenico and I took up baskets and walked to the market to find some food. Instead, we found the square littered with dead bodies, each black with disease and swollen with decay. Booths and carts littered the ground as if there'd been a riot, but I think it was only the plague. That was the first time I saw such a sight, but it wouldn't be the last. That summer, the streets and piazzas filled with the dead and no one came to take them away. No Neapolitan who lived through those months will ever forget the daily horrors that confronted us, nor the certainty that God had deserted Naples yet again.

The city's deputies of health declared an emergency, and their remedy was to organize a procession with Saint Gennaro at the head. But they didn't clear the city streets of the dead before the procession, and I later heard the procession made it only three blocks from the cathedral before it broke up.

Through it all, Mamma and I nursed the sick. When Domenico recovered, we sent him and Bernardo out of the city with my husband. I would have gone, but the day they left I felt unwell and thought it best to stay because I did not want to carry plague to my child. Dear Tristan cried when he left me behind, but I insisted he go to our daughter, of whom we'd had no word since this disaster began.

Though the city was quarantined, and thus theoretically closed, Tristan could afford to bribe the soldiers who kept the city gates. The minute Tristan's carriage rolled out of sight, I collapsed in Mamma's arms. I did indeed have the plague, as I feared, and I suffered most grievously. Mamma nursed me and prayed over me as days turned into weeks. When the worst had passed, I would sit at my bedroom window and look out at the city I called home. By July, the streets were deserted, but for the decomposing bodies and the feral dogs and cats that fed upon them. Mamma went out each day, seeking food and helping those in need. Though no food entered the city and the market had been closed since spring, she and other survivors found food in the houses of the dead. The only reason some of us survived was that so many had already died and there were fewer Neapolitans to feed.

And then, when it was nearly over, the unthinkable happened. Mamma came home one day from a foraging expedition, feeling tired and feverish. At first, I hoped her symptoms were from exhaustion, but alas, my hope was for naught. My dear mamma had the plague.

I will not describe the days I nursed her, nor her suffering near the end. I will say only that once she'd gone to God, I washed her body as tenderly as if she'd been my child. Then I wrapped her in an old curtain—there being no more clean bedding—and kissed her one last time. The worst was dragging her down the stairs and out to the garden. I can still hear the way her head thumped on the steps our way down. My poor mamma, who'd painted such powerful paintings, now lies in the garden, next to Marianella.

By fall, the plague had passed from Naples. I joined Tristan, my daughter (whom we'd named Artemisia), and my brothers-in-art Domenico and Bernardo at Tristan's country house, but business necessities drove us back to the city well before Christmas. Once home, Domenico began working on a painting he calls *Largo del Mercatello*. It is a scene from that day we found only the dead in the market square. I think it shall be a great painting, though I can barely look at it. We hear two hundred thousand souls were lost in the great plague, but somehow they are not half so terrible as the death of the one person who meant the most to me.

I confess that the Mamma in these pages is a stranger to me. I suppose that is true of all children and their parents. We know the adult who cares for us, and because children are wretchedly self-centered, we think our mammas exist only to do so. I had not truly considered the fact that Mamma had a life before I was born or a life that took place outside the constraints of the household. I have always considered my mother an extraordinary woman, but having read her manuscript, I can see she was far more than I ever dreamed.

Yesterday I received a letter from the new archbishop. He wants to move Mamma's body to the Naples Cathedral. He writes that the "Glory of Naples" demands it. I shall think on it, for I know Mamma wouldn't care one whit where her body lies.

As I said, she was an imminently practical woman. And I remind myself that though her body lies in the ground, she is not gone. This much is true of all artists, but none more so than Mamma, who painted like no one before her. She painted the world as she wanted it to be, full of strong women who did what they had to do to survive, and she never asked forgiveness. She painted with great empathy, always questioning the accepted story of the women she painted. I think often of Mamma's Judith, the one where Judith saws off Holofernes's head while blood spurts onto the bed. That Judith did what needed to be done, as did my mamma. I know that as long as there is one Artemisia Gentileschi canvas out there and one person to look at it, my mamma lives on.

Real (and Not So Real) Things

A NOTE ON GEOGRAPHY AND GEOPOLITICAL STATES:

There was no nation called Italy until the mid-1800s. Before that, the Italian Peninsula comprised nation-states, republics, and duchies, some of which changed hands and borders many times. Tuscany was ruled by the Medici family from 1530 to 1737, and Florence was the Medici seat of power. Tuscany was a Grand Duchy (rather than a kingdom) and its rulers grand dukes. The Papal States, with Rome as its capital, cut a diagonal swath across the middle of the peninsula, with Tuscany to the north and west, with the Republic of Sienna sandwiched between. The Republic of Venice was in the northeast, at the top of the peninsula, where it ran into Hungary, while Genoa was on the eastern side of the Upper Peninsula. The Kingdom of Naples encompassed the entirety of the southern half of the peninsula, with the city of Naples on the western coast. There were several more Italian nation-states, including Savoy, Milan, Lucca, Sicily, Sardinia, and Mantua.

A NOTE ON ATTRIBUTION:

Deciding which paintings are Artemisia's and which are not is trickier than one might think. In the Renaissance, many artists did not sign their work, and because she was a woman and was forgotten or underestimated, many of Artemisia's paintings were attributed to other painters. For example, there are two *Madonna and Child* paintings from 1608¬–09 with contested attributions. The earlier of the two was attributed to Artemisia's father, Orazio, but Mary Garrard has re-attributed the painting to the daughter based on the way the hands are painted—they bear the artist's signature dimpled realism. I have used Mary Garrand's expert opinions on attributions and dates. For example, the second *Madonna and Child*, the discussion of which opens **Chapter 1**, hangs in the Spada Gallery in Rome, where it is labeled as the work of G. F. Guerrieri, an Italian painter who briefly trained with Orazio. Garrard and many other art historians agree the painting is Artemisia's and was painted sometime in 1609.

Garrard's re-attribution of the two Madonna paintings, as well as the *Woman Playing a Lute*, are important because Artemisia's greatest early painting, *Susanna and the Elders*, was for some time attributed to her father based on the advanced skill the painting exhibits. When historians discovered Artemisia was several years older than previously thought, pro-Orazio art historians shifted their argument, insisting Artemisia did not have the painting experience necessary for the Susanna (the level of blatant sexism displayed by some modern art historians with regard to female artists is astounding). Garrard and others have proven these naysayers wrong.

A NOTE ON LATE RENAISSANCE / EARLY BAROQUE ART:

The Protestant Reformation greatly affected the European art scene. Unlike the Catholic Church, Protestant churches had little use for religious art, preferring unadorned buildings and public spaces. Protestants particularly criticized the Catholic preference for decorated churches and paintings based on either emotional or pagan themes. The Catholic Counter-Reformation, defined by the Council of Trent (1545–63), responded with new guidelines for art in Catholic countries. Paintings and sculptures were to be idealized, orderly, and sober. Pagan subjects such as Greek and Roman gods were discouraged, as was anything that might encourage lust. Late Renaissance Mannerist painting emphasized idealized beauty and stylized elegance. Raphael and Michelangelo's emphasis on harmony and beauty reflect this style. Caravaggio moved to Rome in the 1590s and revolutionized Counter-Reformation art with his insistence on more natural or realistic paintings of people and events. He also made use of light and dark extremes, or chiaroscuro, and played with shadows in a style called tenebrism. Orazio Gentileschi shifted away from Mannerism in his forties, becoming one of Rome's most notable Caravaggistos. Artemisia followed her father's lead but painted themes significantly more pro-woman than Caravaggio or her father.

Most painters made their paints (or had assistants do it) from materials they purchased at color shops, as Artemisia does in **Chapter 1**. In 1548, Gianventura Rosetti published a book that detailed the best practices of paint- and dye-making, to which I refer in the first chapter.

Lavinia Fontana painted several self-portraits. In one she is seated at a small piano or spinet, and in another she is surrounded by books. Both the spinet and the books would have marked her as a high-born lady of learning. Felice Antonio Casone engraved Fontana's likeness on a medal at Pope Paul V's behest. Fontana's husband, Gian Paolo Zappi, did indeed take care of the household so his wife could paint and earn the family's money. She and Artemisia may have met, but there is no record of it if they did, so I invented a meeting.

Michelangelo Buonarroti the Younger, grand-nephew of the sculptor, inventor, and artist Michelangelo, published the first Italian dictionary in 1612. He was a good friend to the Gentileschis and served as Artemisia's patron when she first arrived in Florence after the rape trial and her subsequent marriage. I didn't want to call him Michelangelo, for fear of confusing him with his more famous relative, so I invented Uncle Michaelo. His granduncle, Michelangelo, was indeed reluctant to paint the Sistine Chapel and critics have noted that his women tend to look like men with breasts. This may have been because, as a gay man, Michelangelo spent little intimate time with women, or because androgyny in paintings was considered spiritual.

Orazio and Agostino Tassi did paint frescoes in the Sala del Concistoro, or Hall of the Consistory, though they have since been painted over. Their paintings at the Quirinal Palace still exist, and in them one can still see Artemisia's image.

The description of Caravaggio's life in **Chapter 2** reveals only a tiny portion of his chaotic life. Artemisia's *Susanna and the Elders* is considered one of the great Susanna paintings, as well as being a visual record of Tassi's pre-rape sexual harassment. It is a remarkably mature painting and thus was long considered one of her father's. Historians recently discovered Artemesia was born two years before commonly believed, thus opening the door for this painting's re-attribution. The conversations between Artemisia, Tassi, and Quorli in **Chapter 2** are paraphrased from Artemisia's trial testimony. Measurement systems varied greatly from county to country in the Renaissance. Florentines had a twenty-three-inch braccio, while the Milanese used a seventeen-inch foot. Romans used a twelve-inch foot, so Artemisia would have measured her paintings in a system recognizable to modern readers. However violent the description of the rape in this book may seem, Artemisia's description of it for the court was considerably more detailed and horrific.

We know a great deal about Tassi's harassment and rape of Artemisia because the court records from the trial have been translated into English. The trial described in **Chapter 3** has been truncated for brevity. In reality, the trial took seven months and Artemisia testified twice, once in March, where she only spoke, and once in May, where she again testified but was also tortured. The trial ended on November 28 and Artemisia did marry Pierantonio Stiattesi on November 29. He was likely related to the Stiattesi who testified on Artemisia's behalf in the trial, though no one is sure. He was a minor painter, or so all the sources say, though none of his paintings survived the test of time. No one knows who Stiattesi apprenticed with, so I assigned him to Frederico Barocci. Barocci lived in both Rome and Urbino and studied with Taddeo, one of Rome's most popular Mannerists of the mid-1500s.

As described in **Chapter 4**, Christina of Lorraine, the Dowager Duchess of Tuscany, informally ruled Tuscany as a dowager in the early 1600s because her son Cosimo II was never strong. She and Cosimo II were important art patrons. Florence's Academy of Drawing Arts, or Accademia del Disegno, was founded in 1563 and made its home at Santissima Annunziata, home of the Servite Order. I named the imaginary friar after Saint Peregrine Laziosi, a noted thirteenth-century Servite. The Cloister of the Dead and church, including its side chapels, are painted with frescoes that would have been there when Artemisia belonged to the academy. Galileo was a member of the academy, as was Cristofano Allori, a portrait painter of modest reputation. Allori did paint a *Judith and Her Maidservant* the same year as Artemisia, though I made up the bit about the contest. Allori's *Judith and Her Maidservant* is considered his best painting and his Judith is modeled upon his mistress, Maria Mazzafirra, while the maidservant is her mother and Holofernes's head is Allori's self-portrait.

Michelangelo Buonarroti the Younger's fabulous palazzo, described in **Chapter 5**, is now a museum dedicated to the works of his famous relative, Michelangelo. You can still see Artemisia's *Allegory of Inclination*, though you will not see it as she painted it. Michelangelo the Younger's great-nephew Leonardo found the muse's nudity embarrassing and had scarves strategically painted over her to cover her breasts and groin. The story of Saint Catherine and Hypatia is accurate, as is the fact that Artemisia painted two Saint Catherines, the *Penitent Magdalene* and the *Anne of Austria as Minerva* for the Medicis, though I had to imagine the circumstances that led to those paintings. Francesco Maringhi was a rich merchant who both painted and acted as a diplomat for the Medici court. He painted the dome of Santa Rita Cascia alle Vergini in 1615–1616. Romantic letters exist between Artemisia and Maringhi, and he did purchase her household goods and return them to her when they were seized for debt. It is impossible to know how physical their relationship was, so I chose to portray it as platonic for several reasons. She certainly never lived with Maringhi, nor did he support her in any of the cities in which she lived. Also, she had no children after her marriage to Pierantonio disintegrated.

Three of four, or perhaps three of five, of Artemisia's children died, and there's some dispute over whether she had one or two living daughters. About 50 percent of all children died of the diseases we now vaccinate against (at least, the smart parents among us). I don't know what killed any of Artemisia's babies, so I imagined the first one died from prematurity, the second from crib death, and the third from cholera.

Genoa was an independent republic from 1005 to 1797. Artemisia's father, Orazio, met Giovanni Antonio Saoli in Rome and followed him to Genoa, as described in **Chapter 6**. No one knows how Artemisia got there and some scholars think she was never there at all. Those historians attribute the Lucretia and Cleopatra paintings to Orazio, but Mary Garrard has good evidence they are Artemisia Gentileschi's. Sofonisba Anguissola was in Genoa at the same time as Artemisia, so there's no reason to think the two women did not meet, but I can't prove it and invented the encounter. Much the same can be said of Anthony (or Antoon) van Dyck, who was in Genoa and knew Orazio quite well. Even today, the van Dyck–style beard is narrow and pointed at the end. In 1625, van Dyck would paint his own *Susanna and the Elders*, a painting very much in the style of Artemisia. The two were friendly enough to exchange letters.

I guessed at Artemisia's style of travel in **Chapter 7**, but barges travel the Po River even today and it would have been the shortest way to traverse Northern Italy. Murano is a separate city on the northern outskirts of Venice. I don't know where Don Giovanni and Livia lived, other than in Murano, so I picked the Trevisan Palazzo, which still stands today, as a model. Its exterior frescoes have long disappeared, but we know they exist from photos taken in the 1800s. Don Giovanni's marriage to the mattress-maker's daughter was a Medici scandal, and after he died the family quickly moved to disinherit his wife. He did die of plague and plague doctors did use leeches, frogs, and cut-up snakes as remedies. Artemisia may or may not have been in Venice when Don Giovanni died—it's hard to tell, so I chose to put her there because it seemed interesting. Garrard makes a good case for the Burghley House *Susanna and the Elders* (as her second Susanna is called) being over-painted by someone else, perhaps Domenico Gargiulo, who would become her long-time assistant. Artemisia's 1625 *Judith and her Maidservant*, now referred to as "the Detroit Judith" after its current location, is one of her greatest paintings, though the second *Judith Slaying Holofernes* is more often reproduced.

The eruption of Mount Vesuvius described in **Chapter 8** is accurate, as are the facts about early Baroque Naples. Considered the most dangerous volcano in the world, Mount Vesuvius is only 5.6 miles east of Naples. Though most famous for the 79 AD eruption that buried Pompeii and three other Roman cities, it has erupted approximately thirty-eight times since then. It has not erupted since 1944. All the art patrons and paintings mentioned in Chapter 8 are accurate as well, though I sometimes had to guess which paintings Artemisia painted for which patrons.

The *San Luigi* described in **Chapter 9** was indeed a xebec—a type of small, fast-sailing ship often used by merchants—that sailed from Naples in the 1600s, though I have no proof Artemisia was on any particular ship. Inigo Jones designed the Queen's House and Orazio Gentileschi painted the ceiling in its main salon. The paintings, which were painted on canvas (rather than right on the plaster, as ceiling and wall frescoes are), were given to the Duchess of Marlborough in 1708 and moved to the Marlborough House in London, where they can be found today, though in poor condition. Greenwich Palace, also called Placentia Palace or the Old Palace, is just to the north of Queen's House and did indeed serve as home to both Henry VIII and

Elizabeth I. Garrard and other art historians agree that Artemisia painted great parts of the ceiling, though only Orazio is credited for doing so.

Queen Henrietta Maria, whom the English called Queen Mary, did indeed keep dwarves in her retinue. Jeffrey Hudson fled England with the queen at the start of the revolution but was exiled when he killed a man who made fun of his size. Hudson was taken prisoner by Barbary pirates and enslaved for twenty years in Africa before being ransomed and freed. Richard Gibson signed his miniature paintings DG, for Dwarf Gibson. He married Anne Shepherd, another of the queen's dwarfs, and the couple had nine non-dwarf children. The *Luminalia* was performed in February of 1638, not Christmas, but I moved it because there was more information on it than the Christmas masque. I found one source that said Orazio died from dropsy, an old word for edema. Edema can be caused by kidney failure or congestive heart failure, among other things. I chose symptoms for heart failure, but no one seems to know what killed Artemisia's father, though he did surely die in London.

I invented Prudenzia's first husband in **Chapter 10**. The only source for her first marriage is a 1635 letter in which Artemisia tells a patron she plans to sell some Pisa property for her daughter's dowry. There's only a 1649 letter mentioning her daughter's second marriage to a Knight of the Order of Saint James, but no more details than that, so I had to invent a guy. Domenico Gargiulo, Bernardo Cavallino, and Viviano Codazzi were all associated with Artemisia's Naples household in the 1640s. Cavallino did paint a number of the backgrounds in

Artemisia's paintings during that time. Though I greatly simplified the revolt of 1647–1648 in Naples, also called Masaniello's Revolt, which led to the brief Republic of Naples, the details in that chapter are accurate. Domenico did go out into the streets to fight the Spanish, and Viviano found the whole episode so upsetting that he moved his family back to Rome.

The plague described in the **Epilogue** killed hundreds of thousands of Italians in 1656. Though the plagues of the 1300s are by far the most famous, bubonic plague bedeviled Europe for centuries. Naples's mortality rates were higher than other cities for just the reasons I described and the viceroy, who must surely go down in history as one of the most irresponsible city officials ever (until the 2020 pandemic when city, state and federal officials all over the United States did much the same), really did jail the doctor who tried to warn the city. Domenico Gargiulo's painting of the market square is considered one of his greatest, along with his painting of the 1631 eruption of Mount Vesuvius. Artemisia Gentileschi died in 1656 in Naples. More than that we do not know, but given the 30 to 50 percent plague mortality (numbers vary depending upon the source), it is highly likely she died of the plague.

Today, Artemisia's paintings hang in the greatest museums in the world, though there are few in the United States. If you're ever in Detroit, go see her *Judith and Her Maidservant with the Head of Holofernes* at the Detroit Institute of the Arts. It's considered one of her finest works, and it is this author's favorite. Speaking of favorites, I am greatful to the lovely people at the Mentoris Project for allowing me the opportunity to write

Artemisia's life. Karen Richardson guided this project through the process and Alyssa Bluhm gave the manuscript a thorough and attentive going over. And as always, my largest debt of gratitude goes to my husband Leo Burke, who fends for himself when his wife falls into the writing hole for hours at a time.

The Playlist

Writers often write to music and the music they choose often assists in the writing. Baroque music encompasses 1600–1730ish (after which comes the Classical period). A lot of early and middle Baroque is operatic or choral, which I find hard to write to—voices distract me. I listened to the following:

MY FAVORITE:

An album of Donne Barocche playing female Baroque composers, including Elisabeth le Guerre, Barbara Strozzi, Antonia Bembo, Isabella Leonarda, and more. And the album cover is a copy of Artemisia's first *Judith and Her Maidservant*. How cool is that?

ALSO:

William Byrd's *Consort Music for Violins*
 Archangelo Corelli's *12 Concerti Grossi* and many, many of his sonatas
 William Byrd, *Consort Music for Violins*

*I will also admit that though Vivaldi is late Baroque, he wrote about a billion pieces for violin and they came in handy when the writing day got long and I ran out of period appropriate music.

ABOUT THE AUTHOR

Peg A. Lamphier has a doctorate in American history she uses to write nonfiction monographs, encyclopedias, and a small pile of novels. A native Montanan (go Bobcats!), she lives in the mountains of Southern California with five dogs, six tortoises, a huge cat, three canaries, one daughter (who's away at college), one husband (who is around all the time), and a collection of vintage ukuleles that she plays with more enthusiasm than talent. When she's not writing, Peg teaches interdisciplinary education at California State Polytechnic–Pomona and American women's history at Mount San Antonio Community College. For more, see www.peglamphier.com.

NOW AVAILABLE FROM THE MENTORIS PROJECT

America's Forgotten Founding Father
A Novel Based on the Life of Filippo Mazzei
by Rosanne Welch, PhD

A. P. Giannini—The People's Banker
by Francesca Valente

A Boxing Trainer's Journey
A Novel Based on the Life of Angelo Dundee
by Jonathan Brown

Breaking Barriers
A Novel Based on the Life of Laura Bassi
by Jule Selbo

Building Heaven's Ceiling
A Novel Based on the Life of Filippo Brunelleschi
by Joe Cline

Building Wealth
From Shoeshine Boy to Real Estate Magnate
by Robert Barbera

Building Wealth 101
How to Make Your Money Work for You
by Robert Barbera

Christopher Columbus: His Life and Discoveries
by Mario Di Giovanni

Dark Labyrinth
A Novel Based on the Life of Galileo Galilei
by Peter David Myers

Defying Danger
A Novel Based on the Life of Father Matteo Ricci
by Nicole Gregory

The Divine Proportions of Luca Pacioli
A Novel Based on the Life of Luca Pacioli
by W.A.W. Parker

Dreams of Discovery
A Novel Based on the Life of the Explorer John Cabot
by Jule Selbo

The Faithful
A Novel Based on the Life of Giuseppe Verdi
by Collin Mitchell

Fermi's Gifts
A Novel Based on the Life of Enrico Fermi
by Kate Fuglei

First Among Equals
A Novel Based on the Life of Cosimo de' Medici
by Francesco Massaccesi

God's Messenger
A Novel Based on the Life of Mother Frances X. Cabrini
by Nicole Gregory

Grace Notes
A Novel Based on the Life of Henry Mancini
by Stacia Raymond

Harvesting the American Dream
A Novel Based on the Life of Ernest Gallo
by Karen Richardson

Humble Servant of Truth
A Novel Based on the Life of Thomas Aquinas
by Margaret O'Reilly

Leonardo's Secret
A Novel Based on the Life of Leonardo da Vinci
by Peter David Myers

Little by Little We Won
A Novel Based on the Life of Angela Bambace
by Peg A. Lamphier, PhD

The Making of a Prince
A Novel Based on the Life of Niccolò Machiavelli
by Maurizio Marmorstein

A Man of Action Saving Liberty
A Novel Based on the Life of Giuseppe Garibaldi
by Rosanne Welch, PhD

Marconi and His Muses
A Novel Based on the Life of Guglielmo Marconi
by Pamela Winfrey

No Person Above the Law
A Novel Based on the Life of Judge John J. Sirica
by Cynthia Cooper

Relentless Visionary: Alessandro Volta
by Michael Berick

Ride Into the Sun
A Novel Based on the Life of Scipio Africanus
by Patric Verrone

Saving the Republic
A Novel Based on the Life of Marcus Cicero
by Eric D. Martin

Soldier, Diplomat, Archaeologist
A Novel Based on the Bold Life of Louis Palma di Cesnola
by Peg A. Lamphier, PhD

The Soul of a Child
A Novel Based on the Life of Maria Montessori
by Kate Fuglei

FUTURE TITLES FROM THE MENTORIS PROJECT

A Biography about Rita Levi-Montalcini
and
Novels Based on the Lives of:
Amerigo Vespucci
Andrea Doria
Antonin Scalia
Antonio Meucci
Buzzie Bavasi
Cesare Beccaria
Father Eusebio Francisco Kino
Federico Fellini
Frank Capra
Guido d'Arezzo
Harry Warren
Leonardo Fibonacci
Maria Gaetana Agnesi
Mario Andretti
Peter Rodino
Pietro Belluschi
Saint Augustine of Hippo
Saint Francis of Assisi
Vince Lombardi

For more information on these titles and
the Mentoris Project, please visit
www.mentorisproject.org

Made in the USA
Middletown, DE
27 March 2022

63210437R00168